Praise for Mary Ann

MW00699127

"Marlowe makes a name for herself in this hilarious and sexy debut. . . . It's filled with frisky sexy scenes set to the backdrop of rock music . . ."
—*Booklist* STARRED REVIEW

"Fun, flirty read about a magical romance . . . a light-hearted pick me up. Eden and Adam's chemistry was so electric, I rooted for them the whole way!"
—*FIRST for Women*

"This love potion romance, which pairs up the lead singer for a rock band with a biochemist who's also an amateur singer/songwriter, is light and fluffy."
—*Publishers Weekly*

"The chemistry between Adam and Eden is instant and electric, and watching them bring out the best in each other gives the story warmth along with the heat. . . . "
—*RT Book Reviews*

"Frisky, Flirty Fun!"
—Stephanie Evanovich, *New York Times* bestselling author of *The Total Package*

"Sexy, engaging and original. I completely fell in love with Eden and Adam. An amazing first novel."
—Sydney Landon, *New York Times* bestselling author of *Wishing For Us*

"Marlowe is a deft, compelling writer with a modern, confident voice . . . A smartly-written, entertaining debut!"
—Robinne Lee, author of *The Idea of You*

Books by Mary Ann Marlowe
Published by Kensington Publishing Corporation

Some Kind of Magic

A Crazy Kind of Love

Dating by the Book

Crushing It
(written as Lorelei Parker)

Published by Mary Ann Marlowe

Kind of Famous

Kind of a Big Deal

Kind of a BIG Deal

MARY ANN MARLOWE

Published by Mary Ann Marlowe
www.maryannmarlowe.com

ISBN-13: 978-1-7334018-0-7 (Paperback)
ISBN-13: 978-1-7334018-3-8 (ebook)

First Paperback Edition: September 2020

Printed in the United States of America

To Elly
The wind and my wings
Shenanigans forever

Chapter One

Noah

I should've struck a better deal with the devil.

It wasn't like I'd gone down to the crossroads and sold my soul all at once. I hadn't needed to; the devil had come to me.

But I'd sold my soul all the same.

I looked around the afterparty to tally up what I'd gotten in exchange. Was this what people called success?

Two women who'd been circling like vultures suddenly flanked me, arms tucked around my lower back—no check that, one hand on my ass, of course—as they tried to squeeze into the shot for a duck-faced selfie. In the phone's viewer, I saw myself, and I didn't like who looked back. The dark circles under my eyes could've been mistaken for smudged guyliner, but the death pallor and ugly sneer were equal parts insomnia and self-loathing.

This was a never-ending parade, all part of the satanic bargain. You get to do the only thing you know how to do well, the thing you love, every night for lots of money. In exchange, you're never in the same city two nights in a row—alone, except when you're with strangers. And after selling your talent on-stage, you're obliged to charm the people who buy the product with the promise of access.

Well, fuck that.

I ditched the groupies and found Shane hiding against a back wall, hamming it up with a different pair of fans.

"Speak of the devil," he said. "These young women were keeping me company until you were free."

He was always moping that I got more action just because he hid behind a drum set while I strutted around like an oversexed rooster, but the truth was, he was never cut out for a string of mindless hookups. That was my area of expertise.

The girls giggled. One said, "Hey, Noah," suggestively. The other echoed her, tucking a strand of hair behind her ear with a coy half-smile that said she'd like to see the back of the tour bus.

I cast them a glance but zeroed in on Shane, my heartrate rising. "I have to get out of here."

Before Shane could protest about contractual obligations, I shoved my way through the remaining crowd out into the wide halls of the arena. Security and roadies clogged the arteries, but I just needed to get to one of the green rooms and breathe for a minute. My shoulder crashed into someone as I barreled down the hall, my vision tunneling. The first door I came to had the name Samuel Tucker pasted to it. As the lead singer of Whip-lash, the much bigger band we'd just opened for, Samuel was likely at his own afterparty.

I took a chance and turned the doorknob.

I froze as I came face to face with Samuel, on a leather sofa, pants down to his ankles, knees canted wide, and his dick in the mouth of Crystal Cunningham.

My girlfriend.

Well. I guess *ex*-girlfriend now.

Samuel's eyes went from slitted with pleasure to wide-eyed what-the-fuck in the time it took me to cross the room and pull Crystal off him, her long straight hair flying out like a cape. Security was faster still and had my cocked arm in a vise before I could take the first swing at Samuel.

As they pulled me from the green room, I snarled at Crystal, "Hey, babe. Don't bother coming back to our bus."

The funny part was, I didn't even really care. I'd been in a mood to punch someone since long before I entered the room, and aiming my rage at Samuel was a pure caveman response to fight for my woman, but Crystal was just the groupie who'd stayed around past the end of one leg of a tour. I felt nothing. I'd given up my soul years ago, and tonight was another down payment on eternity.

Security let me go once they realized I wasn't going to be a problem. I wanted to hit something, but it wasn't Samuel. This existential crisis wasn't new. I strode down the hall toward the exits, pushed open the doors, and kept walking. My name shrieked by teenage girls reminded me I couldn't just hang out here, so I put my head down and ran.

The thing nobody told you about selling your soul was that it wasn't a one-time deal. You sold it again, night after night after night.

By the time my phone started ringing, I'd reached Pennsylvania Avenue. I answered the call.

"Hey, Shane."

"Man, where the hell are you?"

I stepped into the crosswalk. "I needed to get away."

He sighed. "Do you want to tell me what's going on?"

"Not really."

"I know something's up. Crystal came and got her things from the bus. Security was with her."

Jesus. That would make the gossip rags in the morning.

"Noah, man. Come on back to the bus. Micah's hella pissed."

"I want my soul back."

"What even? Where are you? We can come get you."

I glanced up at the white columns of the National Gallery of Art lit from behind. "I don't think you can drive the bus on the Mall."

"Noah, what are you planning?"

"Look, I'll catch a train up to Philly and meet you guys there tomorrow. Go on without me. There's something I need to do."

When Shane didn't answer right away, I knew he was looking for the words to talk me out of the decision my feet had made before I'd even realized where I was going. At last, he said, "If you see Lucy, tell her I said hi."

"Thanks, man."

I hung up and slowed my pace. I might have been rationalizing my actions, but I took it as a sign that we were in D.C. when Crystal opted to trade me in for the bigger rock star. It was a wake-up call to remind me I'd been trying and failing to forget what success had truly cost me. All the Crystals in the world couldn't fill the void Lucy had left when she told me never to contact her again.

Honoring her wishes had been damn near impossible, but I'd done it—almost.

Did it count if I occasionally walked past her house after midnight when the band came through town?

I just wanted to be close to her, breathe the same air under the same moon and all that shit. I had no intention of walking up and ringing her doorbell.

She'd be fast asleep already anyway. As would her husband.

Even before she was out of reach, she'd always been out of my league. Despite that, I'd caught her once, with luck and a bit of charm. How had I been such a fool to think I could put Lucy on hold and find her waiting for me?

Here I was, thirty-one years old, in a band on the brink of finally making it, skulking around like I was sixteen and I could just show up at her door and woo her with a song on my guitar.

That time had passed, my soul belonged to the devil I'd sold it to, and I needed to move on.

The first time I really noticed Lucy Griffin, it was my sophomore year in high school.

That morning, before I left for school, my dad remind-ed me I'd never amount to anything useful. You know, like the head mechanic at the Tire and Auto Center. He said, "Do you expect you can bum money off people on the street the rest of your life?"

First of all, I wasn't bumming money. I was busking.

And second of all, yes. I did. My guitar was the one thing in life that promised me a way out. School surely wasn't getting me anywhere.

For some reason, I kept trying. With him, with high school. It was all a cosmic joke that hadn't yet reached the punchline. Or maybe I was the punchline.

I rolled into school just as the warning bell rang. A group of teens destined for greatness with their perfect GPAs and out-standing extracurriculars blocked my locker. I cleared my throat, and some guy named Todd or Chad shot me a dirty look, like I might be contagious, but he moved. I had a sneer that could frighten any ordinary Bradley. As I collected my books, the group began to break apart, and I noticed her, that girl I'd seen around, too pretty to be anywhere as mundane as a school hallway.

She had this unnaturally black hair. It was rock 'n' roll hair. Sexy as fuck, and way too dark for daytime. Set against her pale skin, she could have passed for a witch. She would have made a hell of a goth or a punk with her coloring.

Except she was one of *them*, one of *that* crowd, or so I'd always assumed.

For a heartbeat, once the group disbanded, she stood alone, and the smile that had seemed so easy a moment earli-er slipped. I saw such unmistakable sadness, recognizable like looking in a mirror, that I froze in place and watched her. I might have missed it, might have missed *her*, if I hadn't looked right when I did, because in the next heartbeat, someone called her name, and that smile went back on like a mask.

The rest of that day, I watched for her. I saw her at the lunch table surrounded by friends, or at her locker. We nev-er exchanged a glance or a word. We were in totally separate worlds, like a double helix, spiraling around each other but never touching. Yet, I sought her out, watching for those signs that she was like me.

But she wasn't like me. She was popular with the right crowds, the academics, the jocks, the preps. I was popular with the outsiders, the losers, the burnouts. We had nothing in common. Except we did. It was a hunch or my imagination or sheer fantasy, but after watching her from afar, I started to see beyond her social manifestation, the face she put on when she thought nobody was watching. I was that nobody.

She might turn out to be someone different, someone who couldn't see past the world she'd been striving to fit into. But deep in my heart, I believed she and I would feel a connection, if only I could get her to see me.

By the end of the day, I told my best friend Shane, "I'm going to ask that girl to homecoming."

When I pointed her out, he said, "Lucy Griffin? You're crazy."

He was right, but I figured I'd never know as long as I remained invisible. And after all, a person can't become *more* invisible. I knew it would take time to make her really see me.

I had no idea how far off the mark I was because she'd seen me already, and she'd rejected me before I ever spoke to her.

Chapter Two

Lucy

Smithsonian parties were always stodgy and refined affairs. The same tinkling piano music or inoffensive jazz bled into the spaces between words as people sipped Prosecco and made small talk about topics that hadn't been relevant in a century, as if we had any idea what Picasso might have intended with his painting *La Vie*.

My feet hurt to my ears, and all I wanted to do was soak in a hot tub. The Uber pulled up to the corner, and I thanked the driver as I got out, fishing in my purse for my keys. Lipstick, gym fob, lollipop, hair tie, fast-food toy of some variety . . . no keys.

I weighed the choice between dumping the contents of my purse onto the stoop outside my door or knocking. The porch light was on, but all the windows were dark. That settled it. I turned the bag over, and everything spilled out. One by one, I put everything back, and there at last were my keys, plain as day. I was convinced my purse contained a portal between dimensions and things appeared and disappeared with no regard to the laws of nature.

Once I shoved everything back into the bag, I stood, wobbling a little due either to the high heels I wasn't accustomed to or the alcohol that I was.

"Steady, there," a voice said through the dark, and I nearly tripped over the first step in my sudden panic to get in the house and away from errant men out this late. "Lucy?"

I stopped. I knew that voice. "Please tell me it's not . . ."

With eyes closed, I turned toward him, willing him not to be there when I finally looked, like a magical creature who only exists when you aren't looking at him. Or like my keys, which only existed when I wasn't looking *for* them.

Before I even peeked, the air around me changed, particles becoming denser with the pull of gravity as celestial bodies approached. The sounds of the night stilled, and though it was the middle of spring, the silence was as deafening as snow falling. A chill skittered up my skin, and I hugged my arms across my chest.

And then when I couldn't stand the torture any longer, I looked up, and he was there. Noah Kennedy. I didn't know if I wanted to punch him or kiss him. He wasn't supposed to be here. My hands shook, and the keys dropped from my fingers.

"What are you doing here?"

He looked like shit. I mean, he looked like he'd been kissed by an angel at birth. There was never a time Noah didn't rival the world's greatest sculptures in beauty. But I knew what demons also lurked, and I could tell they hadn't given the boy any peace of late. That much was obvious from the fact that he stood on my front stoop, after midnight, with no warning, four years since the last time I'd seen him. Four years since I'd told him never to contact me again.

He hadn't. I wondered if that request had cost him as many sleepless nights as it had me.

"You know. I was in the neighborhood, and I thought . . ." One half of his lower lip curled back between his teeth, and my heart broke for him. And for me. But choices had been made.

"And you got lost?"

He laughed. "Or maybe found?"

I rolled my eyes. "Cheeseball." My voice broke, and I swallowed, hoping to hide my nerves. It was like attempting to banter casually with a ghost.

"You were always the smart one." His expression darkened again, and just like that, we were reliving the same conversation we'd been having with each other for nearly a decade. Before we stopped talking altogether.

I was in serious danger of collapsing onto the sidewalk from the combination of high heels and the vapors from this unexpected visit from my past. "Come, sit with me."

He took a seat on the top step, elbows on his knees, hands steepled. "Are you mad I came here?"

I took off my heels and sat a step down, sideways, so my toes pressed into the side of his Converse. I envied him the job that let him wear sneakers. I considered his question. "Mad? Confused, maybe. What were you planning to do if you got here and I wasn't awake—or home. What if I no longer lived here? What if I didn't want you to come?"

He tapped his fingers together. "I didn't have a plan. I hadn't planned to come here at all. I thought I'd probably walk on by. Or maybe knock on the door. I hadn't gotten there yet. Shane says hi, by the way."

I snorted. "Only you could go somewhere with no plan and still arrive bearing messages."

"Did you want me to come?"

That was a more complicated question. I'd known Noah since we were teenagers. Once he'd caught my eye, there was never a time I didn't want Noah to appear out of nowhere, but I didn't entertain fantasies. Noah had his own dragons to slay, and fair maidens could either wait back in the village or suit up and find their own adventures. I was no fair maiden.

I exhaled a four-year-old sigh. I'd missed him, but confessing that would only encourage him to keep showing up unannounced.

He slid forward so his butt dropped onto the next step down. He lifted first my left foot, then my right, and laid them across his knees. Like no time had passed since he'd last touched me, he pressed his thumbs into the ball of one foot and kneaded. And whether because my feet hurt so desperately or because I ached as much for him, I lay my head against the porch rail and allowed myself to be caressed by the keeper of my heart.

A car horn sounded in the distance, and reality came back to me. I pulled my feet away and scooted a little closer. "What's going on? Why are you here?"

In the moonlight, his beauty somehow magnified. He looked nearly elven, immortal, preternatural. I shook my head to rid myself of stupid childish images. He was just a man, not a beautiful vampire. But the way he was looking at me made me consider letting him bite me, turn me, drag me into his nighttime underworld.

And this was a problem because we never did have self-control when our bodies got within sparking distance of each other. He was flint to my rock, but the fire we'd make could consume us—and had already once before.

He dipped his head nearer, and it was inevitable he'd kiss me. It was inevitable I'd kiss him. I glanced up at the front door, wondering if anyone watched. His eyes followed mine.

The spell broke, and he pulled back. "I'm sorry." His hand raked his already disheveled hair. "I shouldn't keep putting you in this position. I swear I didn't expect to find you out here tonight. I just needed to know you were near. How is John? Did you—"

"John and I divorced." I braced myself and added, "Three years ago."

His mouth curved into a hard frown as he processed that. "Three years?"

I nodded and waited for the next logical question—and his irrational reaction.

"And you didn't think to tell me?"

"I considered it." I straightened my spine. I'd been prepared for him to one day appear and demand an explanation for my life's choices. But they were just that. He was out on the road. I had my own to protect. "And I considered every single outcome that might result from telling you, and they were all the same as if I didn't. Besides, it was public knowledge."

He snorted. "Well, not to me. I don't go looking for you online because I—" he squeezed his fists, like he was physically wrangling the demons "—I don't want your ghost, Lucy." He exhaled frustration. "You should have told me."

"And then what, exactly?"

"What do you mean?"

This was the conversation. It was always this conversation. We were going to end up in a nursing home together one day never having resolved this one argument. If we were so lucky.

"Will you come over tomorrow night?" I asked, raising an eyebrow at him. It was a rhetorical question. I knew his answer. His time was not his own. If he could say yes, if he could stay— not for a day or a week—this conversation wouldn't be so futile.

His shoulders slumped, but then he met my brow raise with an imperious eye narrowing. "No, but I can come over *Tuesday* night."

My stomach knotted, and I realized I'd been half hoping for an impossibility. Noah had come back, and I was going to have to make him go again.

"But I asked you to be here tomorrow night. Why can't you come over tomorrow night?"

Defeated, he told me what I already suspected. "I have to be in Philadelphia."

"Yeah." I gave him a wry smile. "That's what I thought."

"You could come to Philly with me." He waggled his eyebrows. "Come up for the show?"

He made it sound so simple. His life took him wherever the wind blew—or more accurately, wherever the tour bus went—and I had to be at work on Monday. It was an age-old dilemma. As long as he chased after that rock 'n' roll drug, he was never really mine.

"You know I can't. Not all of us can take off for parts unknown at the drop of a hat."

His coy expression was eclipsed by that darker, haunted look. "You think I'm always on the road by choice?"

"It's what you signed up for. It's in the job description."

His eyes closed, and I took the opportunity to drink in the face I normally only saw in my dreams. There he sat so close I could actually touch him, and I knew he'd let me. I knew I could have him to myself for one night. It wouldn't be the first time, but it had never been the right time.

As if my thoughts had entered his mind, he whispered, "Three years," and I tensed. He peered at me through a fringe of disobedient bangs, wincing. "Was that because of me?"

What could I tell him? "No, it wasn't because of you. Not directly." That at least was true. Misleading as hell, but true.

"It's why I stayed away all this time." He shook his head. "You never think that one day you'll grow up to seduce a married woman."

I brushed away a hot tear, reminded of how I'd come to him that one night, so upset, crying, and he'd taken me in. That was the last time I'd seen him in the flesh. "You weren't the only one there, Noah. I share in that blame."

"Did you tell him about us?"

"Yes. Of course."

He dropped his head and stared at his shoes. "I wish you had told me. Three years, Lucy. All that time wasted."

I wanted to wrap my arms around him and admit how I'd struggled the past few years. There were so many things I could confess, but I needed to put on my brave face and convince him to go home, move on, and let me try to forget him again.

"It's not wasted. It wasn't going to happen. That night was a bad idea from the start, but that's the story of us, isn't it?"

"No." He took my hand. "That is revisionist history. We were always good together."

I was about to break his heart all over again. I could at least let him have that one delusion. "Yeah, okay. We were always good together. You know, after that initial hiccup."

He snickered. He'd done such a shit job of getting my attention in high school at first, but after that, it had been fireworks. No, it had been rockets. And then grenades. And finally, detente. Here we were in the cease fire.

But it had always been good, even when it wasn't, as long as Noah was here with me. And the only problem with Noah was that he couldn't always be here. And here was the only place I wanted him. So I stood, then bent again to scrabble for my keys.

He got up as well, and when we were more or less eye to eye, he reached up and ran his fingers through the tendrils of hair that had fallen loose from my braid. "God, you get more beautiful every time I see you."

I smiled. Who wouldn't smile at a compliment like that from the loveliest creature God ever imagined? I'd long ago stopped flattering Noah for his looks because it was wasted breath. He wanted to hear he was clever or brilliant, and he was in his way. But he lacked any kind of external proof of that, and he let it define him. He had so much more potential than he knew. So I said, "It was good seeing you again."

It didn't surprise me when he closed the distance between us and tugged me in for what I already knew would be the kind of kiss that my mother warned me against. The kind that un-made virgins. I could not withstand a kiss from Noah Kennedy. In what would probably be remembered forevermore in our history of "Lucy's bad form," I laid my hand across his face like an octopus, blocking his move in the most stunning humiliation. I wished I could have reversed time and found a better way to save myself from the heartache that would follow. But you work with the tools before you.

"I'm sorry." I drew back toward the door.

Noah's eyes widened. "So that's it?"

What had he expected? Nothing changed because he'd shown up on my doorstep.

"You know what I've always wanted." My hand lifted like it had a mind of its own and pressed against his chest. I imagined I could feel his heart beating, and that was the most I could hope for. That somewhere Noah Kennedy's heart still beat. But it didn't beat for me. "Are you prepared to give it to me?"

His lip curled in the most unfortunately bratty sneer. "You want some guy with an ivy league education?"

I shoved him back. "No, stupid."

"You want someone who isn't stupid, like me. That much is clear."

I shoved him again. "You aren't stupid, stupid."

He laughed again, which I took as a pretty good sign that I could pull out of this tailspin and get out of this quagmire without destroying Noah in the process. But he repeated his mantra. "I'm not smart enough for you."

"Use your ears, please." As much as I wanted to keep shoving him until he got some sense, I took his hand and looked him deep in his eyes. "You are exactly smart enough, Noah Kennedy. You could always give me what I wanted. You've never been able to give me what I *needed*. And that is why I *need* you to promise you'll stop doing *this*."

His face dropped, but then transformed into that wild determination he used to get. And he said, "No, I don't think I will."

I chuckled. "Well, it won't be too hard for me to take out a restraining order, so I wish you the best of luck on your continued midnight sidewalk stalking, but as for me, I have to be on *Meet the Press* in the morning."

His eyes widened.

"I'm joking. But I do have responsibilities." I'd promised a guy we'd tour a museum the next day. "So if you'll forgive me, I'm going to go to bed."

And to my extreme shock and dismay, he let me go. I slipped inside, pressing my back against the door, counting to one hundred, then to two, willing him to please be gone when I looked out again because I wasn't sure I could resist that temptation forever, but as long as I could bluff my way through and make him believe it, then I could protect my realm from wandering poets who meant no harm, but left devastation in their wake.

Once my heart had settled into a regular rhythm, I crept up the stairs and entered the bedroom at the end of the hall. I sat on the edge of the wee bed and bent to brush the hair off the overly sweaty head of the boy sleeping there. My son.

I kissed the dewy forehead and whispered, "Good night, Owen. I love you."

And then I stripped off the party gown and slid into my own bed, praying I'd dreamt this entire night.

But if I knew anything about Noah, once he set his mind to convincing me to give him half a chance, he wouldn't relent until he'd succeeded.

I'd be hearing from him again somehow.

The first time I ever spoke to Noah Kennedy, back in high school, he tricked me.

That morning, before I left for school, my mom reminded me to roll the garbage can to the curb, something my *dad* would have done if he were ever home. But we hadn't seen him for, I checked my watch, several months. We'd become a kind of motel or seasonal family situation for him. We got him on his time. Whether we wanted him or not. I was already in a pretty foul mood, and specifically mad at the entire male gender.

"Just a reminder that I'll be late tonight," I hollered back. "I'm on the dance committee!"

I was on every committee. I was in the GSA. I was that honors student, the girl with impeccable extracurriculars. Color guard in the fall, debate team in the winter, and track in the spring. Over the summer, I volunteered for a women's shelter and the SPCA. I studied for the SAT. I had straight As. My entire life was focused on one thing: getting accepted into Georgetown Law one day. My life would look nothing like my mother's. I'd have a lucrative career, and I'd marry someone who would put me first, someone who wouldn't come and go at his own convenience. Every single thing I did was an investment in my picture-perfect future. It would be the mirror opposite of my current home life.

So, like the competitive student I was, I sat in Mr. Spurlock's APUSH class, arm raised, prepared with the right answer to his question about the Stamp Act of 1765. Class dismissed, and the hallway became a free-for-all. I shoved through to my locker, jostled by the stampeding teens. As soon as I had my textbook and *cahier* for French, I spun to head upstairs only to run face-first into the chest of Noah Kennedy who was for some reason leaning against the locker beside mine.

Of course, I knew who he was. Not that we'd ever shared any classes. He'd gone to a different junior high than me, and he hung out with kids from that school. But I knew who he was all the same.

The first time I'd seen him had been at a talent show where he'd dragged out an amp and played a Yes song. His singing was kind of adorably off, but everyone cheered him. He'd played the guitar better than most kids our age. He was also prettier that most boys, even though he never seemed to do anything special. He didn't wear the crisp, clean clothes of the boys I normally befriended, and his blond hair was a wild disaster, like that guy from Duran Duran my mom still obsessed over.

What I knew about Noah came through gossip. They said he was a "troubled kid," though nobody ever explained what that meant, and it left me picturing him doing a stint at juvie. I'd heard rumors he talked back to teachers, had rocky grades, and had gotten an in-school suspension once for fighting. Also, he seemed to be quasi-homeless.

To me, that was enough reason to avoid him. Since we didn't share a single class, it was easy enough to do that.

At least it *was*, before he planted himself in front of me, his long hair half covering his right eye, which was a crime against nature because his blue-gray eyes, framed by long blond lashes, were a work of art.

I started to walk away. I probably should've run, because when he spoke, he opened a crack in my personal space-time continuum.

The first words Noah Kennedy ever said to me were, "I was wondering if you could settle an argument."

Have some pity on me, please. I was on the debate team. I loved to weigh both sides of an argument and make the logical leaps from one point to the next to find the most compelling case. But I was still young and naive, and I couldn't have seen someone like Noah Kennedy coming.

So I tilted my head, ready to provide the correct answer to whatever question he'd pose.

"You see, a friend of mine and I were talking," he went on, with a nod of his head in the direction of the other locker bay across the hall. I glanced around for this friend, but nobody was paying attention to us. Still Noah continued. "And he said that there's no way a girl like you—"

My head whipped back around, and I cut him off. "What's a girl like me?"

"Well, you're going to be valedictorian, right?"

I chortled. That was a stretch. It would be another couple of years before we graduated. I shrugged. "I don't know that."

"And you're also objectively the prettiest girl at this school."

That elicited a full-on dork snort. Oh, my God, he was going to ask me to sign a petition or donate money to some cause. I was such an idiot. I stacked my books in the crook of my elbow, shaking my head at this nonsense, but as I turned away, he touched my arm. "So I take it, that's a no, then. Shane was right."

That did it. My curiosity would haunt me all day if I didn't ask. "Right about what?"

"He said you wouldn't give someone like me the time of day."

I straightened my spine and pointed a finger at him. "That is the most emotionally manipulative statement I've ever heard." I turned to walk away, but then stopped and pulled out my phone. "It's ten-fifteen, by the way. We're late for class."

I was one-hundred percent positive that would be the last conversation I would ever have with Noah Kennedy.

Chapter Three

Noah

The trouble didn't start until I got to Philly.

I'd walked to Union Square without incident. The streets were empty, and I'd lost myself in my thoughts. For the moment at least, I didn't feel angry. Sad, yes, but also determined to get my life back on track. Speaking of tracks, the next available train didn't arrive until after 3 a.m. I boarded a dark and quiet car, searching for an empty row. I probably should've sprung for a sleeping compartment to maintain my privacy, but it was only a two-hour ride, so I took my chances.

Crossing the lobby of 30th Street station as the sun rose, I deluded myself that I might make it out to the taxi stand in one piece.

The first voice was conversational, almost a question. "Hey, that's that guy."

That could have been about anyone. Still I picked up my pace. The doors to the street came into view. But speculation traveled at the speed of a whisper through the crowd.

". . . seen him somewhere . . "

". . . watch ad?"

". . . Micah Sinclair?"

". . . in that band."

I could almost feel them moving toward me, just in case it really was me, even if they didn't know who I was, just in case I was famous. It only took one person to trigger a mob. Nobody wanted to miss their chance at a selfie or an autograph. Just in case.

But that was a minor irritation compared to what came next. And it always did.

Some guy matched my pace and yelled out a question. "Noah, hey Noah. What happened last night in D.C.?"

I glanced over, but the sun filtering in through the huge lobby windows blinded me, and I didn't know if I had the foul luck of crossing the path of actual paparazzi or if some fan happened to be boarding a train in Philly at dawn.

Either way, I had no intention of talking about the previous night with anyone. I curled my lip and leaned into my stride, walking with as much intention as I could display. Nobody would respect my obvious desire to maintain some privacy, but I didn't have to pretend to like it.

At last I pushed out onto the street and hailed a cab. Ducking down into the backseat, I gave the driver the name of the arena, and we were off.

As we flew across Philadelphia, I Googled my own name, looking for any hints as to what the story was, expecting Crystal to have started talking. But her name hadn't come up anywhere. The only real item I found was a local column about the show tonight, with added speculation about why security had escorted me out of the arena the night before. It didn't begin to surprise me that it wasn't accurate, but it would be seed for gossip, and gossip sold papers. That pap might have gotten a tip and staked out the train station.

I texted our manager, Julia, to let her know I was en route. She directed me to our hotel where I checked in and fell face down on the mattress without pulling down the covers or even kicking off my sneakers.

Exhausted, I willed myself to become unconscious, but when my eyes closed, they became a canvas, like the night sky, but instead of stars painting a galaxy across my field of vision, I rewatched my memory of Saturday night, as Lucy turned toward me when I called her name. Her whole body had transformed like a flower opening to the sun. I could always do that to her. But the magic never lasted more than a heartbeat. Her mind always followed behind, dragging reality in its wake. For those few seconds, I'd beheld the Lucy only I knew. Her lips curved with a hint of amusement and a heap of sensuality. It had taken all my force not to run my thumb along her beautiful mouth, even more to resist tasting her. But she'd never let me kiss her. Not yet. Not after last time.

She'd had that incredible black hair tied back in a braid. In my mind's eye, I could reach out and tear the band free. She'd shake her head, and a mane, dark as night would flow over her shoulders. I'd fantasized about dragging my hands through that hair so many times it had become a fetish.

I had to stop thinking about her. My pants were getting uncomfortable, and I needed sleep before the show. I forced my mind to go blank and then, what felt like minutes later, a loud banging on my door forced me to pry my eyes open.

I felt . . . better. For about thirty seconds, and then the world closed back in.

"Noah!" More pounding.

That would be Micah, self-appointed leader of the band. I rolled off the bed and staggered to the door. Before I could even ask him what time it was, he grabbed my elbow and dragged me into the hall.

"Do you have everything?" He didn't wait for an answer and turned down the hall without checking to make sure I followed. Micah had been bossy from the first day he'd joined us, and out of habit, I fell in behind him, after one last gander back at the hotel room where I knew I hadn't so much as undressed.

Micah punched the down arrow on the elevator before spinning back to face me, one eyebrow arched. "So?"

"I don't wanna talk about it."

"I got word Crystal rode over on the Whiplash tour bus. Are you gonna be okay to do the show tonight if she's here?"

I shrugged. "Obviously."

I'd performed under worse circumstances. I hadn't even wondered about Crystal since I'd left the arena the night before. I didn't care where she went. We'd never shared anything more than time and a bed. Crystal spared me the annoyance of dealing with more insane groupies or the impossibility of finding a non-groupie to date like real people did. It was laughably ironic that I was the essence of the sexy rock star I used to imagine I'd be lucky to become, and my romantic options were limited to casual fucking or getting screwed over. I envied Micah for finding a regular girl to fall in love with. Hell, I envied our bassist Rick for his boring-ass married life. At least my best friend Shane didn't have anyone either. We were like monks in a sea of carnal desire.

The elevator dinged, and the doors opened. Micah waited a beat before entering. "So you're okay?"

I ran my tongue across my teeth, sucking back all the bitter things I wasn't going to tell him. Micah hadn't known me back in high school. He hadn't met me when Lucy was mine. He came into my life later. But he'd been there during the years when every tour date in D.C. was followed by storm clouds, back when Lucy would still come to shows and pretend we could do this dance where she'd married some suit, and yet I was supposedly the one living the dream. Micah had been there in the aftermath, too—after Lucy and I had blown past all pretense, after that night I'd foolishly thought everything had changed. All he knew of Lucy was her shadow.

Shane would get it, but Micah could never understand, so I nodded. "Yeah. Don't worry about me."

"Okay." He smacked my shoulder. "Let's go get you something to eat before we need to be onstage."

That was all that mattered. That the guitar monkey show up to do the one thing he knew how to. Micah at least created something with his songwriting. Shane still loved the life of the rock star. Me? I wondered why I'd gotten on that train the night before.

In the elevator, I slipped out my phone and scrolled through my contacts until I found her name. I'd looked at it thousands of times since she'd last told me not to call. What would she do if I texted? Ignore it most likely.

The doors opened, and I made the decision to hit Call as we walked. I braced for her to answer, already planning what I'd say when it more likely went to voicemail.

My heart sank at the sound of three notes in arpeggio followed by an uncaring voice telling me the number was no longer in service. She'd changed the number, and I had no way to call her. Score another point for the Soul Sucker, but I still had one more ace up my sleeve.

I still knew where she lived.

The first time I showed up at Lucy's house unannounced was sometime during my junior year of high school. I'd just bought myself a garbage '97 Skylark—a much uglier car than its ancestor, but one I'd bought with money I'd gotten from busking.

That morning, Dad had bailed me out of jail. He said, "You'll never amount to anything, Noah." He never had anything new to add to that, except that morning, when he told me, "You'll find your things on the curb by the trash." He called me a "fairy" to boot since I hadn't had a haircut in a while.

Mom watched from the living room as I sorted through the pile of clothes, shoes, and musical equipment, shoving whatever would fit into the trunk and backseat of my car. She didn't come out to tell me goodbye, and when I looked back, she was gone.

I knew the charges would be thrown out because busking wasn't illegal, but that didn't stop me from being thrown out on the street as well.

Now, literally homeless, I drove around without a destination. My car was packed with my belongings. I couldn't have slept in it if I'd wanted to. I should have gone straight to Shane's. At least there, I could crash in his basement until things calmed down at home. I spent half my time at Shane's anyway, practicing songs for the two-man band we planned to one day take on the road.

I ended up parked in front of Lucy's house and sat there idling, talking myself into walking up to her door and asking her to run away with me. We could go to New York City or California. Her choice.

Of course she wouldn't go. She had a whole future planned. I didn't want to ruin that for her. I started to put the car in drive and pull away, but her front door opened, and she ran out and climbed in the passenger seat. "Go!" she said. "Drive us somewhere!"

Her cheeks were wet with tears, and I didn't even stop to ask her why. I tore out of there and headed up the highway without a destination. We drove for hours, singing along to a garbage playlist of boy-band music from her phone.

I'd finally gained her attention, if not her friendship, mostly by sliding in next to her at lunch when she didn't have a polite out. She didn't seem to notice how her circle of friends had started to slowly move to a different lunch table. She didn't tell me to leave.

But she made it clear she wouldn't go out with me. She turned me down flat for the homecoming dance for a second year. She turned me down for everything. I once made the mistake of asking her why she wouldn't even consider dating me and got an earful of my inadequacies as she counted off on her fingers: "You skip school. You shrug off your failing grades. You half-live out of your car, for God's sake. You have no plans for college. You scoff at the idea of staying longer than necessary in the vicinity of the school for sports or clubs." She switched hands and kept counting. "Instead, you spend every afternoon playing music with Shane or out on the streets. You aren't serious about your future." And with a beat on the last three fingers she punctuated, "You. Are. Trouble."

The proof was in the fact she was halfway across the state and hadn't called her mom to tell her where she'd gone. By the time the sun was high in the sky, we were overlooking the Atlantic Ocean.

"End of the line," I joked. She hadn't said a word about what was troubling her. We'd only checked in with each other to confirm we both wanted to continue east and east and east.

But here, parked along the boardwalk in Ocean City, I took her hand and asked, "Is it so bad I'm finally your best option?"

She snort-laughed, but then the tears flowed, and she confided in me. "My mom struggles so hard, and she does it all for me. I don't know why she lets him keep coming back. Do you think she does it for me? Like she thinks I need a father figure in my life? Because honestly, I'd rather he never came home."

I understood that all too well. If my dad had abandoned me with my mom, so many things would have been different. My entire T-shirt drawer wouldn't be covering my back seat for starters. But this wasn't about me. "I'm one-hundred percent sure everything your mom does is for you."

She sniffled but looked up at me with the sweetest of smiles and said, "Thank you, Noah. Thanks for taking me here."

"Thank you for coming with me. Now we can be homeless together."

"Seriously though, Noah. This isn't a permanent solution." She flounced a bit so she could face me directly. "I'm really worried about you. You should plan for the future."

"I love it when you lecture me," I said. It wasn't a lie. Her concern touched me. Somehow when she said the same things my dad would, it sounded nicer. Like she actually cared what might happen to me.

"What if you don't graduate?"

"No need to worry. I'm planning to make it big." I gave her the cocky grin that ought to have made her want to sock me in the eye, but usually made her breath hitch in a way that affected me way more than it should. "You'll be begging *me* for money one day."

She didn't laugh. Instead, she let out a breath that trembled with the weight of actual tears behind it. "What if *I* fail, Noah? What if I can't do this? I don't want to end up stuck like my mom working two jobs to break even. What if I don't get scholarships or even admitted to Georgetown?"

"That would be impossible because you're such an epic nerd." I waited for the laugh that would chase away her sad-

ness and added, "Seriously. You're going to do everything you
want."

She breathed in and let it out, and her crooked smile made
me want to wrap my arms around her.

I wanted to tell her how amazing she was.

I wanted so badly to kiss her and show her how amazing
we'd be together.

She thought we were opposites, but we were the same
where it truly counted. We shared the same fear of being in-
significant and anger at dads who made us feel unlovable. We
made each other laugh despite the shit at home. We both wanted
to get the hell away from there.

We were soul mates. This I knew. I just hadn't figured out
how to get her to see it.

I reached over and wiped a tear from her cheek with my
thumb and I dropped my hand onto her shoulder with a little
squeeze. I hadn't exactly planned any of this, but my fingers
were so close to the band tying her hair into the braid that lay on
her shoulder, and I tugged at it. She didn't protest. Instead, she
shook her head as I threaded my fingers in to loosen the tresses.
I'd had fantasies about doing just that.

The way her eyes closed emboldened me, and I leaned over
the console but paused inches from her face. "Lucy, look at me."

Her eyes opened. "Just kiss me, Noah."

What was I supposed to say to that? She might not ask a
second time. But my nerves rendered me immobile, terrified of
wrecking this delicate thing that had finally started. I laid my
forehead against hers, wanting her to know that I cared about
her. She slid her fingers through my hair and lifted her mouth to
mine, our lips fitting perfectly, and I sighed, relieved that I had
something good in my life.

I smiled and said, "So you like me."

She smiled too. But still she added, "You're bad news for
me, Noah."

We ended up walking along the boardwalk, veering in and
out of gift shops that were open and eating garbage fair food,
and when we finally agreed it was time to go back, she handed

me a package. "A memento," she said. "To remember us to-day."

It was a paperweight shaped like a dolphin leaping from the waves. "O-kay." I hadn't ever mentioned that I liked dolphins, but who doesn't I guess.

She laughed. "Would you prefer a snow globe of the boardwalk? Or a T-shirt? There weren't a ton of options, Noah."

"No." I lifted the heavy thing. If anything, I could use it for self-defense. "It's perfect."

It was, too. It was implausible enough that I could never look at it again without thinking about the impossibility of the day I kissed Lucy Griffin.

Chapter Four

Lucy

I gave myself all of Sunday to feel the emotions I normally managed to bury under pragmatism and necessity. I'd mostly lost track of Noah over the years. I mean, I'd sometimes run smack into a glossy photo of him nonchalantly hawking an expensive watch in some magazine when I was least expecting it. If I'd wanted, I could have easily sought him out on purpose, stalking his IG or Googling him, but I'd stopped following his career when I started to find more pics of him with the arm candy he was probably fucking than onstage. I didn't really need to come face-to-face with the reality that he'd moved on, that he'd embraced the whole groupie-on-the-bus cliched rock lifestyle. I couldn't judge him; he wasn't mine.

Still seeing him again in the flesh had stirred up a Pandora's box of desires, and I knew I needed to close that lid. My life would have been so much easier if I'd never met Noah Kennedy.

But as I grabbed Owen's feet and pulled him a little higher before letting his swing fly backward, his face lit with pure joy, and I couldn't wish Noah out of existence. He'd given me my son after all.

I grappled again with decisions I'd made.

I couldn't regret the brief affair that had prematurely ended my marriage. John and I would have split up eventually with or without Noah. But the pregnancy didn't help, and once the DNA test came back, John severed parental rights but left me the town house on the Hill to keep everything simple. Owen never even knew John.

Owen could have known his actual father however. He could yet. The weight of that deception crushed me as I giggled at my son and told him silly things to make him laugh. His blond hair flew back as he swung toward me.

My phone beeped, and I held a hand out to slow Owen's swing before answering.

"I know it's Sunday," the voice began.

I groaned. "Priya—" Any complaint I came up with would be wasted breath. I'd wanted more responsibility so I could prove myself and move up into acquisitions. I knew I'd say yes to whatever she asked. "How soon do you need me?"

I was already lifting Owen from the swing and onto my hip before Priya could say what I already expected. "Immediately."

My lord, this child was getting too big to carry. I signed off and slid my phone in my pocket so I could transfer Owen to the stroller with both arms. He protested, but I produced a juice box and a baggie full of Goldfish. That did the trick.

I phoned ahead to make sure Mom was at home. She opened the door while I clattered in with the voluminous trappings of a small child. I let the enormous shoulder bag drop in the foyer and folded up the stroller as Owen squealed and ran to my mom.

She knelt and pulled Owen in for a hug.

I watched them for a minute, grateful for her willingness to help me out. She'd stayed with me when Owen was born, temporarily at first. Then as I relied on her more and more, she'd up and sold her house and moved in permanently.

And she relished her role in Owen's life. She'd never been so maternal when I was growing up, but then again, she'd had to raise a kid without a dependable partner. I paused. Was this what Owen would think about me in twenty years? We didn't have an ideal family unit, but surely having Nana there was infinitely better than having a dad who wasn't.

"I'm sorry for asking you to pull double duty this weekend. Thanks again for watching him last night."

"Are you kidding? We're going to have so much fun." As Owen ran into the kitchen, yelling, "Nana! Come play!" she said, "Do you want to make sugar cookies?"

I chortled. "Who are you, and where did my mom go?"

She turned and gave me a look I knew too well. "You were out late last night."

"I hope I didn't wake you when I came in."

That expression. Here came the interrogation. "I heard voices outside, so I checked. Did you meet someone at that party?"

"No." I turned toward the stairs to avoid her penetrating gaze, so I could lie without her ferreting out all my secrets. "It was just someone I know passing by."

If she figured out who I'd seen, she'd start pestering me about what I planned to do, whether I'd finally tell Noah everything, and I couldn't even answer that question for myself. I doubted I'd see him again anytime soon, no matter what he claimed, so I could go back to pretending I hadn't stolen something from him. I could return to a world where I might never have to admit my selfish decisions.

My stomach roiled as I shoved the guilt back down. It would pass. I'd find a way to rationalize it away.

"At midnight?" I swore I could hear her shaking her head. "You need to be careful out there alone at night."

"It was okay, Mom. We just talked for a bit." I took the first few steps and looked back. "Oh, and I promised Owen we'd go to the Air and Space Museum today, but we only made it as far as the park. Would you mind?"

"Not at all."

I changed into something more suitable for work, called for an Uber, then headed down to the kitchen to watch Owen attempting to mix the ingredients my mom had put into his bowl. He had a streak of flour across his face and looked perfectly happy.

He didn't look up from the stirring when he said, "Ima have a cookin' show one day."

I came around and gave him a kiss on the forehead, but he didn't even acknowledge I was there. I felt a pang of regret that I couldn't be the one staying home while my mom went into the office.

What a weird thought.

I'd spent many years, not to mention thousands of dollars, on my education, to get me right where I was right now. I'd made sacrifices and dedicated myself to making sure I'd be more and have more than my mom had had, struggling between jobs, at the mercy of an erratic husband's support.

I chalked the momentary wish up to irritation for my ruined Sunday and headed out to catch the Uber.

But that domestic vision persisted, and I imagined what my world might have been like if John and I had ever managed to have our own children. Would we still be pretending to live in marital bliss? Then my mind turned toward the alternate reality I so rarely allowed myself to indulge in. Just for today though. After all, I'd given myself a day to get the feelings under control, to stop missing Noah so badly it made me want to tell the Uber driver to keep going straight to New York City.

What kind of life might Noah and I have shared?

In order for us to make it work, something or some*one* would have had to give. As I saw it, there were three potential scenarios and none of them likely. One - Noah could give up his fly-by-night lifestyle, settle down, get a stable job, and help raise my son. He'd never chosen that route for me; I had low expectations of him changing for a kid he didn't know. Two - I could give up my entire life, move to New York and raise Owen in some squalid apartment while Noah was on the road. Or three - Noah could become a part-time dad, showing up whenever he passed through town. And that was a life I'd rejected long ago.

All of these choices came with other complications, like the tabloids. I'd abandoned my social media ever since Owen was born, only sending pictures to friends and family via email. Having married a congressman, I'd been prepared for some media attention, but I'd never wanted to be the subject of tabloid speculation, and Noah's life was a magnet for paparazzi.

There was nothing safe about letting Noah back in. Yeah, it ate me alive keeping him from his child, and there was probably a special level of hell reserved for me, but what was the alternative? Heartbreak and turmoil for everyone involved.

But my traitorous mind played with the possibilities. What if?

I'd known from the minute he first spoke to me: Noah Kennedy would be trouble. And he always was. But he was the kind of trouble you didn't mind getting into. My most cherished memories always involved a little danger and a lot of Noah.

But that was the crux of the issue. I'd always let him seduce me with his charisma and pretty face, but then he'd be gone, and I'd be the one picking up the pieces. I'd already waited years for him to come find me and promise me a future where we could be together. Life had never followed my lead. And Noah certainly wouldn't.

Instead, Noah found Micah Sinclair. Along with Noah's gift for the guitar and Shane's skilled drumming, they produced a hit song and started touring all over the country. And that's when I knew any kind of life with Noah was no longer going to happen in this universe.

None of that had changed.

Sometimes I wished he'd failed. I wished he'd been ordinary.

But Noah had never been ordinary.

There was this one day, it must have been junior or senior year. It was a Maryland football Saturday.

That morning, Dad had arrived with no warning. He'd come bearing gifts and hearty laughs, asking about all my activities and sugar-talking my mom, as if he'd always been a part of our lives and we were the ones who'd neglected him.

It couldn't last long. He had this routine where he'd remember he had a family, usually as it coincided with a home football game or a gathering of like-minded alcoholics. He'd stay a weekend or a month, collecting grievances like a snowball rolling downhill, until finally, he'd take off as if we were the ones to blame, red-faced, yelling about something my mom had done wrong twenty years earlier.

Dad cracked the first beer just after lunch. He'd bitched quietly about the state of the house, the lack of order or cleanliness. Everything was fine, but he always managed to find something to point out, like he was searching for reasons to be irritated.

I stayed in my room until dinner, a silent affair, punctuated only with unsolicited advice, like, "You ought to grow your hair back out, Sara. It was prettier that way."

If I could have asked him to leave, I would have, but my mom hunched her shoulders and disappeared into herself.

Once Dad had retired to the upstairs master bathroom, I spread my study guides across the dining room table while Mom watched some show she'd been marathoning.

We both sighed in relief at the blessed peace.

I'd just started a practice test when I saw my dad storming toward the front door, shotgun in hand.

Mom and I ran after him, and to my horror, Dad cocked the rifle and aimed it at the porch roof where Noah dangled from the edge, floodlights illuminating a guitar strapped to his back.

My dad had never been the biggest fan of Noah. Not after we ran off to Ocean City together without telling anyone, and my mom had called everyone, frantic with worry.

Of all possible options, Noah had chosen the worst moment, the worst possible window to execute a grand gesture, and he ended up serenading my dad who was sitting on the toilet. His plan might have gone entirely unnoticed had he simply stood at the end of the driveway with a boombox blaring Peter Gabriel, but no, he decided to go the Romeo route. At any other time, and any other window, it would have mostly been a failed attempt at wooing. But my dad was rarely in the mood for a little romance, and so now, he aimed directly at the poor misguided boy.

When I screamed, Noah startled and lost his grip, tumbling off the roof into a thicket of box hedges. The guitar snapped in two with a hollow twang, but Noah jumped up and brushed himself off, cradling his elbow.

My mom stood between the man and the boy, finger raised at my dad, demanding, "Put that fool gun away!"

I glanced over at Noah, expecting him to look as terrified as I felt, expecting him to flee at the first distraction. But he stood tall and locked eyes with me, biting back a smile, and I started to laugh.

That was the day I fell in love with Noah. It was us against the world.

While my mom and dad bellowed at each other in the yard, I snuck over and grabbed Noah's hand and dragged him after me to his car. We took off into the dark, my bare feet on his dashboard, music from his radio filling the car, and our relationship leapfrogged from a couple of ostracized goofballs to something closer to kindred spirits.

I knew he'd throw my life's plans into complete disarray, but as much as I tried to resist this troubled boy's charms, I needed him in my life.

After that we were inseparable, sitting together in the cafeteria at lunch, walking to class whenever Noah showed up for school, waiting for him to get out of detention. He was the worst sort of trouble, but he was fun. And I loved hanging out with him. I loved kissing him.

When I finally agreed to let Noah take me to a dance two-and-a-half years after he'd first asked, he somehow managed to make even prom a complete disaster—and a magical memory of why I loved him.

He'd led me under the streamers and swimming spotlights to the middle of the dance floor. The girls who used to be my friends made way for us like we were lepers. Another loss I never minded. When Noah pulled me in tight, I smiled into his neck, breathing him in. He smelled so intoxicating, as always. He was this secret that I'd discovered, and I didn't mind if we always kept it that way.

The music in the school gym was corny and perfect, and we kissed in public as if we were all alone, pressing against each other and rocking our bodies like foreplay, like nobody else existed. I craved more. With Noah, I always wanted more.

So when he drew back and gently kissed my cheek, I more rasped than whispered, "Let's go."

He didn't need another minute to decide. The back seat of his car was hardly conducive to the way I was feeling, but I hiked up my dress, straddled him, and was in the process of loosening his tie when someone pounded on the window and yelled, "Ride that train."

I told him, "Ignore it. Let's just go somewhere else."

Noah couldn't let the insult go and flew out of the car to chase down whatever asshole had interrupted us, but they were long gone.

When he came back, I adjusted my dress and climbed out of the car, saying, "Well, you just blew a sure thing."

Nothing about fighting turned me on, not after the way my dad had treated my mom up until he finally stopped coming home altogether. Fingers crossed on that.

I went back into the gym, unsure who to ask to drive me home, and ended up hunkering down on a bleacher, alone, crying. Shane found me and wrapped an arm around me, asking, "Are you okay?"

I wasn't. I was mad at Noah for letting anger override passion, for letting his ego over my honor ruin a moment that was for us. I was mad at the idiot who started it, of course, but mainly, I was mad that I'd be going to Georgetown in three months, and Noah had no plan at all except for some half-baked idea to drive up to New York with Shane and scope out the scene.

The whole thing made me realize it was time to break up with him. We could use the summer to wind things down and move on.

Suddenly, a commotion stirred the crowd, and I glanced up, a tear still hanging on my lashes, to find Noah strapping a guitar over his neck with a nod to the band. When he started singing Taylor Swift's "Love Story," complete with "I'll be the princess," I started to laugh so hard, I nearly threw up.

And well, after that, who wouldn't have forgiven him? After making him grovel for another week so he'd never make the same mistake again of course.

I grabbed Shane's hands and pulled him up so we could wave our arms in the air and dance like assholes while Noah performed onstage for a receptive audience. Noah shot me a cheeky grin, called back to the band, and transitioned straight into Jason Mraz's "I'm Yours." He was so talented, so charming, so sexy, so goddamn sweet, he tempted me to reconsider all my future plans, to throw away my scholarship to Georgetown and follow him wherever he went.

But when he sang the lyric "our time is short," reality came crashing in. Noah and I couldn't last. High school couples never worked out long term, and we'd never made sense together anyway. There was always the chance Noah would hate New York and come home, but one glance at him onstage proved otherwise. I couldn't shake the feeling that we'd go our separate ways and eventually look back at this time in our lives and wonder: What happened to us?

It hadn't taken as long as I'd expected.

Chapter Five

Noah

The Philly show went off without a hitch because of course it did. The only time I know who I am and what my purpose in life is is when I have a Gibson in my hands and Shane's belting out a four-count behind me. I can get lost, man. It's the one time I remember why I gave up so much else. I forget about the fans. Their cheering is nothing but an accompaniment to the screech of one long guitar solo. I forget about the travel. I could be anywhere. A stage is a stage everywhere you go. I forget about Lucy. That's the best part of the gig. I make love to the neck of a gorgeous instrument, and for that window of time, I know exactly what it's like to speak to God.

Then the last note dies, and we race off the stage from the sublime into the profane mayhem that surrounds the show. It's like coming down from outer space. Gravity feels heavier. Heat and humidity suddenly register. Roadies hand us water bottles, and we immediately pour them over our heads, tilting back to catch whatever we can in our mouths. Managers push and pull us to wherever they've promised our bodies, usually to interviews with music reviewers or other industry professionals. VIP ticket holders get to take pictures with us, absorb our sweat, give us their germs. And then we're in an afterparty, and I'm talking to someone who looks exactly like Crystal, but her name is Lisa or Monica or Jewel, and while she's getting a picture, she's copping a feel. Sometimes they just want to touch me. Other times they want to use me as a prop for a lewd Instagram photo. I bought an athletic cup after some lady thought it would be freaking hilarious to slap her hand over my dick as the flash went off.

Philly came and went like this. Then we climbed on the bus and headed to our last show of that leg of the tour which was supposed to be in Newark, but we never made it there.

I mean, we made it as far as the parking lot. The roadies had started unloading our gear when Crystal showed up with her bags slung over one shoulder and stood outside our bus like she expected to climb right on. Micah blocked her way as he was descending the stairs. I leaned against the side of the bus, not bothering to ask her the obvious question. I let my face do the talking. It said, "*You want to explain yourself?*"

She huffed and dropped everything at her feet. "Well? Are you going to be mad about this forever?"

I stepped a little closer and gave her my full attention. "Yes."

She shot a hand toward me, and I moved out of her reach. "Noah, I'm back."

The setting sun lit her hair aflame, and I swore she looked just like a succubus from hell. Beautiful, but possibly missing a soul. That was something we had in common.

"Does Samuel know you're no longer traveling with him?" The realization dawned on me. "He kicked you out, didn't he?"

"No." She played the pouty victim like a pro, doe-eyed and remorseful. "I missed you."

Sadly for her, I just didn't care. "You better hurry on back to Samuel, or you're not going to have a ride."

Micah took the cue, and as he exited the bus, he made a circle in the air with his forefinger, signaling to the driver to shut the doors.

Crystal made a cry of frustration and grabbed her belongings. She hollered back, "You've got a tiny dick, Noah. I always hated sucking it."

I cackled.

That would have been the end of that, but Samuel Tucker, the man himself, came all the way over to have words. Apparently in order to get back in his good graces for the time being, she'd crawled back and started trashing me hard enough to make it an issue.

Micah gestured me away, like I really gave a crap about any of this, but I let him because I also didn't trust myself to play nice. As they huddled together, talking seriously, they both turned their heads in my direction and nodded. When Micah's shoulders slumped, I knew this was not going well. With only one show left to open for Whiplash, I couldn't believe they'd send us packing.

Rick came over and stood beside me. "That does not look good."

Shane emerged from one of the arena doors, saw what was transpiring, and shot me a quizzical glance. I shrugged. In that moment, I wasn't sure what outcome I wanted. Performing was a drug I craved, but I was also bone-weary. I wanted a few days in my own bed.

Not to mention, I was tempted to turn right around and go back to D.C., but Lucy wouldn't want to see me. She'd rightly point out that I had to be somewhere else in a week. Some college town. Some new string of tour dates as the headlining band. Some festival. Just a never-ending circus. If only I could call her, talk to her, plead my case, maybe I could steal some of her time. I didn't know if she'd want to talk to me, and I didn't have her new number even if she did.

But I had an idea how to get it—a way that would let me find out if she was ready to talk at the same time.

Micah yelled, "Pack it up!" over to the roadies and came back to the rest of us.

"And?" I asked.

"Samuel's not upset, but Crystal's threatening to go to the gossip rags and air a whole lot of dirty laundry if he lets us stay on. Since it's the last show anyway, he said he'd rather part ways than deal with cleaning up his image."

Now that it was said and done, I didn't feel the disappointment I was anticipating. All I felt was relief washing over me. The stress of touring had been exhausting. "Can we head home now?"

We were so close, Micah didn't even phone ahead to warn his girlfriend Jo he'd be back in less than an hour. "Come over with me," he said. "Let's go surprise her."

Rick didn't wait for us to board the bus before saying, "Later on," and taking off for parts unknown. He was such a weird dude, and I wondered every other day whether we could find another bass player. On the in-between days, I wondered if the band could find another lead guitarist. For the next week, we'd be in town, rehearsing for yet another set of tour dates, and those were the killer days when emptiness threatened to bury me. As much as I hated the nonsense that surrounded touring, there was the chance to perform. At least when Crystal was with me, I wasn't so lonely during those long nights back home.

If only Lucy could see that being together part of the time was better than her total eclipse method, I could find some reason to carry on. Back when I'd first come to New York, we'd managed a long-distance relationship, and I assumed for too long that it was working okay. Then one day, I came to find I'd been replaced by some guy who had all the qualifications I could never attain: education, respectability, money. And the fact he could be there for Lucy on any random Tuesday. Well, I'd eventually found my way to the money, but the rest was simply out of my control. What was I going to do, go to Harvard without a high school diploma?

All the while, I'd been doing my best to make time for Lucy, but that clearly hadn't been good enough.

And yet, my replacement had vamoosed, despite all those qualities she'd found so important. Maybe there was a hope that he hadn't been enough in ways that maybe I could be.

This time around, I wouldn't let her forget about me so fast.

♡

The day Lucy broke things off the first time should have been the best day of my life. We'd just signed a contract with a record label, and that night, I called to tell her the good news.

Up until then, Lucy and I had been making the long distance work for years while she went to school and Shane and I paid our dues.

Shane and I had this scuzzy apartment in Brooklyn no bigger than the backseat of my car. It had a certain smell in the entry that could only be described as "urinal cake." Shane suggested we bleach the place once after discovering an unidentifiable mass in the corner. We were hoping it was a decayed mouse.

We'd started out playing the streets and barely scraping by. But then we got a lead on a gig in an actual hole-in-the-wall club in Gowanus as a Black Keys cover band since there were only the two of us. When we started to make a little cash, I discovered I could take a train to D.C. for eighty bucks round trip on weekdays. Lucy and I emailed, texted, videochatted, called, and even snail-mailed the really gooey stuff in the meantime.

I thought we were holding steady, and it was just a matter of time before she'd follow me up to New York, and we'd be together again.

I hit speed dial as I slipped out of the apartment into the stairwell for a bit of privacy. Shane and I were practically married we spent so much time together. I looked forward to the day we could get a bigger place. Or if I was dreaming, our own separate places. Mine would be as far away from Shane as I could get. Not that I didn't love him, but I was really going to murder him soon.

Lucy picked up, and the sound of her voice when she said, "Hi," made me want to skip the news and go straight for the dirty talk.

"So we signed a contract today."

"Oh, yeah? That's great news." She must have been half asleep because I could hear the lack of an exclamation point in her tone.

"Micah came up with the band name. What do you think of Theater of the Absurd?"

She snorted. "Kind of highfalutin for a rock band isn't it?"

"I thought you might like it since you're into all that early twentieth-century art stuff."

"Noah, the Theater of the Absurd was a literary movement. That's why it has the word 'theater' in the name."

"Micah has these ideas for making our shows more theatrical anyway."

"Does this mean you've hit the big time?"

I sighed. "Hardly. We go into the studio to record some songs, and then the manager lady wants to send us out for some tour dates stretching all the way across the country."

"Oh. So you'll be on the road for a while, huh?" Her disappointment carried across the distance. I felt it, too.

"We don't leave for a bit. You could come up here. I could show you around."

"Well, I mean . . ." She exhaled. "I've got class until the end of May."

"But after that, you'll be done with grad school, right? Why don't you come out on the road for a week? It would be a blast. I'd love for you to meet Micah and Rick. Well, mostly Micah."

"My internship at the museum starts right after I graduate."

I slumped. There never seemed to be any give in our situation. "At least promise you'll come out to see us when we pass through D.C. You haven't seen us perform as a band, and we have this whole new sound. It will be fun!"

"Of course. I can't wait." She didn't sound convincing, and I knew she was annoyed that things had been so difficult for the past few months.

"I'm sorry I haven't been able to come down to visit for a while. We've been playing all over town, trying to save up the money for a van to tour in. And work out the kinks in the act, too. But I miss you. I wish we were closer."

"I miss you, too."

"Yeah?" I sat down on the grungy step, wishing again to go somewhere private. With a glance down the stairs, I said, "Tell me how much," in my lowest sexiest voice. This was how we'd made the time pass during the weeks I couldn't swing a trip to see her. Or lately, when she was too occupied with classes for me to visit.

I bit my lip, waiting for her to tell me something seductive.

It had been too long since we'd played. I blamed Shane and his ever-present presence in the apartment. I considered kicking him out for an hour so I could say naughty things in private where it didn't smell so pervasively like piss.

Before I could even decide to stand, she said, "Noah, I can't."

"Oh, you were trying to sleep, weren't you? I'm sorry—"

"We need to talk."

I didn't like the sound of that. "About?"

She paused, and in that space, my mind ran wild. I wanted her to tell me she'd changed her mind about staying in D.C. I braced for the unimaginable.

"A guy I know asked me out on a date."

My stomach lurched. "That can't be the first time someone's tried to hit on you." After all, girls hit on me after every show. I'd figured out ways to slip around them and avoid the uncomfortable situations.

"It's not."

I laughed, pretending the ground wasn't shifting under my feet. "So what's the big deal? Tell him you've got a boyfriend."

"That's what I need to talk to you about. I don't see how this is going to work."

The door below opened and clanged shut. Voices rose through the stairwell accompanied by stomping that sounded like my heart felt. "What are you saying?"

"I'm saying our lives are going in opposite directions."

"You're breaking up with me? You're seeing this other guy?"

"I haven't told him yes. But, Noah, I think I'm going to. I'm sorry to tell you over the phone. I was hoping I'd see you soon, but that's the problem. I never do."

I turned to face the wall as the couple rounded the corner and had to squeeze past me. I didn't want them to see the tears streaming down my cheeks. "What then? You finally met some smart guy in grad school, huh?"

"No, actually, he's a friend of a friend. He's nice."

"So that's it? Just like that?"

"This can't come as a surprise. We can't go on like this."

I scoffed. This wasn't how our story was meant to go. I wanted to jump on the train and get down to D.C. to prove to her I could be there, but the truth was, I couldn't because we had to be in the studio in the morning, and the guys were counting on me.

"I love you, Lucy." I wiped my nose with my shirt sleeve. "I'll always love you."

"This isn't the end. You'll see." I promised myself I'd fix this as soon as I had time. The band would do this tour, and then I could swing down and woo Lucy back. Maybe it would be good for us to take a break. I could focus on the music, and she could realize that nobody else was right for her.

"I'm sorry, Noah." She sniffled. "You're going to do great things. I hope that you'll let me know when you're in town."

"Sure." I was already planning it. "I'll put you on the guest list."

When we hung up, Shane said from the doorway, "Sorry, I didn't mean to eavesdrop, but I came to find you. You okay?"

I nodded. "It's just another setback."

He laughed. "Sure thing."

But the thought of Lucy with someone else clawed at my insides, and I knew I'd need every bit of distraction the next few months of recording and touring would bring me to honor her request and give her the freedom she needed.

I figured, once the band was on solid ground, then we could see where we stood. I just didn't know it would take so long.

Chapter Six

Lucy

Exiting the National Gallery of Art onto the Mall in the late afternoon always gave me such a special sense of place. To my left, the Capitol bustled with activity, a reminder that unlike the museums flanking it, that historic building breathed with the vibrancy of current events. To my right, the Washington monument stood as a reminder of who we were as a country, where we'd come from. Visitors from all over the world took advantage of the richness of this one magical place.

When I was a kid, I never tired of taking the Metro in and losing myself in all the rich history of our nation's capital. As long as I could remember, I'd dreamed of attending Georgetown because I loved being so near all of this. When I'd finally started college, my long-term ambition had been to continue on to Georgetown Law and then to work in government.

Noah derailed even that simple plan without meaning to when he suggested I take an art history elective.

For him, it had been a question of taking the path of least resistance, but he'd been right. I did take the art history elective. Then another. Soon, that certainty I'd go to law school became clouded by teachers asking me if I'd considered going into museum studies. It all made so much sense, it was like someone had laid breadcrumbs for me to follow them, and Noah had come along as the path ran cold and pointed me in the right direction.

But he hadn't come with me. He always disappeared like the figment of a dream.

I shook off the memory. It was Monday now, and my self-imposed time limit for dwelling on Noah had run out. I cursed him for showing up and disturbing the peace I'd managed to find, consoling myself in the knowledge he'd become so consumed by his music, he'd forget about me again until the next time he passed this way. I should have moved when I had the chance. I still could, but I didn't want to put Owen through that.

As I neared the steps to my town house, the air seemed to spark with residual wormholes traveling from the past with details from Saturday night I'd already started to forget—like the way he'd smelled. Noah always had a kind of post-concert funk like Pigpen from Charlie Brown, but where someone else might find that horrifying, I never mistook that rock 'n' roll cologne for him. It was just the life he carried around with him. Underneath that scent, when I stood close, when he shared my breathing space, there, a single whiff could unlock things time had tried to erase. With a sniff, I breathed in a potent elixir that could dredge up a memory of the two of us, snuggled in a sleeping bag on the camping trip we somehow convinced my mom to let us take. There wasn't much sleeping.

As I climbed up the stoop to my door, as if the time warp could carry sound, a man's voice said, "Lucy Griffin?"

I spun, surprised at how much I hoped to find Noah there again, but it was just a young man in a delivery uniform. He held out a clipboard toward me. "Are you Lucy Griffin?"

I nodded and signed, hoping he hadn't tricked me into a signature for a ballot initiative. He thanked me, then opened the door to a van double-parked on the street and retrieved a vase filled with purple lilacs. A sob broke of its own accord, and I wondered if I was starting to turn into one of those people who cried at commercials. They were just flowers.

But they could only have come from one person, and this was intended to prove he wasn't bluffing the other night. I didn't know how to feel about that. I wished I only felt renewed resolution to wait him out. But in truth, he'd lit a match with this gesture, like the night he'd serenaded me, setting fire to a secret pleasure I'd never admit.

My mom called from the top of the stairs. "Lucy? Do you need a hand?"

I waved her to go back inside, but the damage was done. She'd want to investigate the flowers. As I carried them inside, I tried to rid myself of the various things I held in my other hand so I could snatch the card out first. No such luck. Mom grabbed the vase from the crook of my right elbow and set it on the kitchen table, plucking the card from the holder as she stepped back to admire them.

"Are you sure you haven't met someone? These are beautiful."

Thankfully, she handed the card over without a word. I slipped it from the envelope and snorted when I read it, which was an unfortunate reaction since it only encouraged Mom to steal it and read it aloud for herself.

" 'I've lost your phone number. Call me.' " She repeated, "Call me? This isn't a local number." Her eyes narrowed. "Isn't 212 New York City?"

Shit. Nothing got past her.

"Must have been sent to the wrong person, huh?"

It was worth the effort. Mom flipped over the envelope. "Then why does it say Lucy Griffin?"

I put the card back in the holder, ignoring her.

"Lucy?"

Note to past self: *Eat the card.*

"Does this have anything to do with the man who was here Saturday night?" She tilted her head.

I sighed. "They're from Noah."

Her face pinched. Not much, but I saw it. The judgment. "What are you going to do about it?"

"Nothing?" I looked at her for a reaction, but she took that moment to master her expression. "I don't know, Mom. I expected him to go back home and things would go back to how they always were."

"And how were they always, Lucy?"

Whose side was she on, anyway? "I'm better off without him. Didn't you say that?"

She glanced toward the living room where Owen sat on the floor, surrounded by Duplo Legos, and said so low I almost didn't hear, "I worry about the boy."

I snorted. "You think this would be better if he had someone showing up here once in a blue moon? If he got his hopes up every time the phone rang or there was a knock at the door, always watching for a man who never comes?"

"Are we talking about Owen now? Or you?"

"I stopped getting my hopes up years ago, Mom. Noah will give up soon enough." I'd just have to stifle any unwanted longings he unlocked in the meantime.

"But what if he doesn't?"

My stomach soured.

I couldn't entertain the thought. I'd made a perfectly safe world here for Owen, and Noah could never casually enter into our arrangement. It would be a disaster.

Of course, Noah would probably walk right back out once he found out how badly I'd deceived him, and that was a whole extra level of pain I didn't want any of us to suffer.

"I don't want my son to live with half a dad. I know from personal experience that it's a new heartbreak every day."

She nodded. I knew she understood. "I'm sorry that I didn't cut your dad out of your life entirely. I do get it."

I didn't want to argue with her of all people about this. "I'm not blaming you. You couldn't have known." But I'd lived with the reality of her decisions, so I did know. I knew the emotional cost of waiting for someone who parceled out commitment on birthdays and holidays.

She eyed the flowers. "Maybe there's hope for that one yet?"

I almost laughed. The flowers would outlive his attention. As if flowers could ever replace a person. "Hope is a brutal master, Mom."

Hope was what had kept me waiting and waiting for Noah to settle down until I had to face the fact that he'd always choose his music over me.

We used to make things work even long distance for a while, back when I was in college, when I thought his music was a hobby he'd tire of. The transition from high school hadn't been easy on either of us. I should have broken it off sooner, but instead it was like we were going seventy-miles an hour and the car came to a complete stop, but our bodies continued forward, unaware that a crash was inevitable.

Noah was always scraping together enough money to take the train down from New York. He'd just show up at my dorm, night or day, and he could always flirt his way inside, befriending everyone like he was practicing for the meet and greets of a rock star life.

One afternoon, it must have been my second year, I'd had a meeting with my adviser. We'd reviewed the courses for pre-law, and I just needed to decide on my elective. It was weighing me down more than it should have.

I walked back to the residence hall, deep in thought, but as soon as the heavy security door clicked in place behind me, someone called out, "You have a guest in the community room."

My face melted into a giant grin. Noah and I talked and texted constantly, but seeing him in the flesh was like breathing oxygen again.

Fortunately, my roommate was in class all day, so we spent an hour doing all the things we talked about doing to each other on our late-night phone calls that left us frustrated as hell. Then we headed out for food, strolling across Georgetown, hand in hand, stupidly in love and casually taking every moment for granted. It was such a clear beautiful day, blue skies, with a slight chill in the air and his warm hand in mine.

Not for the first time, he said, "Come visit me for a change."

I sighed. As if that were an option. I had my own narrow concerns. "I've got to figure out my course schedule for next semester, and I need an elective."

He stopped dead in the middle of the sidewalk. "You should study art history."

I laughed at him. "How is that remotely practical?"

He grew so serious. "You said you need an elective, right? Wouldn't that be an easy A for you? You're always dragging me to museums."

I shrugged. "It's not a terrible idea."

At the corner, he started bouncing on his toes, pointing me toward a music store where he dragged me inside and picked up a guitar to show off. He sang "Lucy in the Sky with Diamonds," and I told him to stop because he was embarrassing me. But he wasn't really embarrassing me. The customers in the shop applauded his skills, and I beamed with pride that he'd been performing only for me.

He'd gotten so much better so fast, like playing grungy gigs was the real education. He sounded like a professional. And holy God did he look the part with leather bracelets hanging from his wrist and his hair defying all logic. More than one girl checked him out, like he might be someone famous. More than one boy too.

But he was mine—temporarily.

His evident progress made me a little sad because, selfishly, I kept waiting for his little two-man band to fail, so he would come home to me. He was supposed to finally grow up, get his GED, attend community college, and maybe find an office job. Then, he was supposed to promise me a future where we'd be together. I worried I could wait years for him, but he would follow his own dreams.

Soon the day came to an end as it always did, and I forced my heart to close a little to save myself from the pain of losing him to New York once again.

Chapter Seven

Noah

Micah was turning into an old man before my eyes. He'd bought a boring-ass town house in Brooklyn a couple of years ago, after selling a couple of songs that became hits for other bands. It was like he just knew he'd settle down with a nice girl from Georgia one day. And that's exactly what he'd done. He was already nesting. It twisted me up with envy.

And really, it pissed me off how quickly he'd moved from dirt-bag afterparty groupie slut to homebody, leaving me pulling double duty with the cock chasers on tour. Occasionally Shane could pinch hit and distract a few girls, but with no Micah to balance the center of gravity, the fame fuckers all eventually circled me.

What? Was I expected to be a saint?

When we'd first started performing, I'd avoided the one-night stands and let Micah indulge in all the whoring. It wasn't until Lucy made it clear we were no longer an *us* that I dove headfirst into the sex part of rock 'n' roll. I mean, my girlfriend *dumped* me. Once she was actually married, could I be blamed for taking comfort in the hot girls fawning over me after shows? It fed my vanity and gave proof to the band's mounting success.

Once I'd dabbled, I quickly became a connoisseur of the girl fan. Boy fans were another matter altogether. A few offered to take me home, but boys mostly just wanted to *be* me, wanted the life that looked so compelling from the outside. Girls, though? There were so many, and it was too easy. I'd wake up with a name and a phone number Sharpied on my hip with no recollection of who the name belonged to.

When Micah met Jo, the attention all got astronomically worse for me. That was when I decided to try to imitate Micah by taming one of these girls and keeping her beyond her natural expiration date. But apparently, Crystal had set her sights higher than me.

Micah had been far luckier. Jo had crashed into his life when he was least expecting her, and although he'd had reason to doubt her motives for wanting to be in his life—I mean she *was* a paparazza at the time—she'd turned out to be his perfect fit. Nothing had ever come that easily for me.

But I liked Jo, and it was nice to be able to pause for a moment in their happy home for a quick dinner with my found family before transitioning back to an empty apartment. I didn't exactly miss Crystal, but I would miss the company. Maybe I should get a cat.

Shane, Micah and I settled around the kitchen island as Jo rummaged in the fridge for something to feed us, apologizing. "I didn't expect you all here tonight."

Yeah, another reminder that we'd been unceremoniously kicked off a tour. Would the humiliation never end?

Behind me, the glass door to the porch slid open, startling the hell out of me, as a gorgeous redhead stepped into the kitchen.

Micah said what I was thinking: "Well, hello."

The girl's eyes widened as they bounced from Micah, then to Shane, and then to me. They lingered on me.

And I recognized that look. That was the look of a girl who kept a magazine photo of me on her bedroom wall. That was the look of a girl who would come home with me if I crooked a finger. I confess, my dread of being alone put the thought in my head. But the last thing I needed right now was another shallow fuck. I was through with girls who got stars in their eyes when they gazed upon me, like I wasn't even really there.

Sure, I could use her to hold off the pain for a few hours, but she could never fill the gaping chasm where my soul used to be. I'd already tried filling that void with all the wrong things. My only hope now was to hold out for the one I believed could slake my thirst.

Jo ran through introductions, as if this girl hadn't already known exactly who we were. I winked, and her whole face turned bright red in a way that reminded me of Shane.

"Gentlemen, let me present my newest coworker and a brand-new resident of our fair city, Layla—" she paused "— shit, I've already forgotten your last name."

"Beckett. Layla Beckett."

I saw with horror the exact moment when it happened, when my best friend saw a girl he might want to pursue. He gave her a shy smile.

Oh, Jesus. All Shane needed was to fall ass backward in love with a girl who fetishized rock musicians, one who'd clearly already fantasized about climbing in bed with me. Hadn't he been paying attention? Hadn't he been there to witness Crystal toss me over for a bigger catch? This dance had become as familiar as breathing.

As we waited for pizza delivery, Jo started asking us about the tour. "How was it traveling with Whiplash?"

I grumbled, and Micah said, "Noah doesn't want to talk about it."

Jo winced. "Oh, right. Sorry. How long are you home?"

She avoided the topic of our ouster from the last stop, possibly to keep that news from Layla. Probably to avoid ruffling my feathers.

Micah answered, "We have to head back out on Sunday."

Jo's shoulders slumped. "Okay, then. I'm glad you got home early."

The love she showed for him made me happy for Micah, but it rankled me so deep I couldn't stand it. And when she kissed him, like they still had all the sparks of first love, all I could think was how unfair the universe could be to let some people have everything while others only got pieces.

It made me wonder about the girl currently sending heart eyes over at Shane.

To girls like Layla, our world appeared glamorous, and we all looked so fascinating. But she didn't know the first thing about the realities of this life. More than likely, she'd get her fix of musician fucking, become disenchanted with everything, and return to her regular life with a lot of memories she'd dole out as anecdotes to impress her friends one day. That, or she'd come to like the life just fine, and start looking for someone higher on the food chain. Like Crystal had done.

Shane had to know a girl like Layla would be one or the other. And if she was a fame fucker, who would be next in line? That would be me. It was always me, and Shane hated me for it. Not because I ever let one of his groupie girlfriends seduce me, but because they always eventually tried to.

It became my top priority to find out how easily she'd switch teams on him. I faced her. "So, Ginger Spice. Where did you say you're from?"

"I didn't. I'm from Indiana."

I thought about that. Indiana. Indiana. That was a while ago. It was . . . "July. We were in Indianapolis in July."

"Uh-huh."

Shane piped in. "Oh, yeah. Maybe Layla was there."

"Yup. I totally was." She bit her lip, saucy little flirt that she was.

"Sure." I hoped she was lying.

"No, I really was." Her big innocent eyes nearly threw me off.

Hmm. Coming to our show wasn't incriminating in itself. "So, where did we play then?"

"You played the Lawn at the White River State Park. Chain Smoke opened for you."

I didn't even remember that much. I looked at Shane. "Is that right?"

Micah and Shane cheered for her correct answer, as if this wasn't proof the girl had groupie tendencies.

Once my spidey senses tingled, I couldn't stop. I couldn't stand the looks Shane shared with this interloper all through dinner. I kept pecking at her to try to get her to show her hand but only ended up pissing everyone off. I was just trying to protect Shane from inevitable heartbreak. He was such an easy mark, and when a girl that pretty showed him any interest, he was a sitting duck. Why was I the bad guy?

I could only hope to drag his ass away before it was too late, so as soon as he pushed his plate back, I said, "Let's hit the road, man. I'm beat."

Outside, he punched my arm. "What the hell was that?"

"I don't know what you're talking about." He should have thanked me for saving him. I'd gotten him out before he'd asked for her number.

"Were you trying to flirt? Or do you think everyone is Crystal?"

It hit too close to home.

"Sure. I was totally flirting."

"You need to grow up, Noah." He skipped down the steps ahead of me, and spun to the left, heading down the sidewalk toward his own place without looking back.

I didn't worry. We fought all the time. I had his interest at heart, and he'd forget about this girl by tomorrow. It was for the best.

Maybe I should have told him what was really eating me. I slid my phone out of my pocket and opened the call history to verify I hadn't missed anything. I'd sent Lucy the flowers over an hour ago. I'd paid extra to get the delivery driver to wait until she came home to make sure she got them, and again for receipt of delivery. She would have read my note.

Still nothing. How long did I wait until I gave up?

I'd already let Lucy go once before. It was maybe six years ago. She'd started seriously dating some guy, and before I had a chance to win her back, she showed up at one of our gigs and dropped a bomb on me.

That night, I'd texted her: *Hey, reminder, we're playing at the Black Cat tonight. I know it's late for a weeknight, but I'd love to see you! Bring John with you. I'll leave your names on a guest list.*

Shane poked fun at me for checking in on Lucy every single time we passed through D.C. but what was I supposed to do? She'd meant everything to me, and even though it took a while to get over the shock of her dating other guys, she was still a close friend. So maybe I visited her at the museum every time I came to town. And sure, whenever she came to a show, I played better than usual.

I hadn't seen her in a while though. She'd missed our last few shows, but that night I saw her in the crowd. She looked hot with her hair all down around her shoulders, eyes closed, dancing with her arms over her head. When she glanced up, I winked at her and shredded my guitar to show off.

I thought I was being extra cool by inviting that Chad she was seeing to come along with her to the show. He bounced a little out of time with the music, swaying more than dancing, but I was glad he'd come. I wanted to see who I was competing against.

During a break, I found them in the crowd, shook his hand, and leaned in to give Lucy a hug. "Thanks for coming out. It means the world."

"I'm glad I got a chance to see you tonight." She grimaced weirdly before saying, "We have some news."

She glanced over at the guy. He had on a suit, and not ironically.

I shrugged. "Yeah?"

She lifted her hand, displaying a prominent diamond. "John's asked me to marry him."

"Oh," I said. "That's—" I looked from one to the other and mustered up a happy face. "Congratulations!"

"He's going to be running for Congress, so this will be public information shortly. I wanted to tell you face-to-face."

My smile held, but the words that slipped out were, "Do you love him?"

Both of them gave me the hundred-yard stare, like I'd shit on the floor.

"That's . . ." Lucy grabbed me by the arm and dragged me against the wall. "Look, I can hear your preconceived judgment, but John and I share the same goals. I know it all looks really ordinary to you, but I want to build my career and my family here in D.C."

"Do you love him, Lucy?"

"Yes." She didn't sound convinced. "I think you'd like him if you got to know him. He's kind and funny."

I bit my lip so I wouldn't add, "and boring." Instead, I sucked it up. "It's your life. If he's what you really want, I wish you all the best."

She wrapped her arms around my neck and spoke right into my ear. "I'll never love anyone like I've loved you, Noah. Understand I needed more than a phantom boyfriend in my life. I need a grown-up relationship."

What was I supposed to say? I fully respected her decision to marry someone who could offer her so much more than I could. I really did. Still, I couldn't say it didn't hurt to know she'd go home with him, and I'd go back to a lonely tour bus or a nameless fuck.

And I'd spend the rest of the night remembering how her eyes couldn't hide her desire for me when she'd seen me onstage. I knew that look because I'd seen that look in the eye-fucks of fan girls who'd later shared my bed.

So I hugged her back and said, "Good luck, Lucy."

She let out an enormous sigh. "Thank you."

I gritted my teeth and pushed her back. "Look. I've got to run. I need to go grab a bottle of water. We're supposed to be back onstage in five."

"Yeah. Of course."

She went back to her fiancé, and before the next set ended, Lucy was gone.

Chapter Eight

Lucy

I fished the card out of the trash.

Again.

One of these days, my mom would get there first and carry the bag out to the curb.

Every time I pulled the card out, I read it. Throwing it away at this point was symbolic; the number had seared itself to my brain.

I saw it in my sleep. I dreamt I dialed it.

In my dream, the phone was already in my hand, ringing and ringing. When he finally answered, he said, "What do you want?"

I woke up in a sweat. What did I want?

After a week, I put the soiled card in the shoe box I kept in my closet. When I'd been married to John, I'd hidden that shoe box inside another bigger box that held the huge art history books from grad school I couldn't part with.

The box was filled with letters Noah had sent me from New York, all written in that jagged script. I opened one and unfolded it, smiling at the promises it held, all the fiction we'd once believed.

That was the first moment I nearly broke down and called. I hated him so much for making that possibility a reality. It was as cruel as setting a plate of chocolate cookies in front of someone trying to cut sugar from their diet. Noah was my sugar. Delicious but so, so bad for me. I knew eventually I'd need a nibble. I'd think I could take a small taste—just call and hear his voice again. But it wouldn't be enough, and he'd amp up the stakes, whispering the words he'd once written to me in those letters.

I've never loved anyone else.

My soul craved that kind of understanding, to succumb to the power of that emotion once more before I died.

The devil on my shoulder prodded me, asking me, "What's the worst thing that could happen?" It wasn't like anything could get any worse between us. We'd already broken up. We'd already had a fling that ended with a four-year split. How could I be faulted for wanting to give it another chance? I'd never recovered from the hurt the last time, so what was the harm of stanching a wound for as long as he could give me?

If I could have lived with stolen moments, our problems would have been solved. I might have contented myself with a one-nighter here and there if I only needed to worry about myself, but my last one-nighter with Noah had forever changed my priorities.

Part of me always figured that maybe one day, in our old age, we'd both retire and could finally share our lives.

Or maybe we'd be reincarnated.

And those thoughts left me sad. Why couldn't we take our happiness now?

Was I rationalizing? Or was I making sense?

I picked up my phone and saw his number in my mind. Where was he? Probably in some college town with some college girl in his bed. Or the girl he'd been rumored to be dating. And that was another reason I couldn't call him.

What was I thinking? Of course he'd move on. A week for Noah might as well be an eternity.

"Mommy?"

I sighed. Nap time was over. "Coming, baby."

I dropped the phone on my nightstand and went in to pick Owen up, cradling him to me. I did have a part of Noah anyway.

And that was the other complication.

If I called, if I let Noah into my life, I'd have to tell him about this child. And it terrified me on so many levels.

Owen squeezed my neck tight, letting me stand up with him spidermonkeyed around my waist. I carried him like that downstairs and deposited him onto the sofa. He bounced on the cushions until I shot him a look to remind him he wasn't allowed to jump on the furniture.

"Where Nana?"

My mom was practically raising him lately. Since she'd moved in, she'd been more spouse than John had ever been. "She went out. You want to go see the dinosaurs today?"

I packed up his stroller with emergency snacks and toys and led him out to the sidewalk. A trip to the Museum of Natural History would keep me occupied long enough to shake off the temptation I'd nearly succumbed to. Maybe another week, and I'd have forgotten about the number altogether.

But as I unfolded the stroller and watched Owen climb in, Noah's number played inside my mind like an ear worm. Like one of his band's catchy songs that I could never escape no matter how hard I tried.

Maybe I'd go back to yoga and meditate this desire away.

Owen swung his feet, rocking the stroller as he whined, "Let's goooooo."

I needed to take the advice of a toddler and move on. I would do it.

Just as I started pushing Owen up the sidewalk, our mailman turned the corner heading toward us. I waited another minute so he could hand me my stack of bills.

Owen wiggled, and I asked, "Do you want to walk?"

That quieted him for a moment. I should have been making him walk. He was big enough now, and most of the other moms I'd met at parks had weaned their kids from the stroller at three. Owen would be four in December. Maybe I was babying him. But he was still a baby to me. Plus, he was too heavy to carry, and there was no way he wouldn't get tired halfway to the museum.

The mailman saw me and waved, passing by several houses as he flipped through envelopes in his bag. He said, "Phew. So glad to get rid of this one."

I laughed, confused. "What?"

He handed me a stack of junk mail, then used both hands to unload a rectangular package. The weight of it caused my hand to drop several inches before I adjusted. He tipped his hat and headed back up the sidewalk. I crammed the envelopes into my bag and followed the way he'd gone, pushing Owen with one hand while I wondered at the object I held.

My first thought was that it could be a paperweight. I was coming up on my fifth year working at the National Gallery. Maybe I was getting some recognition.

My next thought was that it was some random promotional item, though it seemed an elaborate and costly way to market.

Neither of those possibilities rang true because the packaging was hardly professional, like brown grocery bag paper, and my name and address were hand-written in black Sharpie. No return address was listed.

This fact birthed a hope I didn't even want to acknowledge as possible.

I pushed the package into the bag, a mystery to resolve later, and picked up the pace. The weather was perfect for strolling, and Owen pointed out everything, narrating our walk, like a live-action Richard Scarry book while I modeled correct pronunciation absently.

"Lellow twuck."

"Yup, that's a yellow truck."

When we got to the museum, I unhooked Owen so he could climb the stairs. Our goal for the day was to visit the hall of fossils and come face to face with ancient history. It was like a cosmic metaphor for my life. I had skeletons, too. Of course, five minutes into the museum, plans changed immediately when Owen announced that he needed to pee, so we made a U-turn to find a bathroom before disaster struck. Owen shouted as he pointed up at the elephant. I turned to look up for barely a second and my face slammed into the shoulder of someone who'd positioned himself there. I stepped back, apologizing, and heard a male voice say, "Lucy?"

This was becoming weird.

"Oh." My eyes focused in on the man in front of me and then on the woman beside him. "Hello, John."

Speaking of coming face to face with ancient history.

Owen tugged on my hand, and I worried he'd break free and run into the crowd, but for a moment, I stopped and studied the tableau before me. My ex-husband, his new wife (newer than me anyway), and their daughter asleep on her shoulder. This wasn't awkward.

John gave me a once-over, and habit compelled me to brush down the front of my jeans as if I'd been caught wearing a wrinkled skirt. I returned the appraisal, taking in his relaxed Saturday attire and the hint of silver at his temples. The last few years in politics must have aged him a bit. He still looked as handsome as ever. I forced a smile.

"How've you been?" he asked, like we were at a high school reunion.

I didn't have a prepared answer for that. What is one supposed to say in such circumstances? Owen yanked, and the urgency of the situation took over my instincts.

"Great. But I've got a kid who needs the potty."

He nodded. "We'll have to catch up sometime."

Did his wife's smile tighten?

I managed, "Nice seeing you," before Owen succeeded in pulling me after him while I replayed that minute in my mind like an afterimage. I knew John had remarried. I'd never had the occasion to meet his wife. She was a little younger than me, but probably not by much. Definitely boobier. I glanced back for a refresher on that, but they'd moved on.

At the door to the women's restroom, we encountered a line.

"Can you hold on a little bit more, buddy?"

He crossed his knees together and made a sad little grunting noise as if that would help distract him from wetting his pants. It had been a while since we'd had to deal with accidents in public. Night was a different story. I didn't want this to become a problem, so I said to the women in line, "Excuse me, but would any of you mind if my son went ahead?"

The lady in front of me gave me a judgmental glance. "Just use the men's room."

Another woman added, "Can't his dad take him?"

Wouldn't that have made things easier?

I glared at them both but bent down to Owen's level. "Do you think you could be a big boy and go into the other restroom on your own?"

I didn't dare take him in there myself.

He knew how to do it all. He'd have a hard time washing his hands, but we could come back to this restroom for that.

He nodded vigorously, so I held his hand and let him disappear into the men's room. Alone. And it made me feel powerless. There were always going to be things I couldn't control as he got older. I couldn't be there for every big moment in his life.

Oh, no. I suddenly realized I hadn't made sure he only needed to go pee. I closed my eyes and said a brief prayer to whatever gods controlled defecation to please, please hold off on the shits until this afternoon.

I hovered outside the door, feeling like a creep. To appear less fixated on the men's room, I grabbed the stack of envelopes out of my bag and flipped through them, separating out the trash to toss. When I put the remaining bills in my bag, my fingers brushed up against the package that had arrived earlier. I wrapped my hand around it, uncomfortably aware that it was about the right size to contain a dildo. But it would need to be made out of crystal to be so heavy. Curiosity won out and I lifted it from my bag to study it. The postmark said Brooklyn. My heart began to beat faster.

I glanced over at the men's room, wondering if I should go in and check on Owen.

A man approached the door, and I stopped him. "Hi. My son is in there. Would you mind asking him if he needs me?"

The man's face registered disgust, but he was too civilized to say no. "Sure."

I waited a beat, and finally Owen came out. The man followed and said, "He was having a hard time reaching the sink. I gave him a boost."

"Thanks." I nodded to dismiss him from his service, then bent to make sure Owen's clothes were on right. "Good job, buddy! I'm super proud!"

"What's that?" he said, pointing at the package still in my hand. "Can I see?"

"Um." I had no idea what was in the package. What if it really was a crystal dildo? I suspected I knew who'd sent it. Surely, he wouldn't have sent me a sex toy out of the blue as a sign of his eternal devotion. "You know what? Let's go get something to eat."

Owen bounced a little. "Cookies?"

"We'll see what they have."

I steered him toward the cafe which at least had a shark on display, so I could call this an educational side trip. I got myself a coffee and a gelato for Owen. As he ate, he hummed a jaunty little tune, happy as could be.

"What's that you're singing, kiddo?"

"It's the poopy song." He giggled like he'd said the funniest thing in the world.

"Does it have words?"

He started scatting in the way he would when he'd make up songs. "Boop boop da doo. Loo loo doopy doo. Boopadoo. Poop." He started laughing again.

"That's hilarious, Owen."

While he was occupied with singing and eating, I slipped the package onto my lap and peeled at the seam, hoping to get the tape off without loudly ripping the paper. The ambient noise in the cafe and museum at large would likely cover it, but just in case a life-sized rubber cock dropped out, I didn't want to take my chances.

The paper fell away to reveal a navy box, about the shape and size to hold a Precious Moments figurine—on the other end of the morality spectrum. The flap slipped out easily enough, and I turned the box upside down with my hand underneath to catch whatever might materialize.

To my great shock, it was a bronze dolphin attached to a craggy rock base. The dolphin was chipped, but it had once been beautifully painted in a cobalt blue and white with lovely gold flecks across its back. I knew this because I'd given it to Noah that day we'd driven to Ocean City. I couldn't believe he'd kept it all this time.

"Ma'am." A woman stopped by our table. "You dropped something." She pointed toward the floor where a folded page of stationery lay.

"Thank you," I said as I bent to pick it up.

In case I'd been in any doubt as to the origin of the rather uniquely ugly statue, the jagged handwriting on the page confirmed my suspicions.

Lucy,

When you gave me this, I had nothing to offer you. You already had the world at your feet, and all I had was me. I thought I could become someone worthy of you. I thought if I had enough money, enough talent, enough success, I might be enough.

I've managed to garner money, a bit of talent, and some definition of success.

What more do you need? Tell me. I'll find it and bring it to you.

Noah

My heartbeat pulsed in my fingertips as I stared at his question, mouth agape. Oh, Noah. What more did I need?

Time. I needed his time.

How could he not have figured that out?

Had he really thought I wanted him to make more money? Be more successful? More talented? More educated? Anything other than home with me?

I set the dolphin on the table, wanting to lose myself in the sentimentality of the gesture, but then I glanced at the wrapping with the stamp from Brooklyn on it.

It was sweet of him to remind me that he loved me from afar, but that wasn't really loving me, was it? That was no different than obsessing over a rock star in a magazine. Or obsessing over a rock star in my memories.

If it was only *my* life that hung in the balance, I might take the risk. The worst that could happen would be another broken heart. But I had someone else's heart to protect.

I put the letter and dolphin back in the box and the box in my bag, then pulled out the wet wipes. Owen had managed to get chocolate on the bridge of his nose. He was reaching his tongue out past the corners of his mouth to get whatever he could reach, but I got there and cleaned him up with an ignominious swabbing across his face.

"Come on, little guy. Let's go look at bones."

He latched on to my hand, and as he dragged me through the exhibit, I kept my eyes peeled for John, hoping not to run into that bit of my own history again quite so soon. We'd managed to split amicably enough, but I had enough ugly memories to last a lifetime.

The first time John and I fought because of Noah, it had been after a show. I must have been about twenty-six at the time.

That night Noah's band opened at the 9:30 Club. It was a huge milestone in their career, one more piece of evidence they were about to break out. I was thrilled for him, and of course I wanted to go out and see him, but convincing John to go was complicated. He'd started to worry about getting recognized in places like nightclubs. I could have told him it was the rare concertgoer who would be able to identify a congressman from Virginia.

But I'd missed Noah the past few times he'd come through town, and I insisted on John's attendance by threatening to go alone. John really didn't like me to go out alone.

So we went, and we had a pretty good time. Better than we'd had in a few months. Or so I thought.

Noah came out to the merch area to sign things, and I had to get into a line to finally say hi and give him a hug. He was sweaty and disheveled, like he'd just gone through a car wash, but the girls around me whispered and giggled and took pictures of him when they weren't standing on tiptoes to gape at Micah who had a line of his own to contend with.

In those days, I'd convinced myself that seeing Noah as infrequently as I did would be enough, like he was a favorite painting I could hang on a wall and look at safely once in a while without it reaching back out and biting me.

John griped about the crush of bodies and suggested we hit the road, but I held firm. "It's only going to take a few minutes."

Fifteen minutes later, we made it to the front where Noah smiled wide and opened his arms for a hug. "You should have cut the line!"

As if.

His smell was so familiar, so Noah, and I fit so easily against his chest, but I broke away after a moment, sensing John standing at my shoulder. I leaned back and said, "Congratulations on the gig!" I didn't mention all the memories I had of coming to this venue with him, like the night he'd dragged me out to see Amos Lee, and I'd fallen in love with those songs while Noah stood behind me, arms wrapped around my waist, swaying back and forth. I still sometimes listened to those songs now and remembered those perfect moments.

There was too much history and too little time. I became increasingly aware of all the people waiting their turn. I'd just wanted to lay eyes on Noah and make sure he was well.

Noah held out a hand to John, and as they shook, John told him they'd put on a hell of a show. Realizing everyone else had come up to ask for a picture or an autograph, I suddenly had the uncanny feeling of asking to sit on Santa's lap as an adult. I blurted out, "It was so good to see you. Let's get coffee soon."

John tugged my hand, and I let him pull me toward the exit.

Outside, as we waited along the crowded sidewalk, waiting to be picked up, John scanned the street, grousing, "Where's the damn Uber?" As if we were waiting for a getaway car.

At last the white Civic honked twice from the corner. We rode in silence, and I convinced myself it had been a long day, and we were both tired. We were always tired.

But when I asked him, "Did you have a good time?" he snapped a curt, "I need a drink," at me, and I knew there was more to his mood. I chalked it up to stress. His job put him under a lot more pressure than he'd expected. Campaigning had been exciting and fun, but the actual work came with a steep learning curve. I knew he'd settle in, and then we'd iron out the wrinkles and get back to normal.

As soon as we entered the town house, he poured that drink and drained it in one pull. And then he turned dark eyes on me.

"You made a fool of yourself, tonight," he said.

The words landed right between my shoulders, forcing me to instinctively hunch up, a reaction I'd seen in my mom a thousand times. He was searching for a fight.

"For enjoying a concert?" I laughed as if I hadn't noticed his tone. I wasn't going to play. "That was a great show. The band really sounds better than ever, don't you think?"

"You know what I mean. Your tongue was practically hanging out of your mouth."

He'd never acted jealous of Noah or anyone else this way before, but he wasn't entirely wrong. I'd been utterly mesmerized by Noah onstage, because *my* Noah had gone from the boy who'd climbed onto my roof with a junky guitar to a bonafide rock musician, and he'd been incredible. I could totally understand how groupies were formed.

But what I'd felt was pride, nothing more than that. I hadn't flirted with Noah or even lingered in the hug, though honestly, I probably could have. I needed a hug, and was it wrong to miss my best friend?

"Can we talk about this tomorrow?"

He shrugged and headed up to bed.

I probably shouldn't have brought John with me to the show, but if he was in the mood, he'd find another pretext. It wasn't really even a fight about Noah. It was a fight about us.

We'd slowly had to face the reality that we'd married for all the wrong reasons: convenience, ambition, loneliness, security. But then we'd tried to start a family, for all the right reasons. We both wanted to raise a brood of children. We'd put our names on the preschool waiting lists. We'd dreamed of taking them to the museums and the playgrounds nearby. Of course, starting a family was what upwardly mobile politicians did, and we'd already planned the photos of our three children in a pumpkin patch on the glossy fliers that would appear in the mailboxes of John's congressional district. It just so happened the picture-perfect political family life matched my own visions, and I desperately wanted to make that dream a reality.

We hadn't planned for the possibility that family wouldn't just happen.

I'd done everything right. I'd set aside the wild and unpredictable boyfriend and found a stable, upstanding man who was the polar opposite of my own father. We'd bought the town house on G street near great private schools and had dinner together every night at six.

We just needed the kids.

But month after month, my period came, and we'd started to consider whether a fertility clinic was in our future. And then whether we even had a future. Shared grief led to blame led to fighting.

That was the basis of our ongoing argument. Noah's existence didn't help, and I decided that I needed to pull the plug and stop going to see his shows. It could only make my life easier not to have to face the path I hadn't traveled every single time I saw him.

Chapter Nine

Noah

Festivals were always a nightmare of chaos and noise and dirt and people. While we waited to perform late in the day, I considered going back to the hotel since sleep had eluded me for days if not weeks, but the silence of the hotel only amplified the silence of my phone.

She hadn't called.

Maybe in my arrogance or revisionist history, I'd embellished Lucy's reaction to me when I'd seen her two weeks ago. Maybe she'd found it easier than me to shake off the memory and go back to whatever she considered normal life. Is that how she let four years pass without a word?

I lay on a fold-out chair in a quasi-air-conditioned tent, hoping I might manage at least a nap while the energy of rock shows on multiple stages drowned out my thoughts. At least back here, we weren't constantly assaulted by fans. Shane had suggested we go watch the other bands perform, but I was in no mood to pose for pictures and sign autographs. The whole day was a waste in my opinion.

A couple of voices disturbed my rest. I narrowly opened one eye, still playing opossum, and caught the backside of Shane leading Jo's friend Layla out toward the crowds. I sat up, pissed off that he'd brought her all the way up to Boston, giving her everything she was clearly after. I couldn't believe Shane hadn't learned his lesson from my experience.

I went back to the bus to hide until show time. My joints hurt from playing five consecutive nights in a row. I opened and closed my hand, hoping to work out a cramp that had been bothering me all day.

For about an hour, I may have caught a catnap, but no sooner had I drifted off than my phone buzzed and Micah alerted me we were needed onstage.

I'd never adjusted to the abrupt transition from emptiness and boredom to power and electric energy that occurs on long festival days. One minute, the time wouldn't pass. Then the world bent into fractured sound and motion while magic flowed through my veins. Words could never capture what it means to *be* music.

My hands only started hurting again once we'd left the stage after the final encore. The high of performing hadn't worn off when one of our handlers corralled us and gave us instructions to take care of nature or clean up before going right back to work at an afterparty.

When I was younger, I'd imagined rock stars having crazy parties after the shows. They'd stay up all night with interesting people, trashing rooms, getting high, and having sex. Shane, Micah, and I certainly would have loved to lead that kind of life when we'd first started out. But when we were touring with a dilapidated van from dive to dive, we didn't have the money for a hotel room, let alone the means to trash one. When we'd started earning enough money to stay in hotels and travel in a bus, we found we were too exhausted after all our post-concert obligations to do much of anything except the fucking. That, and we put our money in mutual funds.

And now as I stood at another afterparty, surrounded by a buffet of beautiful young women, I just wanted to go to bed. To sleep. Not that my lack of interest would stop the women from trying. One girl who looked familiar enough to make me wonder if I'd slept with her at some point stood for a selfie with me, then spun to face me, arms around my neck. She had on a shiny lip gloss and smelled like strawberries. I did remember her then. I couldn't place where it had been, somewhere we'd stayed for a night. She'd followed us to the hotel, and I hadn't turned her away.

I glanced around looking for Shane, and when I caught his eye, he nodded once, understanding. It was time to go. But instead of coming to my rescue, he said something to Layla and left. Layla hovered by the bar, watching me, and I wondered if she'd make her move. I hated to hurt Shane, but he should know right from the start what she really wanted.

There was no time like the present.

I extricated myself from Brandy or Delilah or Candy and headed toward the bar, aware that Layla's eyes followed me the whole time. I veered over toward her, waiting for that look, the one that gave away the lust and ambition. As I drew near, I watched for her pupils to dilate or her tongue to dart out to lick her lips. When she did none of these things, I put an arm around her shoulder and drew her closer. Here was her golden opportunity to proposition me.

But instead of leaning in for the kiss I'd never intended to deliver, she backed up. "What the hell, Noah?"

Maybe she was leery because I'd been a little mean to her when Shane had brought her around to rehearsal earlier in the week. A charming apology would fix that. I faced her, placing a hand against the pole just behind her, my lips close enough to speak directly in her ear. "Layla, I'm sorry I was being a total dick to you before."

She shocked me further with an expression of disgust. "You're kind of being a dick now. What are you doing?"

Her scowl was so righteous, it reminded me of myself when fans got too handsy. I honestly thought she might shove me, and it surprised me. Not much around here surprised me anymore. Maybe Layla hadn't been using Shane to get to me. I relaxed a bit, relieved.

To be honest, the realization also brought an unwelcome pang of jealousy. I pushed down the immediate lizard-brain reaction. Shane deserved happiness, even if that meant I'd be left alone as the ironically eligible bachelor.

I still hoped she could liberate me from . . . Amanda or Beverly or Miranda. Despite Layla's attempts to maintain her space, I created the outward appearance of a possible hookup while bringing her into my confidence. I hoped I could trust her. "Look. I just need your help for a minute."

"What are you talking about?" Shit, she was still pissed at me.

I shot my eyes toward the thinning crowd. "Did you see that girl earlier?"

She nodded.

"She's someone I got involved with once, and she will not leave me alone."

"So, why don't you just leave?"

Good question. I would, but I had some historical experience with that particular fan. "She'll follow us to the hotel."

"And? How's this my problem?"

I almost laughed at myself for thinking Layla would ever take a chance with me. If she'd wanted to seduce me, she was doing a piss poor job of it. "If she thinks I'm leaving with you, she'll find someone else to harass."

"There are perhaps a dozen other girls here who would happily leave with you. Why me?"

No sympathy at all. I needed to change tactics; she was my ticket to freedom. I stepped back so she could get a good look at me and shared my truth. "I'm completely exhausted. I haven't slept well in weeks, and I just want to get out of here without having to deal with any drama."

She just arched an eyebrow at me. "Noah, what's Shane going to think if I walk out of here like that with you?"

Damn, had Shane found someone who truly liked him with no other motives? I might have kissed her on the lips if she wouldn't have slapped me. I ran a finger through her orange hair, so much like my best friend's. "Maybe I was wrong about you."

She snarled, "Noah."

Her possessive anger got me to realize that maybe I'd been wrong. About Layla. About the kinds of women who might want to be with a musician. I'd cut Lucy out of this world because she'd always protested about her schoolwork, her job, her responsibilities. I'd never pushed against her excuses because she validated my belief that the world could be divided into neat groups of people. I didn't belong in her world, and she didn't belong in mine.

But we'd managed to juggle both when we'd been kids.

I needed to formulate a new plan.

The first step was to mend fences with my best friend's girlfriend. I'd been pretty rude to her all week. "I guess you think I'm a jackass. For what it's worth, I've been aiming my anger at Shane and Micah because they're my brothers, and they have to put up with me. I didn't mean to get my assery all over you. Apologies?"

"I think Shane could use the apology more than me."

Fair point. But now I had a scheme to execute, and I definitely didn't want to be dealing with any other women tonight. "Will you just come with me? We'll find Shane and then we can all go to the hotel together. That's all. Okay?"

She shrugged. "Fine. But don't ever touch me again."

And that was the moment I gave my rare but official seal of approval to one Layla Beckett.

At the hotel, the two of them lurched for the elevator like they couldn't even wait to get upstairs before pawing at each other. I hooked a left and headed for the bar, dreading the empty room upstairs.

I kept my head bent, hoping to avoid any unwanted attention. I could get laid if that's all I was looking for, but what I needed was a double bourbon to take the edge off my energy and help me sleep.

Hotel rooms were a lonely hell.

In all the times the band passed through D.C., Lucy only came back to my hotel room one time.

That night, the band pulled into town exhausted. We were on back-to-back tours. Our shows were selling out in the U.S., and our agent was trying to get us on a European circuit. If we could hitch our wagon to a larger act and open for them, we could be playing arenas any day now. It was thrilling, but I really needed about two weeks to recuperate. My hands hurt most nights, but I couldn't complain. We were so close to breaking out, we could taste it.

I sent the customary text to Lucy, inviting her to the show, but expected her to turn me down. She hadn't come out the last time we passed through. I'd read the signs and figured she probably didn't need me dropping in to visit her at the museum either. But I sent the invite nonetheless.

During the show, I searched for her and her husband, and when I didn't see them, I felt a weird relief honestly. I wanted to see her, of course I did, but as tired as I was, I needed all my focus to put on a great show, and watching her hang on some other guy would have thrown me off my game. Micah had lit into us the last time we took our foot off the gas and put in a lackluster performance.

As we were loading equipment into the trailer, I stopped to stretch and yawn, ready to fall into bed. Straggling fans hung around trying to chat us up, get autographs, get our hotel keys. And that's when she appeared, looking lost and hurt.

For the record, as far as Lucy went, I had behaved admirably from the first time she'd told me she'd started dating the Chads. I'd raged in private, but I understood, too. I couldn't be in two places at once, and I'd chosen the band for now. I couldn't expect her to wait forever while I chased a dream that required my full attention. I'd always assumed it was a temporary sacrifice, but the rock gods don't make bargains lightly, and the devil requires blood sacrifice. I was paying for my hubris.

It had been my own damn fault that I'd lost Lucy.

And so I'd kept my vow to respect her marriage. Even when I'd visit her for coffee, neither of us had so much as flirted with the possibility of crossing that line into infidelity. I no longer texted her unless I was in town, and I never called her.

I would have continued that valiant streak that night, but I could never stand to see her crying.

She said, "Everything's a mess, and I didn't know where else to turn."

I wrapped an arm around her and led her up to my hotel room, intending nothing more than to comfort her in private away from the curious bystanders and cameras. We'd talk, and then I'd send her back home and re-start the count until I might see her again.

She said, "My mom thinks everything's perfect, but John and I bicker constantly. He left tonight and never came home. It isn't the first time, either. What if he's seeing someone else?"

"Where did he say he went?"

"Tonight, he didn't say. He just walked out while we were arguing."

"What?" This man was living the life I couldn't . . . "Do you want me to go beat him up?" I probably would have if she'd asked, though I doubted my aching fists would have done much damage.

She shook her head. "I shouldn't have come here. I'm sorry. I shouldn't lay all this on you of all people."

"It's fine," I said. "I'm here for you, for whatever you need."

She stared at her hands and said so quietly I almost didn't hear, "The fighting sometimes makes me doubt I found the polar opposite of my father after all."

My heart broke for her, so when a tear rolled across her lips, I brushed it with my thumb, not really meaning to touch her in any way intimate. And when a strand of hair stuck to her tear-stained cheek, I tucked it back behind her ear. I told myself I only wanted to heal her, help her, stop her from crying.

Her hand clamped over mine, trapping my palm flat against her cheek. She met my eyes and said, "I've missed you so much," on a sob.

People say: *It wasn't supposed to happen*, and now I understand how one innocent choice could lead to a complete breakdown of my will power.

Maybe I was making excuses to touch her. Or maybe I thought I deserved a brief respite from my long penitence, all that time wanting her and never acting on it. Either way, it was wrong of me to let it go on from there. But it was wrong of her to let me think it meant something.

We'd put ourselves into a situation where I might kiss her forehead, where she might lift her face, close her eyes, and press her mouth to mine.

Her lips tasted salty from the tears, and she might as well have been the ocean for how I fell into her. I'd dreamed of kissing her, just like this, slow and easy. Just the two of us forgiving each other and wanting to express a deep and abiding love that had never truly faded.

Nothing felt more natural than peeling her shirt off, and when she straddled me and kissed me like she needed me, I might have allowed myself to believe in the possibility that we could start over somehow. When I covered her body with kisses and slid into her, I was certain this was a prelude to her leaving her husband for me, even though she'd never even suggested it.

That was also my own damn fault.

I had no plan to whisk her away, and it didn't matter anyway. In the post-sex haze, she stood up, got dressed, and suggested, like a sucker-punch, that she'd made a mistake.

"It was entirely my fault," she said. "I needed a friend, and thank you for being here for me, but this was a bad idea. I've got to go home and find a way to fix my marriage. This can never happen again." As she opened the door, she gave me one lingering look and frowned. "Please don't contact me, Noah."

At least her voice cracked when she blew up the last bridge that connected us, when she blew a hole in the middle of my chest.

In the aftermath, I chose to be grateful I had that night with her to remember. I knew it would take time to heal, but it had been an unexpected gift. The band would leave for Pittsburgh in the morning, and that wasn't the life she wanted anyway. It had been sheer fantasy to start imagining a life she'd never chosen.

So I did as she asked. I let her go. I gave her a chance to fix her marriage and hope that she'd come find me if things didn't work out.

And then she didn't.

Chapter Ten

Lucy

"Mom, I told you. He's way too big for the highchair."
I lifted Owen and helped him into a booster seat strapped to
the big chair. I buckled the belt and slid him closer to the table.
He immediately went to work on the dinosaur-shaped mac and
cheese. The kid loved his dinosaurs.

"Well, then why do you keep it?"

It was a reasonable question. Honestly, I hadn't donated
it yet because I hadn't wanted to admit that I wouldn't need it
again. But obviously, my prospects for a baby brother or sister
for Owen were waning.

Sure, I had social outings, even the occasional date,
though most of those were with people I met through work.
At my age, most of us came with baggage. I had a kid. They
had insurmountable student loans and a video game addiction.

Since I no longer had the luxury of considering a guy for
his boyfriend qualities without also measuring his potential as
a dad, my pool of potential suitors generally boiled down to

actual dads. And most of those hadn't divorced until their kids were closer to my age.

I hadn't given up entirely, but realistically, the highchair wouldn't become a permanent fixture.

The phone blipped as soon as we'd all sat down, and I slid it over, ignoring my mom's scowl. She didn't have to stay for supper, and Owen wasn't expecting sparkling conversation. He'd gone right back to humming a tune that consisted mostly of bouncing between two octaves while he danced his dinosaur into his mouth one at a time on their slow march to extinction.

I unlocked my phone to see who might be trying to contact me. A text from an unknown number read: *It was so good to see you again.*

My spine went stiff. Had Noah found some other way to reach me?

A second text followed. *We should meet for coffee sometime and catch up.*

Something was off. I checked the area code, and a light bulb went off. John must have changed numbers.

The sudden whoosh of disappointment that it was John and not Noah surprised me. Did I really want Noah to hunt down my phone number?

It wouldn't have shocked me if he'd managed to. He'd gone to great lengths in high school to convince me to change my mind about him. I might never have relented if he hadn't made my dad so angry that one night when he serenaded me. That weird moment together altered our chemical makeup in a way that would tangle our spirits together irrevocably.

But that kind of mischief hadn't been without a price. My dad forbade me from seeing Noah ever again.

Lucky for Noah, my dad was the one person I'd always disobey.

So why was I sitting here wishing he'd managed to find my number on his own?

I stared at my phone, wondering if I ought to respond to John's text. What would we have to talk about? We'd spent years together, and I didn't have a single memory that made me laugh like that one night my dad had nearly murdered Noah.

My mom cleared her throat in a way that decided me, and I put the phone to sleep. "Do you remember the night Dad nearly shot Noah?"

Her fork clattered to the plate. "Lucinda Rose, that *never* happened."

"It *did*. Don't you remember? It was October. I remember we had pumpkins on the porch. I think Dad had come home to go out to watch a Maryland football game, but that could have been another weekend."

Mom narrowed her eyes as if she was trying to visualize it. "Was this when you were prepping for the SAT?"

Another detail jarred loose. "Yeah. I always wondered why I was studying on the weekend. I had the SAT coming up, I think. Maybe the PSAT."

"Was this your senior year?"

"No. Junior." I smiled. "Jasper was in the house howling the whole time."

"That dog never stopped howling."

"Do you remember? Noah tried to serenade me, but Dad went out front with his 12 gauge."

"Oh, I'm sure he only meant to put on a show. Your dad was all bark."

How could she remember him that way? What normal person would even point a gun at a sixteen-year-old?

I let the topic drop and turned to Owen who was squirming to be free. "What did you and Nana do today?"

He stilled, only his face twisting while his eyes rolled up, like he needed to access his memories from the outside. "Uh . . . We made a painting."

I wished I could capture the sound of his voice. Maybe I should make more videos with him. I took out my phone and opened the camera. I hit record. "Tell me about your painting, Owen."

"It was blue." The way he said it sounded more like *bleeyou*, and he went with that into another song. "Blioup

blioup," he sang. But he continued. "And the people were
lellow and they had hats." He still couldn't say yellow,
but he'd corrected most of his words, so I smiled and let
it slide.

"What kinds of hats."

His hands went up to show me. "Round."

My mom got up and started clearing the table while I conducted my interview. "Where were the people going?"

He bounced again in a little dance, shoulders twisting. "To
see the monkeys."

So matter of fact.

Mom said, "Oh, I forgot. Here's the mail," and dropped it
on the table next to me. It annoyed me because I was obviously
capturing this all for posterity. Granted, I never uploaded my
videos anywhere, so it didn't need to be perfect. Still, I was a
perfectionist.

When Mom asked if he wanted to give her a kiss before
bed, my interview came to an end as Owen started pushing
against his straps. "Out!"

I released him, and he ran over to give her a big hug. I
slid the envelopes on the table aside, one after the other. Coupons, credit card offers, a reminder to get my eyes checked. A
hand-written address stood out. The stamp looked legit, not
presorted mail. The postmark said Brooklyn again. This time
there was a return address.

My breathing increased.

I tore open the envelope so fast, my mom paused halfway
through collecting the dishes. "What is it?"

A blank piece of paper fell out, folded over a long rectangle of card stock. I picked it up to examine it.

Theater of the Absurd would be playing the 9:30 Club in
D.C. on Saturday. And I had a ticket to the show.

I laughed at myself for earlier thinking that incoming text
had been from Noah. As if he'd settle for a lame text when he
could find more dramatic ways to talk to me.

"Um." I turned it over, as if the other side would shed light
on this new quandary.

Mom plucked it out of my hands. "Did you order this?"

"I didn't even know they'd be back here again so soon." It drove home how unpredictable his time was and why I'd finally taken a break from him before.

"Says it's this weekend. Do you need me to babysit?"

I laughed. "I'm not going."

"Well, why not?"

"Mom, I really don't see the point."

She crossed her arms. "You haven't given that boy a chance in, what, six years now?"

"You're keeping track? You never even liked him."

"I didn't like all the sneaking about."

I huffed. "We never sneaked around."

She shot a glance at Owen as if to counter my argument with proof to the contrary. Low blow.

"That was one night. John knew whenever Noah came to town. I wasn't hiding it."

"I'm not saying you should marry him, but you think I don't see the way you looked at those lilacs?"

"I don't know what you mean." I pushed my chair back and continued gathering up the dishes, hoping she'd take the hint. It was giving me a headache trying to maintain logic over emotion, and I didn't need her taking Noah's side. It had taken all my self-control not to call him. I needed her to bolster my courage to resist his stubborn seduction.

"If you don't go and find out if there's anything there, Lucy, you're going to come to regret it for the rest of your life."

I spun to look at her then. "What would you know about that?"

She frowned. "More than I care to talk about."

I suddenly realized she'd loved someone. Someone she regretted. "Who was he?"

She snorted. "It's not important now. But I do wish I'd given it a chance. It might have come to nothing, but at least I would have known." Her shoulders relaxed, like she'd decided to stop fighting. "It's the not knowing that will kill you."

I couldn't argue with that. "But what if I do know? Every time the band gets a little bigger, their definition of success gets farther out of reach. This is his life, Mom. He's never going to settle down."

She picked up the ticket from the table and examined it before shooting me a look. "I've always held my tongue, but Lucy, don't you think it's time you let the boy's father know?"

My temples throbbed. That was the million-dollar question. One I'd never have to answer if I didn't go to the concert.

"I will tell him when it's best for Owen. Not for me. Not for Noah. Not for you." I picked up the ticket and shoved it into a drawer. Out of sight, out of mind.

She shook her head. "One day, you're going to realize that even the choices you make with the best intentions can be the wrong decisions for your child. And for you."

I rolled my head back and stared at the ceiling, frustrated that I was having to argue about this with her of all people. Then again, she'd continued to take my dad back over and over, never learning that every time he came home, our perfectly ordered world shattered to fit around his needs. And when he left, he left nothing behind but tears and anger.

But for my mom's sake, and because my headache threatened to turn into a migraine, I said, "I will consider going to the concert to see what Noah wants. But that's all I can promise at this time."

It would get her off my back, and hopefully she'd forget about it until it was too late anyway.

That was unlikely.

My mom had been the only one I had to turn to the night the pee stick turned blue.

That night, I'd sat in the bathroom, staring at the sudden change in my circumstances, wondering: How could something happen in one night with Noah when it hadn't in years with John? Did God have a sick sense of humor?

That should have been news to celebrate, and had it happened a month earlier, I would have been elated. Except a month earlier, John had started sleeping in the next bedroom.

I had to show John the pregnancy test, so I mustered my courage and went down to his office.

His first question was: "Is there someone else?" I couldn't blame him. I might have lied, but he said, "I'll get a paternity test either way."

"It was an accident, John. It didn't mean anything." But that wasn't entirely true. It had meant something. "It was one time. It's in the past now." I wasn't sure if I was trying to convince him or myself.

He paced the floor while I sat at the kitchen table, waiting for him to decide my fate.

A year earlier, John might have forgiven the infidelity, but a year earlier, I wouldn't have cheated. Six months earlier, he might have considered this a miracle baby that would fix our troubled marriage, but the truth was, now our relationship was beyond repair.

He balled his fist and feinted a punch at the wall. "This is an unforgivable threat to my career."

I kept my voice neutral. "I never planned this. We could raise this baby together. Nobody needs to know."

"This will complicate my future political viability."

"Only if you let it."

He had a reason to be angry, but he hadn't said the first thing about how this had made him feel, only fake arguments based on a faulty premise. He was just test driving his excuses to end a marriage that had run its course.

When he packed a bag and left me alone in the town house on the Hill, I considered calling Noah. I did. He had a right to know, but it would be an impossible decision for him. His band had just left on a month-long tour of Europe, opening for a big-name rock band. Everything they'd worked for was starting to happen, and Noah would be focused on his career right then.

I knew he'd come straight home to me at first, out of obligation. I trusted him enough to know he'd do that for me. He'd find a way, for a while, but there was no way Noah would drop everything to raise a family with a girl he hadn't been romantically involved with for years. I knew this in my bones.

I'd been lucky enough to hold him in my arms for a time, but Noah was like the wind: hard to predict, impossible to catch.

I didn't want that for my child.

I'd always been the pragmatic one. Not—as Noah would twist that—the smart one. I was the one holding down a home. I was the one who'd stayed in one place, creating the stability I'd always wanted, the permanence I wanted for my children. Meanwhile, Noah hadn't even tried to contact me since that night. Granted, I'd asked him to stay away for the sake of my marriage, but I hadn't expected him to follow through so easily.

On the edge of my bed, I held my phone, considering every possible future, but in every scenario, I could only come up with one common picture: Noah would never settle down. And I'd never go on the road with him. We were an impossibility.

And so I made the only decision I could live with and turned my phone off.

One day, when our child was old enough to understand, I'd tell them both. I hoped my child would forgive me. I was sure Noah never would.

Chapter Eleven

Noah

I was going to murder Shane before this slate of shows ended.

He'd been whining now for days about his whittle fee-wings.

As cool as Layla had turned out to be, my initial instincts had been right all along, and Shane was dismayed to discover she wasn't just a groupie, she ran a motherfucking fan site, one where she had, as I'd suspected, once drooled over pictures of me, among other musicians. When Shane found those photos, he finally reacted the way I'd wanted him to before he'd fallen in love with her.

The irony was that I no longer thought of Layla as a groupie, even if, on paper, everything defined her that way.

But Shane had clearly never learned the lessons experience had taught me the hard way. I'd give anything to have what he had with Layla—but with Lucy of course. Here he was, willing to blow everything out of proportion and risk this one chance at happiness, as if life would give him another shot. And as much as my own misery loved his company, I couldn't stand to watch him make rookie mistakes.

"You're being a moron, Shane."

"Uh—she has a stash of pictures of *you*, asshole." Shane pulled out his phone like he was going to show me the evidence.

Micah yelled from the front of the bus, "Would you both shut the fuck up?"

I just wanted to get to D.C. It had actually been thanks to Layla I'd gotten this stupid idea to send Lucy a ticket to the D.C. show, but now I was wishing I hadn't. When she didn't show up, I'd have an answer I didn't want. If I hadn't sent her the ticket, I could have pretended she didn't know I was in town. I could have dropped by on her unannounced again.

That was my dick thinking.

I started in on Shane again to take the edge off my anxiety. "You finally find a girl who doesn't know how ugly you are, and you throw it away?"

Micah walked back. "I told him to give her a call and work it out. He almost did. But he chickened out."

"I didn't chicken out," Shane protested. "It's complicated."

Micah laid a hand on Shane's shoulder. "It's not complicated. Do you want the girl?"

I hated Shane a little for taking what he had for granted. A girl who truly loved him, who didn't mind that he was a musician, that his life was eaten up by touring, and he was beating his chest. He looked at his feet. "You know I do, but—"

"But nothing. You do realize you're the one who fucked up, right?" Micah never pulled a punch.

Good lord, Shane could be a twatwaffle. I punched him. "You know, Shane. I tell you this all the time, but you are your own worst enemy."

He smacked my hand away. "No, you are."

Micah shook a finger. "Stop it, both of you, or I'll turn this bus around right now."

Micah's phone rang out a notification. He read a text, then said, "Shane, check your phone."

I laughed out loud when I saw that his phone was connected to the very girl we were talking about. How much had she heard?

Man, was I ever jealous at the unfairness of our worlds. He could butt dial his girlfriend while I couldn't even find a way to talk to Lucy short of sending out messages in bottles. Or driving down to be near her like a psycho creeper.

I sent up a silent prayer: *Please let her come to the show.*

We got into D.C. at around five and went straight to the hotel to get some sleep. I did try, but between nervous worrying and the extreme exhaustion, I only managed an hour or so. I finally gave up and took a shower. I might have started primping earlier than usual. Shane teased me for being a pretty girl when he woke up and found me trying on different shirts.

I should have punched him in the nads, but I held up the shirt I liked best. "What do you think? Black right?"

"I think Lucy's never once cared what you were wearing. I doubt she's ever even noticed."

On the bus the night before, somewhere around three a.m. after he'd hung up with Layla without having resolved their issues, I'd confessed to him what I'd done. He'd only said it had taken me long enough.

I'd given him the only advice I was good for. "Don't screw things up, Shane. If you love that girl, swallow your pride and do whatever it takes to win her back."

My ship had likely already sailed. When had I made the fatal mistake? When I went to New York?

No, not then.

For a while, she tried to make it work. All through college, she wrote heart-felt letters and sexy talked over the phone. It wasn't ideal, but I always assumed she'd graduate and then join me in New York. Sure, we each had to pay our dues for a little while, but then all that waiting would pay off.

Everything had changed the night I called to tell her about the record deal, the night I'd told her we'd be going on a nationwide tour. That was when she decided to stop giving me any more chances.

I should have taken a train to see her that night.

"Get your ass in gear," Shane said, throwing on a Henley and running a wet hand through his ginger mop. "We've got soundcheck, then dinner."

I did a sweep of the room to make sure I had everything and headed to the elevator.

Micah and Rick met us in the lobby, and we all walked across the street. We'd played this venue dozens of times. It was legendary, and when I was in high school, I'd seen The Black Keys, Sufjan Stevens, My Morning Jacket, and a ton of other musicians perform here. Playing this stage always felt a bit like coming home, but at the same time, daunting. The impostor syndrome was always peak when we played these iconic venues.

Soundcheck entailed taking a gander at the stage to make sure our gear had made it. There'd be an early entry VIP photo op that we needed to come back in time for, but until then, the place was empty and we had time to eat. I gazed around the vacant area where I hoped, later tonight, I might see a pair of pale blue eyes, a shock of raven hair, and raspberry lips I could suck on for days.

I ought to have been angry with her for pushing me away, for never letting me know she was free again. And I was. I was livid. But more at the knowledge that life was fleeting, and every minute she'd kept her freedom secret was another minute we'd lost.

Inhale. Exhale. *Let it go.*

There was nothing to do about that now. And I still didn't even know if she wanted to be with me. I checked the time. I'd find out in a matter of hours, and it was eating me alive.

My head fell back. I was such a fool. She'd never show.

And tomorrow would be step one on my twelve-step program to get Lucy out of my system.

Again.

♡

Lucy

I couldn't go in.

Young kids crowded around the front of the venue, and I couldn't get out of the Uber.

"This is the club, ma'am. You getting out?"

I could have the driver take me back home. The show had already started. I'd stalled so long leaving the house, I might have missed it. The club doors opened, and a trio stepped out. Were those people leaving?

I slammed my head against the headrest three times. My mom's voice in my head nagged me to get out, go say hello. I didn't have to stay. This wasn't a marriage proposal.

But I'd nearly kicked the habit. One more hit would start the addiction all over again.

If I was being perfectly honest, when it came to Noah, I'd been a dry drunk for years. Pretending otherwise only left me white-knuckling moments like this.

The fact that he wanted to see me sent a thrill through me. He'd seen me less than a month before, so he knew what I looked like now—older, heavier—and still he pursued.

I opened the door. Then I closed it, breathing deep to regain my courage.

"Ma'am."

"Okay. Okay. Don't get your panties in a wad." I stepped out of the car and closed the door in one smooth move. The driver hit the pedal instantly, sensing perhaps my total ambivalence. Now that I was stranded, the only option seemed to be entering the den of iniquity.

Music hit my eardrums, almost painfully. Had I gotten so old that music hurt me now? I stopped and let the déjà vu of the venue wash over me.

I stood outside the door, deciding whether or not I wanted to re-open an old wound.

Nobody owned me. I could go in or go home, but it was entirely my choice. I stretched my fingers out, then clenched my fists.

Curiosity won out, and I handed my ticket to the woman at the entrance.

"ID?"

I presented my driver's license. While she clacked on her keyboard, I scanned the scene. I hadn't been to a club like this in ages, and I didn't like how old it made me feel.

"Lucy Griffin?"

"Yes."

"I have instructions to give you a VIP pass." She held out a laminated plastic badge hanging on a ribbon necklace. "You have access to all the areas of the club, including the green room."

"What's a green room?"

She smiled with a shake of the head. "I've never given one of these out to someone who didn't know what that was." She motioned to another employee to take her spot. "Follow me. I'm Lana, by the way."

We entered the club, passing the merch tables I remembered from when I'd come out to support Noah. T-shirts advertised the band with images that didn't mean anything to me, abstract art or perhaps they were album covers. Signed pictures of Micah and Noah hung on the wall along with the rest of the commodities, their very images for sale. Women draped over the counter, likely waiting their turn to flirt with the band members. I irrationally wanted to punch them all in the eye.

Lana urged me to continue on, through the undulating crowd, toward the stage where four dynamic guys performed, lit by stage beams from every direction. I stopped, frozen by the view.

Micah had both hands wrapped around a microphone, eyes closed, singing like every woman in the audience was his lover. Rick stood to the side, still, playing his instrument like he'd collect a paycheck later and disappear. Shane's arms flew so fast they were a blur.

And there to my left, Noah destroyed his guitar with a talent I'd often thought he'd extracted from the defiled bodies of rock legends past. I'd seen him perform many times, though the last time had been years earlier, and he'd somehow evolved beyond the talent he'd had back then. Now, he and his guitar appeared to be fused, and I couldn't tell if he was playing the guitar or if the guitar was playing him.

Lana tapped my shoulder and pointed toward a hallway on the other side of the stage. I shook my head and spoke loud enough to get past the music. "Thanks, but I came here to watch the show."

She shook her head again. "You're different."

With that she abandoned me in the middle of a sea of bodies.

I should have left. Nothing good would come from staying. I promised myself I could slip out before the show ended, before Noah knew I was there.

People jostled me as they danced, though many kids had phones out and were either looking at screens or trying to get pictures or video of the show. I saw Micah or Noah multiple times like they were part of an art installation.

And no wonder. They were at the height of their powers: beautiful, alive, full of talent. I'd been to concerts and could tell the difference between a band that had peaked and one that was headed for the top of the charts. Noah's sheer potential was proof that he and I would never live in the same world.

The song came to an end with cheers from the crowd. The transition from one song to the next rippled through the audience as people slipped out to go to the bathroom or worked their way to or from the bar. It should have been my cue to turn around and leave.

As Micah strummed his guitar, he talked about what a pleasure it had been to play the club, how great the fans were, and announced, "This will be our last song."

Definitely a sign I should go. Instead, I inched through the pockets left open by the shuffling in the audience, drawn closer by the need to watch Noah while he wasn't watching me. I understood the urge to get out my phone and hit record. This was a vision that should be preserved for all of humanity to enjoy, hung on a wall in a museum, next to works by Vermeer.

When I was a good twenty feet from the stage, I paused. The music vibrated through my whole body, pounding at my eardrums. Shane set a blistering beat, and I could never understand how he didn't keel over from a heart attack midway through a set. On the opposite end of the energy spectrum, Rick nodded subtly to the rhythm of his own bass, cool as if he sat in a recording studio. As always, Micah owned the stage. I hadn't seen him this close in years, but he'd grown more handsome, more confident, and he held the audience in the palm of his hand.

Then there was Noah, shredding his guitar like it was therapy. The stock tipped up, and he raised a knee, looking every bit like the rock star he'd been destined to become. His eyes opened and roamed across the sea of worshiping faces until they found mine.

And he stopped playing. Right in the middle of the song. He lifted the strap over his head, set the guitar on the stage, and dropped the neck like he'd forgotten it was there.

More phones came out, as the audience tried to figure out what was happening. And then Noah jumped off the front of the stage.

As he pressed through the crowd, Shane quit playing, stood up, and walked off stage left, as if this entire thing had been planned. As if it was normal to stop a song midway through.

Micah's guitar stilled, but he kept singing, and Noah had almost reached me. I looked around for a way out.

Rick's bass went silent, and just as Noah reached me, Micah said, "Good night!"

The crowd erupted in cheers and calls for an encore, but Noah had me by the hand and was dragging me out toward the entrance.

"What about the encore," I yelled.

He pressed his mouth to my ear, tickling me with his breath. "Micah can do a solo acoustic set. The crowd will love it."

We pushed through the lobby. Lana's eyebrows flew up at the sight of us.

"Where are we going?" I asked.

"Anywhere that isn't here."

Once we were out through the front door, he took a sharp turn left but kept his pace, hand tightly clenching mine. Without slowing, he said, "You never called."

"No, I didn't."

"But you came."

"I nearly didn't."

We turned another corner, into a kind of alley, and he kept walking until he got about halfway down the side of the building, where he stopped and spun me to face him.

"Why didn't you call?" He backed me up like we were waltzing.

"I didn't want to encourage you." My shoulders hit the brick.

"Why did you come?"

"You sent me a lure." My breath came out on a ragged tear. "A junkie can't resist her drug of choice."

His tongue dragged across his lower lip, and he raised a hand up, fingers threading into my hair, sliding around the back of my neck, and I shivered.

"You think of me as a drug you have to resist?"

His eyes settled on my mouth, and I tilted my head up, praying futilely that he had more self-control. My muscles tensed in anticipation and longing, and treacherous hands lifted up to find the hem of his shirt. I clenched the fabric in my fist, so damn tired of wanting what I couldn't have.

I nearly broke down and begged, but he reached his limit first. The press of his lips to mine was slow, languorous, nearly tentative, but intentionally so. My eyes closed, and my shoulders relaxed. I slid my hands inside his shirt and touched skin that felt like coming home.

He tilted his head slightly, parting his lips, promising the kind of kiss that would unlock my every resistance.

A voice broke our trance. "Hey."

Noah drew back, confusion in his eyes. I glanced over at two opportunistic girls approaching. One placed a hand on Noah's shoulder. "Wouldn't you rather get two for one?"

Oh, sweet Jesus. I straightened my shirt and stood taller. "You want to ask me again why I resist?"

He shrugged the girl off and took my hand again. "Come with me."

I followed. I'd follow him wherever he led me. I knew he wouldn't take me to his hotel room. He couldn't. Not after last time.

Though, the cave woman in me wished he would.

Chapter Twelve

Noah

I didn't know where I was taking her. Away. To Mexico. To the bus. It didn't matter. I needed to get her alone. She'd come to me. She was finally here, and I didn't know where I was taking her. I hadn't thought quite this far ahead.

Until I saw her in the audience, I hadn't allowed myself to believe she'd come.

We crossed a street toward a bar near the venue. A couple of people held up phones and shot pictures, and I considered dragging Lucy back to my hotel for some privacy. I knew how much she hated this whole side of my life, the crowds, the frenzy. I assumed that was why she rarely came to my shows once we'd moved to these bigger venues. Before she'd stopped showing up at all.

I didn't want to scare her away when she'd finally come to see me, so I needed to get her somewhere calm, somewhere we could talk honestly. Maybe I could get her to tell me what I'd done so wrong to keep her from contacting me for years.

Thankfully, the bar was a total dive, dark with neon lights advertising cheap beers on the wall. I led Lucy to a booth at the far end and slid in, praying none of the fans would follow or post anything about my whereabouts on social media. I figured we had maybe ten minutes if we were lucky. It wasn't like I was George Harrison after all.

A waitress sauntered over. "What'll ya have?"

Lucy used to be a gin and tonic girl. I glanced at her. "Tanqueray still?" She nodded, and I said, "Two Tanqueray and tonics."

Across from me Lucy's face shone red, then blue as the neon sign above us transitioned. She chewed on her lower lip, and I lost my train of thought, mesmerized by the shape of her mouth, the raspberry decadence that I'd once taken for granted. I doubted there was an inch of my exposed skin that hadn't experienced that naughty mouth. If my pants had grown uncomfortable from kissing her out in the alley, fantasies about our long-lost past weren't helping that situation.

I laid my hand across the table, palm up and waited, a little nervous. She gave me a wicked grin and placed her palm across mine. I curled my fingers around hers. I might worry Lucy would reject me completely, but I'd never had to worry she didn't like me. She'd been fighting against that current since I'd spoken the first word to her.

"You were telling me why you decided to come tonight." I squeezed her hand. "Honestly, this time?"

"My mom made me."

Her nonchalant shoulder shrug didn't fool me, and I actually snorted. "Your mom hates me."

She shook her head. "She's getting nostalgic in her old age."

"Old? She can't be more than sixty." She'd been a nice-looking lady for a mean battle ax. "How is she?"

"Good. She's been a help since John left."

"A help with what?"

She drew her hand back as the waitress appeared with our drinks, and I let her take a sip, assuming she'd answer the question, but she asked me something else instead.

"Why did you send me the ticket?"

"Isn't that obvious?"

"And the flowers. And the dolphin. Why are you trying so hard to get me to call?"

"You're kidding me."

"No. I'm really not. It's been a while."

She couldn't be serious.

"It's only been a while because you misled me. You let me believe you were still married all this time. Remember when you told me to go away? I assumed those two things were related."

Her pretty mouth twisted. She fussed with the stir stick in her drink. "They were and they weren't. My marriage fell apart slowly, and then . . . Well, then it happened fast."

"When you came to see me that night—"

She raised a hand. "I take full responsibility for what happened."

"It takes two." I'd thought it did, anyway. "But you regretted it, and I never did."

How could I regret the last memory that had sustained me through my soulless existence? A real moment in time. If nothing else was true, that night had been. I'd had her in my arms, and she'd said things to me that I'd never expected to hear her say again. The only thing I regretted was that it had given me a hope that made the aftermath so much more painful. And it left me half a man, half here, half in a past I could never return to.

"No?" She ran her thumb along the side of her glass as the condensation rolled down. I envied the glass. "Not even now?"

"For myself? No. But I really am sorry for whatever it screwed up in your life. I understand why you'd think it was a mistake."

Her eyes popped up to lock with mine. "I didn't say that."

"If it wasn't, why have you been working so hard to shut me out of your life?"

She sighed and tilted her head, like she needed to find an answer that wouldn't matter now. "By the time John and I finally divorced, you'd already been out of my life for months. I thought it would be easier if it stayed that way."

"Easier for who?"

"For me, obviously. And by proxy, for you. We were never good for each other."

"Says you." How could she even think that? "Besides we used to be friends, and I've really missed our friendship."

"I miss you, too." She whispered it like a secret. "But the problem is, we were never friends. You were always fire, and I was always dry wood. One spark between us, and we consumed each other. That's the way it's always been."

I scoffed at her ignorance; she'd been the spark. "You seem to forget all the times we met, just like this, just to talk, even while you were married. Wasn't that friendship?"

Her laughter was tinged with bitterness. "That was denial and self-sacrifice."

"Yeah, well, that's become irrelevant now, huh? So tell me, since you have all the answers, what do I have to do to get your phone number, Lucy?"

"I don't get why you want to resurrect something long dead."

Dead? Had she forgotten the kiss she'd just given me in the alley, not fifteen minutes before? "You can assume I'm not going to quit asking. I was thinking of subscribing to some kind of woo of the month club."

"Which you'll be sending me from where exactly?" She reached for her purse, and I thought she'd relented. But the strap went over her shoulder. "Look, it's been great seeing you again. This has been a fraught trip down memory lane for sure, but I can't do this."

My hand shot over and encircled her wrist. "What is it that scares you so much about me? Is it the paparazzi?" I glanced back at the entrance of the bar, which so far still hadn't been breached by hordes of selfie-hunting teens. "Is it the fans? Is it me?"

She narrowed her eyes. "It's none of that. And I'm not scared of you, Noah. How have you never figured out that what I want is something stable. Something permanent. You can't promise me where you'll be in two weeks. You can't promise me I can have you when I need you. What I want from you is your time."

It was like she'd thrown cold water all over me. "Oh, Lucy, I gave you all the time I ever had."

"That's what I mean. You could give me every minute of your free time—" she waved at the bar around us "—and this is what it looks like. Stolen moments. Even when I had you, I saw you almost never. How is a person supposed to have a relationship like that? How can a person plan their life when the one they want to plan it with is so unpredictable and never there?"

That was all? Time? "Can you honestly tell me that you ever got as much time from your ex-husband as you did from me." Her eyebrow rose, like I was speaking gibberish. "Sure, he might have been there next to you, physically, but was he really always with you? Did you ever command his attention the way you've always captivated mine?"

She started to speak, and I saw the arguments rise up and then die on her lips as she thought about it.

"Listen. I'm gonna make you a deal, okay?" I reached over to take her right hand in mine, like we were shaking. "Go home and think about the time you spent with John. Then think about all the time you've spent with me. Don't count the hours or the days. Count how often he was actually attuned to you, listening to you, talking to you, writing letters to you when he couldn't be right there with you, planning for weeks to find a way to be in the same physical space with you, making sure that you were always the focus. Do that, and if you can honestly say that everything I've given you over the years was lacking, don't even bother to contact me. I'll be out of your life for good. But if you decide that my time has been concentrated, but valuable, I'm just asking you to give me a call, text me, email me, friend me on Facebook, tag me on Instagram. Do something so we can stay in touch. So we can get to know each other again."

Fuck, a tear rolled down my cheek, and I couldn't believe I was falling apart in front of her. I had one last thing to say. "Because I would like to be friends, Lucy Griffin. And I would like to have a place in your life. Seriously, what do you have to lose?"

Lucy

What did I have to lose? The Uber ride home lasted an eternity of doubt and second guessing.

When I finally got home that night, once I'd checked on Owen, I did a search on Theater of the Absurd's tour schedule. I'd never wanted to look at their tour dates laid out like this before because it made me sick. Every one of those dates was an opportunity for Noah to meet another girl and take her to bed. I couldn't shake off the memory of that pair of girls casually offering to sleep with him in that alley. How many girls had he kissed the way he'd kissed me the night before?

A bead of perspiration broke out on my forehead at the memory. If we hadn't been in a public place, if those girls hadn't interrupted us, if Noah had invited me to his room, there was no doubt in my mind, I would have had a hard time telling him no.

How much harder would it be for any of those lovesick fan girls?

But that wasn't the crux of my problem with his schedule. I'd given up any control over who he spent a night with when I'd cut him out of my life. My main problem with the schedule was practical: Every one of those cities wasn't anywhere close to me. And every time I saw him, I'd spend the next several days mourning his loss.

I'd come home thinking about what Noah had said, about getting to know each other again, about how much of his time he'd devoted to me. What did I have to lose by letting him back in my life? Right in front of me, on the computer monitor, was the answer. It was cold objective fact that as long as Noah was in Denver, Colorado, he couldn't also be with me.

There was a week-long break coming up between dates. I hadn't had a week straight with Noah since high school. But surely, he had rehearsals or other obligations that would keep him in Brooklyn. He couldn't just move here.

And I wasn't about to move there.

Even letting him back in as a friend seemed pointless from the get-go.

But nevertheless, I did ponder the question he'd raised. I started to calculate the quality of time he'd showered on me versus the quantity I'd had with John. Noah was right that time with John hadn't always been *time* with John. John was either campaigning, fund-raising, glad-handing, or once in a while governing. We went to parties and traveled back to his district in Virginia. There were times he wasn't home, but frequently, I went along with him for the photo op. I had my own role to play as the wife of a congressman. It had been somewhat amusing for a while at the beginning, when John had been a freshman congressman. We'd been so idealistic, partners in the way I'd always imagined a marriage.

An image suddenly surfaced of some random day after we'd been married about a year. John had met me in George-town for dinner. As we walked along the sidewalk, he talked on the phone rapidly while I glanced around at all my old haunts, reminiscing about my college years. The music store on the cor-ner remained, and I stopped dead to stare in the store window, just wanting to wallow a bit in nostalgia for that day Noah had shown off on the demo guitar. His ghost haunted Georgetown.

I was pulled back to reality when John tugged me forward. He didn't ask me to explain my thoughts. He just said, "Come on. We have reservations."

Maybe Noah was right that time couldn't be measured in physical company. Maybe that moment in the music store had more potency than a distracted date with my husband. But on the other hand, at dinner that night with John, I'd had someone to talk to about my day. I'd had someone to hold my hand and make me feel less alone.

Mom tapped on the door, and I told her to come in. She sat near my feet, like she'd done in high school whenever she launched into her never-ending lectures about education, sex, and life. In that order. "School," she'd say when I was a teenag-er, "can take you farther in life than any man ever will." She'd been talking about her own past mistakes but somehow had foretold my own future ones. Still, it was because of her I'd gone to a prestigious college. My earliest memories were of my mom playing "games" with me that I only later realized were educational. They'd been fun, and I'd learned to read before I could tie my shoes.

This version of Mom simply sighed and said, "Well?"

I shrugged. "He's going to stop stalking me."

Was that disappointment in her expression? "Did you tell him to stop?"

"Not exactly, but I think I made it clear there's no future for us. Not with things the way they are."

"And you told him how things are?"

"You mean about Owen?" I had considered it, but everything had only confirmed my doubts. "It wasn't the right time."

"So that's it, then?"

I picked at the hem of my blanket, deciding how much to tell her. "That's it. Unless I change my mind."

The corner of her mouth turned up ever so slightly. "You were always so stubborn."

"Was not."

"All through school, nobody could deter you from a single-minded goal. You were going to graduate, go to law school, make a ton of money, and finally move away home for good."

"As I recall, those were your goals. You pushed me as hard as I ever pushed myself, but it was never my goal to make a lot of money, and I never intended to move far away."

She snorted. "Oh, but you did. You never let me hear the end of it. How you'd live a different life than how you'd been raised. You once even toyed with the idea of moving to New York City. Do you remember that?"

It rang a bell. "That may have been the year I got obsessed with *When Harry Met Sally.*"

"Well, everything you did was for a purpose, an end goal. I'm pretty sure you joined the color guard to have an extracurricular activity on your college application and not because you wanted to be in the marching band."

That was true.

"And of course I supported your hard work. I always wanted more for you than what I'd been given. If I'd had a college degree or any marketable skills, it wouldn't have been so challenging to raise you practically alone."

"You did your best, Mom." It had only recently become obvious how much she'd sacrificed for me, and I'd never shown her the proper gratitude when I was a teen. "I wish it could have been different for you."

"But you see? That was why I was so worried when Noah started coming around back then. He was the only person who could ever make you pull your nose out of a book and see past the horizon. He'd cajole you into doing things that at the time took years off my life. That day you skipped school without telling me where you'd gone? I'd been about to call the police. I considered doing it anyway. I thought that boy was going to ruin you."

"He nearly did, Mom. I flunked an exam that week. My physics grade never did recover. I thought for sure I'd wrecked my scholarship chances."

"And yet, what I failed to see was how much he was enriching your life in ways that your studies never could. Oh, you learned a lot and you've got a wonderful education, but you weren't having any fun. Not until Noah came along."

"That's precisely why he's so much trouble, though."

"Trouble comes in many forms." She was full of pithy word bombs tonight. "Don't you think you could use a little excitement in your life? You're living like a sequestered nun, and I'm hardly romantic company."

Who was this woman?

I shook my head. Sure, Noah was exciting, when he was there. "Christmas only comes once a year, Mom. It's not practical to stare out the window, waiting for Santa the rest of the time."

"Hmm . . ." She left that hanging.

"What?"

"Nothing." She cocked an eyebrow. "I just find it interesting that you compared Noah to Christmas of all things."

"You know what I mean."

"Just because it isn't always Christmas, do you want it to never be? Do you want to miss out on something special because you can't have it all the time? I notice you manage to drink a glass of wine only sometimes."

"That's a great analogy, but where Noah is concerned, I have a drinking problem. I can't stop with him. And the forced withdrawals are a bitch."

"Which is all the more reason you should consider calling him. You two could talk without it always being so dramatic. Why does it have to be all or nothing?"

"Is this your way of trying to get me to tell him about Owen?"

"You know everything doesn't need to be so black and white all the time. Talk to him. See how you feel after you've given him some time. You're always bitching about time. Don't you think you owe some of that to Noah? You might be surprised by what the future holds if you stop walling it off."

I scoffed. "I have hardly walled off the future. I've planned and worked for exactly where I am."

"Is this really the life you've worked for? Raising a child with your mom?"

"You know what I mean."

"Right. You've wrangled yourself a career and a house. But are you happy with that?"

"Yes." I was. I was pleased with what I'd achieved. I loved my work and my son. "I am."

"Okay." She patted my leg. "Ask yourself that question again in about ten minutes, after you turn the light out."

Blushing with horror, I shooed her out of my room. But when I turned off the light and lay in bed, my arm spread out, seeking the space where nobody but Owen had slept in years. I'd plastered up the hole in my heart from the lack of a man in my life, and I didn't want to start demolishing that barrier for fear of what might lay beyond.

I didn't need a man to be happy.

But then I remembered his kiss the night before, his hands in my hair, the taste of his lips, the feel of his skin, and my heart began to pick up its rhythm, pounding like it had when I'd stood in the middle of that loud concert hall. The beat moved south, and so did my hand, fingers seeking out relief from a visceral need I didn't want.

Chapter Thirteen

Noah

Of all my dumb ideas, promising Lucy I'd stop bugging her forever was probably my worst.

I lay across all the seats on one side of the bus, nursing a headache and trying to blot out the blinding light filtering through the orange curtains. Long daytime bus rides were a nightmare, and our next gig was several states away. Several long states. Right after D.C. we'd headed to Lexington and had to be all the way to Kansas City by dinnertime. We'd been on the road for hours, and I was so sick of it.

I was sick of the motion of the bus. I was sick of the claustrophobia. I was sick of Rick's stupid face. I was sick of the never-ending stretches of farmland. I was sick of being hurtled to destinations far and wide.

And today, I was sick of Shane whining about his own wretched state of affairs.

"What if I played a song for her?"

I groaned and rolled onto my side to face him. "Where do you intend to do that?"

"I'm just thinking out loud."

I'd serenaded Lucy once before with mixed results. "I don't recommend climbing up to her window."

"I could do it at a show. If I could get her back to one."

"That's the trick isn't it. If you could get her to a show, you wouldn't need to grovel. Maybe you could record yourself singing something, then email it to her?"

He twisted his lips. "Yeah, maybe."

I wasn't the one to be giving advice. I'd self-deported from my own love life, and now I had no reasonable way back in. Once I'd given Lucy total control, I could only wait for her to make a move. And it was killing me. I'd almost rather she sent me a cease and desist letter so I could start managing my emotions.

At least she'd had the courtesy to do that last time, and I'd survived, though it wasn't easy to go from boyfriend, to friend, to lover, then suddenly to nobody.

That last time, I'd coped with her silence in various ways.

First, with alcohol. Booze worked to a point. I'd steered clear of harder drugs because it seemed like such a cliche, and I didn't want any future documentary about the band to be a tragedy about addiction. But I did drink. I'd been hard to tour with for about a year after Lucy had told me to stay away. That was the hardest year.

Next with girls, obviously. It's easier to forget someone isn't in your life when you replace them with someone else. Trouble was, Lucy wasn't someone I could replace. If I could have done that, I'd be through with her already. I would've taken that easy out a million times over. My life would've been so much easier if a Jo or a Layla had crossed my path in New York, but nobody had been compatible enough to make me completely forget Lucy.

Music was always the best escape, but we only performed at most a few hours a day, and filling the other hours required imagination.

Therapy had helped me work through a bunch of other problems I'd been having, like anger at my dad for all the times he told me I wouldn't amount to anything. It was my therapist who convinced me to build a relationship with someone instead of moving from bed to bed. But therapy couldn't take away the emotions I most wanted to eradicate.

Finally, time had been the key. By the third post-Lucy year, the wound had healed nicely. I didn't think about her on a daily basis. I didn't Google her or try to search out her image on social media. And then Crystal arrived.

The best thing about Crystal was that she was nothing like Lucy. I thought that meant I'd grown and was no longer holding women to an impossible standard. But the trouble with Crystal was that she was nothing like Lucy.

First, Crystal was super interested in the band. That should have thrown up a million red flags. But at that time, all the girls we encountered were by definition over-invested in the band. That was why they were there.

Second, Crystal wasn't super interested in me. I mean, she liked to be with me. I could take her from tour stop to tour stop, and she loved that life. She loved our music. She loved sex with me. But when I talked to her about things that interested me, she yawned. To be fair, I'm not quite sure what interested her. Other than purses. She freaking loved purses.

Third, she didn't make me feel any particular way. I never hurt because of Crystal. And that was a positive for a long time. I never put my heart at risk with her. She was safe. She was anybody.

And if she hadn't gone and cheated on me, she'd still be here, and I wouldn't have opened my veins again by going to see the one woman who personified pain, the one woman who could shred me with a look.

It had been incredibly stupid of me to walk back through that door. But it had been even stupider to walk back out.

I glared at Shane through slitted eyelids. At least he still had some hope of winning Layla back.

My phone beeped, and I sat up to pull it out of my bag. I didn't dare to hope for anything and prepared for a reminder I had a dentist appointment coming up or an upgrade to my data. Anything to guard against disappointment.

I unlocked the phone and opened the text notification.

Hey. I'm opening a channel to talk.

"Holy shit," I said, jumping up out of my seat. "Holy fucking shit."

"What?" Shane sat up now, alarmed.

I paced to the front of the bus, then turned around and paced back. "Holy shit. She texted me."

Rick started laughing. "Maybe you can ask her to homecoming."

Shane shot him an eat-shit glare. "Shut up, Rick."

"What do I do? What do I say?" I dragged my fingers through my hair, completely freaked out by what her text might mean.

"What did she say?"

I showed him the text. "She isn't saying much. But I have her number now. Should I text? Should I call? I should totally call."

"You should calm down first." Rick slid down the row of seats closer to us. "She took this long to decide to let you know how to reach her, so you know she's probably completely unsure she's made the right move. So chill out."

He was probably right. He'd been married as long as I'd known him, so he must have done something right at some point. But Lucy wouldn't expect me to chill out. She would have known that if I got her number, I wasn't going to play it cool.

"Right," I said, still considering dialing her number right away. Then I realized I had zero privacy on that fucking bus, nor would I for another three or four hours. Then we had a show. Then fans to meet. And after all that, it would be incredibly late on a Sunday night.

Instead, I spent the next five minutes typing a text, then deleting it, then typing something nearly identical or dramatically different and deleting it. At last, I wrote:

Do you remember the first thing I ever said to you?

It was innocuous. It was open ended. It invited a response. I thought it was a great way to start a conversation.

And two seconds after I sent it, I wished I could recall it. Why hadn't I just said *hi*?

I poked at Rick to get him to move over, then lay back down on the bench and crossed my arm across my eyes, willing myself to die.

Lucy

What the fuck had I done?

I stared at my phone like it was an alien creature. I'd been sitting in the cafeteria with Farid, discussing a possible series of lectures about Dadaism. Farid made an off-hand comment that fired a synapse.

He'd said, "And I don't see any reason why I couldn't talk about the evolution from Dada to Surrealism," which would have been innocuous enough, until he added, "Of course, I wouldn't go as far as Absurdism."

"Of course not," I'd said, but my brain had already hiccuped. "We have some Dalí pieces we could show. What did you have in mind?"

He gathered his things. "I don't know." He paused. "Hey, did Priya say anything to you about the collection we're borrowing from the Cooper-Hewitt?"

"No. Why would she?" The Cooper-Hewitt was a design museum in New York, but as a part of the Smithsonian, we had a cooperation.

"There's a Van Gogh she wanted evaluated. You sure she hasn't mentioned it?"

"First I've heard."

He nodded. "We'll discuss the lecture series again soon."

Of course that left me sitting there, alone. I wondered what he'd meant by Absurdism. I opened my phone to Google. I'd studied every period of art, but my specialization had been in early twentieth-century, focusing primarily on the Impressionists and Post-Impressionists. My search results took me to some more modern artists, a lot of philosophers, and of course, the Theatre of the Absurd—the existentialist dramatists, not the band.

It seemed too weird a coincidence that I'd be staring at my ex-boyfriend's band name just days after watching them perform. Maybe I was rationalizing. I don't know. Maybe if I hadn't memorized that damn phone number, I would have had time to reconsider my next moves. Instead, my fingers had typed the number, like I was sleepwalking.

Now I stared at my phone, hoping maybe I'd mistyped. Maybe I hadn't just given Noah a direct line to me.

I was about to turn it off and shove it in my purse when the notification dinged, and I squeaked.

What had I unleashed?

Could I just ignore it?

I did the mature thing and blew a raspberry at the stupidity of the situation. It was just a text after all. How bad could it be? He'd probably just say *hi* anyway.

I slid open the message, and the museum cafeteria fell away . . .

I was back at my locker that day when he'd come up with a cockamamie excuse to talk to me. He'd nearly made me late for class, rudely implying that I was somehow too good for him, too snobby to give him a minute of my time.

Speaking of late, the lunch hour had slipped by while I considered what or if I should respond to Noah now.

I heard my mom reminding me that there was no commitment in talking and laughed at the simplicity of her advice. All bets were off when it came to talking to Noah. Noah could sell hot dogs to a vegan.

But Mom was right about one thing: I didn't have to decide on forever. Just the next few minutes. The trouble with that logic was that I'd used it for years to rationalize saying one more yes to Noah when I knew better. He was the captain of shenanigans, always sailing me into choppy waters, and I'd follow along because he'd somehow steer us to sandy beaches with beautiful sunsets, and I craved the adventure he promised. But sometimes the ship would run aground on rocky crags, and I'd find myself pregnant and alone because neither of us could ever say no.

Every single moment with Noah could change my entire destiny.

As I walked back to my office, pondering the perfect reply, I passed through the sculpture hall, then took a right to detour through Gallery 83 where I found Priya before Van Gogh's self-portrait.

Van Gogh fell into my area of expertise, but I fell under Priya's direct supervision. "What's this I hear about the Cooper-Hewitt?"

"Ah, Lucy." She gave me her full attention. "Nothing to worry about. I was thinking of sending Farid up to take a look at a drawing they have in their collection."

"It's a Van Gogh?" Why was she sending Farid? "I assume it's the *Bateaux de sable à quai.*"

Her eyebrow rose. "You know it?"

Of course. "I know *of* it. I'm aware of any post-impressionist works that reside at our sister museums." It was literally my job to know that.

"But you've never seen it first hand?"

"I've actually never been to New York."

She snorted. "How is that possible?"

Instead of answering that question, I crossed my arms. "Why would you send Farid?"

I didn't want to go myself, but it was insulting she'd asked a specialist in post-modernism instead of me.

"I didn't think you'd be interested in traveling. You've turned trips down in the past."

"Well, I had an infant in the past. He's old enough to go with me or I can arrange for care. I can't imagine I'd be gone longer than a couple of days."

"Right." She screwed up her mouth and said, "Yes, okay. Then we'll arrange for you to go."

Only after I'd won the principled debate, did I stop to contemplate whether I actually wanted to go. New York City was Noah's territory, but I'd seen his tour schedule and knew he'd be away all week and this weekend as well. I could get in and get out without any risk of caving in and asking him to meet me.

"Excellent. When do I leave?"

She slid out her phone and tapped open the calendar. "Let's see. They've set up a time, looks like a week from Friday."

A week from Friday? Noah would be in Brooklyn then. I squeezed my fists together.

Priya smiled. "You could catch a show while you're there."

I double blinked. There was no way I could back out after my protestations without looking flaky and unprofessional. "Sure."

Noah wouldn't need to know I was in town unless I told him. And I could practice the same will power that had kept me from ever jumping on a plane to go see him since he moved there.

But my imagination had already begun to fill in like a drawing slowly taking shape. Whenever I'd ever pictured New York City, I'd always placed Noah on those streets. It was going to be impossible to erase that impression, and now I was beginning to see myself sketched in alongside him.

Priya turned back toward the Van Gogh, saying, "Great. We can meet this afternoon to discuss it further. Are you free around three?"

"Yeah. See you then."

I glanced at my phone to check the current time, and then I knew how to respond to Noah. I opened his text and wrote: *Shane was wrong. I gave you the time whenever you asked for it.*

My phone buzzed seconds later, and I thought, *Geez, Noah, calm down.*

The text read: *Can you meet me in the sculpture garden in ten?*

Huh? I scratched my head. Noah was literally halfway across the country. But then the confusion cleared as I noticed the texts above and remembered John had tried to contact me the week before. It must have been urgent, so I texted back that I could be there and headed outside, worried about what could be wrong.

What if he'd been diagnosed with a fatal illness? I picked up my pace.

When we were married, the proximity of our jobs had made it so easy to meet for lunch or just go for a walk. I had a sense of déjà vu strolling into the sculpture garden to find him sitting on a bench in his shirtsleeves, a smile on his face that he'd lost near the end of our marriage. My eyes narrowed. Something wasn't right.

"John." He patted the bench, and I slowed my pace. "Is everything okay?" He didn't appear ill. In fact, he looked perfect, like the polished politician he was. But he'd always been great at pretending. I'd once watched him confidently glad-hand a group of campaign donors while recovering from a rotary cuff tear. I approached with caution.

"It was so nice to see you the other day," he began.

"Yeah."

"You look great."

I froze in place. "Uh-huh."

He beckoned me over, and I disregarded my qualms as overreaction. Was it so weird to want to just catch up? We worked in neighboring buildings. We used to meet in this very spot once upon a time.

As I took a seat, he tilted his head, eyes softening, and said, "I've missed you."

"Okay." Alarm bells were ringing.

"You look really great."

I glanced at my nonexistent watch. "Did you want to talk about something specific?"

He took my hand, or he tried to. I yanked it back, glancing around to make sure nobody in the vicinity had seen us. "You're a congressman," I whispered. "And you're *married*."

"We have history, Lucy."

"But we don't have a future."

"No, but we could have a present, from time to time." The look on his face left no question to his intent.

Blood rushed to my ears. "You can't be serious."

"It's nothing we haven't done before."

"But we were married then, John. To each other?"

He laughed bitterly. "I don't remember that being an obstacle to you before."

Direct hit. I opened my mouth, searching for a proper response. I'd had an affair, so did that mean I had no right to object to cheating? What had happened with Noah was under different circumstances. It was unplanned, an accident. Except Noah and I had history. We'd also had history, but no future.

I suddenly realized I'd probably said some variation of those exact words when I'd tried to excuse my behavior at the time. "I don't know what to say, John. I'm sorry for what I did. It was wrong."

"I didn't come here to relitigate the past." A devilish smile curled his mouth, reminding me of the early years with him, when things were easier, when I'd convinced myself I loved him. "But since you brought it up, maybe you could make it up to me."

My gut clenched, and I scooted away. "No."

"That look on your face? I recognize what you're thinking. Judging me for even making the suggestion. But I'll leave you with two thoughts. The first is that how you're feeling right now? Multiply that out and you'll know how it felt for me all those years ago. The second, once you calm down and think about it, is that we're both adults who enjoyed each other's company once before. We could be discreet. I know you're alone—and lonely. And I'm not quite . . . satisfied at home."

"No," I said louder as I stood. "Don't contact me again."

I wished I felt more righteous as I walked away, but he'd convicted me of my hypocrisy. It wasn't as though I'd propositioned Noah, and he'd never suggested anything close to John's disgusting invitation to *enjoy* each other from time to time. It *was* an accident, but Noah must have hoped it was the start of something.

Maybe it should have been.

I walked up the steps to the National Gallery, turned into the ladies' room, and threw up in the trashcan.

Chapter Fourteen

Noah

Lucy's text finally dinged on my phone.

Shane was wrong. I gave you the time whenever you asked for it.

I puzzled over her message. What did she mean, whenever I asked for it? Yeah, she always met me when I came to town, whenever I passed through, but she'd never once come up to meet me when I'd asked.

I read it again.

Could it be an invitation? Did she mean I could ask for her time now and she'd give it?

Jesus, I felt like I was in high school again, just trying to make sense of her.

I recalled the first time I spoke to her, when I'd tried to manipulate her into noticing me and gotten her attitude in return. That day, I'd told her she was the most beautiful girl in school, which was true, but it wasn't the thing I'd first noticed about her, or the reason I was drawn to her. Her pretty face didn't hurt, but no, my curiosity about her started long before my fixation.

I stared at her text message again.

Fuck it. I'd never known how to choose caution when it came to Lucy, and I wasn't going to start now.

I typed out: *I've got all the time in the world.*

She replied right away. *Sorry. It will be a few minutes, but I'm on my way. I had to run by my office first. See you in five.*

What?

Another text followed. *Shit. I was responding to someone else.*

Then silence. I tried not to let it bother me, but she was quick to text someone else, someone she was rushing to see. That old familiar sense of jealousy crept into my veins. Out on the road, so far away, I used to always worry I might lose her to any one of the smarter college guys she saw on a daily basis, but my paranoia had been unfounded until that one night when she broke up with me. I'd never forgotten the acid taste of it on my tongue even if it had relented over the years. Once I'd allowed myself to accept that she'd chosen a different man, I'd swallowed back the primitive notion that she was mine.

I hadn't even tasted that adrenaline when I'd caught Crystal with Samuel.

It was an ugly feeling, and it made my thoughts wander toward whiskey and pistols. Not good.

If I'd learned anything over the intervening years, though, it was that Lucy was not mine. If I could win her back, then that would be all right, but if I couldn't, I needed to be able to walk away. I could never make her do what she didn't want. And if she wanted someone else, I didn't have to like it. I only had to respect it.

Still, my hands clenched into fists, and Shane took one glance at me and moved to the back of the bus.

As we were pulling into Kansas City, my phone rang with an incoming call from Lucy's number. I hit the green answer button faster than I'd done anything else in my life.

"Hello?"

"Noah?"

The sound of her voice was like music. I settled back against the bench. "Hi, Lucy."

"Where are you?"

I glanced outside as if I'd see anything other than highway. "On the bus. We play Kansas City tonight."

"I know." She laughed. "I saw your schedule."

That was . . . interesting. New.

"I'm sorry about before. I wanted to explain, but it would take too long over texts, and something weird happened."

"Yeah?"

"Yeah. I got a text from John earlier. He wanted me to meet him." She paused, and I waited. "I thought it must be important. I've barely seen him lately. I ran into him a couple of weeks ago though."

"Okay." I schooled my voice to neutral, but I was worried about where this was headed. That guy had done what I'd never been able to do. He'd captured her once.

I reminded myself that I didn't want a captive. I wanted free-spirited Lucy.

"So I met him, and oh, God, this is so awful. Maybe I shouldn't have called. I'm just . . . I need to tell someone this, and I can't."

"You can tell me."

"He said he missed me, that he wanted to see me sometime."

My stomach knotted. This was too reminiscent of that earlier phone call. "And what did you say?"

"What do you mean, what did I say? He's married, Noah! I mean, not that I would want to see him if he wasn't, but what the hell?"

I laughed. It was the wrong reaction, but it was such a relief to hear her angry so I didn't have to pretend I wasn't.

She started laughing, too. "It isn't funny."

"Oh, I know." Still, I smiled. "What happened next?"

"He told me that I shouldn't have a problem with marital infidelity, you know because—"

"Because of me?"

"I nearly slapped him. I mean, how dare he think I owed him an affair or something? How dare he think that what happened with you had been some kind of sleezy hookup?"

"It wasn't?" I recovered fast enough to change my tone. "No, it wasn't." I was just glad she hadn't thought so. I'd sometimes wondered. We'd never spoken of it again, never gotten the closure of a postmortem.

"Of course not. It was wrong. It was stupid. But I hadn't gone out and intentionally set up a side fling." She sounded righteously angry, and I much preferred that to sad. "And it got me thinking about how quickly John broke things off with me back then, how he'd wanted to keep things as quiet as possible, even giving me the town house when he could have blamed me for adultery and left me with nothing."

I knew about none of this, but I listened.

"Then he was quick to remarry. In retrospect, suspiciously so. I'd always assumed he needed to have someone by his side for his campaigning, but now, I wonder. Is it possible he'd been cheating on me all along? I mean, it doesn't absolve what I did at all. I'm not trying to find excuses. But doesn't that sound likely?"

It did because in my experience, everyone cheated on everybody else. My dad, my last girlfriend, most of the musicians we went on the road with. But I hated to think that someone had broken Lucy's trust, that someone would take Lucy for granted. "Well, if he did, he was a fool."

"Cornball."

She grew quiet, and I didn't know what she needed me to say, so I waited.

Finally, she sighed. "You know, I hate to admit it, but you were right."

"How so?"

"What you said about quality time. Even when John was with me, he was always mentally somewhere else. And when he wasn't there, he was probably literally with someone else."

I knew how that felt. "I'm sorry, Lucy. You deserved better."

"And the stupid thing—" Her voice cracked. "The stupid thing is—" She was clearly on the verge of crying, and it was breaking my heart that I couldn't be there to wrap my arms around her. Though that was how things started that last time. "I told you to stop contacting me because I thought it would fix things." She sniffled. "I thought I could salvage my marriage, but I ended up losing you instead, and I've missed you."

"You couldn't lose me, Lucy." I looked over at Shane who had one eyebrow dipped like he thought I was full of shit. I turned away from him and faced out the window. "I'm here whenever you need me."

Unfortunately, the bus pulled into the venue parking lot as soon as I said that. We'd need to start unloading the instruments before going to get something to eat. I listened to Lucy's ragged breath even out before I dropped the news on her. "Do you want me to call you later tonight? I have to work for a little bit now."

She laughed, but it sounded like the remnants of a sob. "That's okay. Thank you for listening. I need to get to a meeting anyway. Shit, I'm a mess."

"Lucy?"

"Yeah?"

"Whatever time I have? It's always yours."

"I know that." She exhaled. "I just wish it could be time with me. I wish it could be more."

"I just want it to be more than nothing."

Rick made a choking sound. I was going to punch him in the gonads later.

"Thank you, Noah. And—"

"And?"

"I'm sorry I've been a terrible friend."

I wished I could say I understood, but I couldn't recover the lost time. "Can we start from here?" I didn't want to scare her, so I added a caveat. "Can we try being friends again?"

"I'd really like that." She sounded calmer. I'd done that.

"I'm gonna text you later, okay?"

"Okay. Bye."

I hated hanging up on that call, but the bus doors had opened, and Micah was starting to bark orders. My legs had cramped anyway, and I needed to stretch out. Once off the bus,

I looked around at the parking lot that looked like any parking lot. Several chain restaurants across the street could have been anywhere. The venue had a different name, a different marquis, but it was another stage, another concert hall. A different face greeted us at the door, but he gave us the same marching orders to come back and meet a different set of VIP fans who would take the same pictures and tell us the same stories.

But in a few hours, I'd get to lose myself in my music. And then I'd find the perfect thing to text to Lucy. And maybe she'd write me back. So I had something to live for for another day, and that was enough to get me by.

Lucy

Noah: *You awake?*
Lucy: *Yes. In bed though.*
Noah: *Well, that's a nice image.*
Lucy: *How would you know?*
Noah: *How would I know what you look like in bed? I know what you look like. I know what a bed looks like. I can use my imagination.*
Lucy: *Your imagination is dangerous.*
Noah: *My memories are dangerous. My imagination can barely keep up.*
Lucy: *It's been a while.*
Noah: *That could be rectified.*
Lucy: *See? You are dangerous.*
Noah: *Maybe I'd just like to read you a bedtime story or sing you a lullaby.*
Lucy: *Mmm-hmm.*
Noah: *Scout's honor.*
Lucy: *That's awesome, Noah. Considering you were never a boy scout.*
Noah: *Technicalities.*
Lucy: *How was your show?*

Noah: *Like every other show.*

Lucy: *Where are you now?*

Noah: *Hotel for tonight. We leave for Denver in the morning. On the road all day. If you want to text me, I'd love the company.*

Lucy: *Oh, now I see why you wanted my number . . .*

Noah: *You're on to me. I've been hounding you for your number to fulfill my super-secret plan to get you to talk to me. So busted.*

Lucy: *I'll be at work, but I can text when I have free time.*

Noah: *I've missed this. I've missed you.*

Lucy: *I've missed you too.*

Noah: *I *miss you* now.*

Lucy: *There's a solution to that, you know.*

Noah: *You could come on the road with me.*

Lucy: *Nice try.*

Noah: *Can I call you sometime?*

Lucy: *. . .*

Lucy: *Yes.*

I put my phone on my nightstand, smiling despite myself. It was nice to feel wanted, to feel desired. It was nicer to have a friend who'd known me as long as Noah had. If only I could believe he could be content with that.

John's words from earlier echoed in my mind: *We could have a present, from time to time.* The very idea nauseated me. I didn't want to be anyone's part-time lover.

I hadn't even told my mom about the conversation with John, and I hadn't decided yet if I would. But Noah had once been my confidant, and he slid back into that role too easily. I worried I might begin to rely on him. I worried I might fall back in love with him. And nothing about our situation had fundamentally changed. We were talking now when we hadn't been before.

Was he right? Did it matter that he wasn't physically here when I could talk to him wherever he was? Would it matter to the kid in the next room if he bonded with his dad and then wondered why he was never around? Would it be worse for him to wonder why he didn't have a dad?

I wrestled with these questions constantly. The only out-come I'd ever dreamed of was one that could never be: Noah living here in this town house with us, raising Owen like a regu-lar dad. I couldn't picture Noah settling anywhere besides New York. I certainly couldn't picture him falling into a static paren-tal role.

My mom was right that he could surprise me yet, but there was no way I was going to jump to the chase. We took things slow or not at all.

"Mommy!"

The cry came from down the hall, and I was up in seconds.

"Mo-hommy!"

I ran into Owen's room. "What's the matter, baby?"

"The montoo."

"Shhh." I slid into his bed and hugged him to me. "There's no monster. I'm here."

He babbled a little, and I realized he'd never completely woken up, so I lay there, listening to him breathe. And the next thing I knew, it was morning. My alarm was blaring back in my bedroom.

"Shit," I said, without remembering where I was. Little ears picked up every swear word so fast. I peeled Owen off me and stood, stretching until my back cracked. He hadn't had a nightmare in ages, so I wondered what had tripped this par-ticular wire. Usually it happened when I hadn't been present enough, and I resolved to make sure I spent as much time with him as I could, but my time wasn't all mine. I needed to be at work in an hour. He needed to be at daycare before that.

That line of thought made me remember Noah's comment about giving me what time he had. Maybe in some ways, I was no different, giving Owen parts of me when he wanted me all the time. At least my mom substituted nicely. But reality required that I go to a day job. And Noah had a job as well. His time simply divided into differently sliced chunks. He was right that I got him one hundred percent of the time when he could spare a moment. But fitting his free time into mine hadn't always been easy. I had classes. I had work. John's time lined up with mine. John's life had made sense to me. Noah had always felt like a choice between abstinence and indulgence. All or nothing.

What I'd never really stopped to consider was that Noah's *some* outweighed John's *all*. When I had John every single day, it was just half measures. Looking back, I wondered how I'd been satisfied with that.

It had started with self-prescribed expectations about what I thought I needed in a man.

John had asked me out on a proper date in an upstanding, traditional way. He'd taken me on predictable dates to movies and dinner. I must have been starved for normalcy, for something that looked like romance as portrayed on TV or in books. But while John courted me, Noah had swept me off my feet. Maybe I liked the control I thought I had with John. With Noah, I was pulled by the undercurrent and never had an option of coming up for air. John had given me space to breathe. And in comparison, it had felt safer. But now I knew better. Safety had been as much an illusion as time.

Owen stirred, and I started the morning routine, getting him to the toilet right away, then giving him a choice between this or that to wear to school. "I don't wanna go," he said. And I couldn't blame him. I didn't want to go to work that morning either. The dark cloud of John's proposition the day before had colored the exterior of my workplace in a miasma of gray.

I considered calling in sick, but I'd promised Priya I'd contact the curator at the Cooper-Hewitt today and coordinate a time to see their exhibit. "Hey, big boy, how would you like to go on a trip?"

It wasn't something I'd even considered until that moment, but maybe he'd love to go see Central Park. I didn't even know what New York City had for kids, but maybe we both needed to get away.

"Go where?" He still said *where* like it had two syllables. *Whey-ah*. I wondered if he'd been swapped with some child from the deep south.

"New York City. Have you heard of that?"

He scratched his belly under his pajama top. "It's the museum."

I wracked my brain to figure out how he might have heard of the museum before I remembered he'd seen the movie *Night at the Museum* and he knew that took place in New York. "That's right, buddy. Would you like to go see the big museum?"

He nodded with a big yawn. "Uh-huh."

"Maybe Nana would come with us, huh? What do you think?"

Now he was bouncing. That was good. "Okay, so I need you to help me get you ready for school today."

Thankfully, he complied, and I patted myself on the back for managing just fine on my own.

Chapter Fifteen

Noah

Buoyed on my resurgent friendship with Lucy, I thought I had all the answers.

Shane needed to mend things with his girlfriend, and when Micah suggested maybe he could make a big gesture at the Denver show, I encouraged him, fed his foolish notions, lent him courage. And then he did it. He came out from behind the drums, got Micah to ask the crowd to record Shane as he performed a song—poorly—on guitar. But he did it. I was so proud of him for getting out of his own way and going for it. It was something I might have done back when I'd been trying to convince Lucy to give me a shot.

I was sure Layla would be thrilled to get serenaded at a live show, even if she only saw it on video. A fan girl like that would eat that up with a spoon—or so I assumed. But I kept underestimating Layla. After a week dragged on with the video showing up on hundreds of YouTube channels and no word from Layla, I watched Shane's hope slowly fade.

I thought, *There but for the grace of God go I.*

Any wrong move and Lucy might also dive underground, and I was convinced that if I fucked things up this time, it was my last chance.

Despite Shane's moping, I was having a pretty amazing week.

What with Shane shaking things up, Denver had been a cool show all around. We had a long drive to Memphis but didn't need to be there until Thursday, and Lucy texted periodically which made the time pass deliciously. After we played Memphis, we had a short three-hour drive to Nashville, so we pressed on through the night and had a lazy day sleeping in at the hotel.

Our last leg of this tour took us to Atlanta. After that show, we splurged on plane tickets and flew home on Sunday, letting our tour bus and equipment follow us back.

We had a little over a week at home, and I started making a plan to get on a train down to D.C. for the next weekend.

When the plane touched down, Micah said, "Hey, Adam's having a cookout. You wanna come over? Jo's heading over. Layla might be there, too."

We all looked at Shane. He shook his head. "I'm gonna go home. If she wanted to talk to me, she would've called already. It'd be too awkward."

"You want company?" I asked.

"Nah. Go have fun."

After performing, the next best thing about being a musician was the band family. I might be lonely at home alone in my apartment, but the guys kept me busy between rehearsing and hanging out. Rick took off to go back to the family we rarely saw, but Micah and I called his car service and headed home to Brooklyn. My empty apartment would wait.

We arrived in the middle of some kind of drama. The girls all sat across from the TV, comforting a crying Layla, who had somehow only just seen the song Shane had written for her. From her reaction, I patted myself for correctly predicting Shane's big gesture would be a hit. A week ago, I might have been bitter about how lucky he'd been to find her, but now, I couldn't help but grin at the hope of young love.

I took out my phone right away and texted Lucy. *What do you have planned Friday night?*

I didn't expect a response right away, but I'd barely settled into a patio chair when my ringtone went off.

Why?

I'd considered surprising her, but a week of anticipation would be a lot more fun. *Thinking of having a real date night.*

You can't come down.

My heart skipped a beat. We'd been chatting every day, and while my efforts at flirting hadn't met with the same level of bantering I was hoping for, we'd at least kept the lines of communication open. Because she'd always been at work when I'd been traveling, I hadn't taken advantage of her promise to let me call. That ended now. I hit Call.

She picked up right away.

"Why can't I come down?"

A sigh. "I won't be here."

"Oh." She hadn't mentioned a trip, but maybe she'd only been humoring me for the past few days. Maybe she hadn't let me in at all. "Where you going?"

She cleared her throat. "I'm uh . . ."

I watched as Micah wrapped an arm around Jo while he talked to our host Adam. Adam's wife Eden sat in a chair behind him, baby asleep in her arms. Adam's band Walking Disaster had been headlining the types of venues we'd been opening, and yet despite the pressures of touring, he'd managed a whole family somehow. It could be done.

Lucy hadn't answered, so I prodded. "Yeah? Mid-May trip to Paris?"

She laughed, but her voice wobbled. "I'm going to visit another museum. Check out a Van Gogh they have."

"Oh, cool." I'd never known her to travel. It was a good sign. "What museum?"

"Oh, um. You wouldn't know it."

"Try me."

"It's a design museum actually."

"Why does a design museum have a Van Gogh?"

"Well, it's a sketch. They have a drawings collection."

"Who does?"

"The museum."

"What museum?"

"It's a Smithsonian."

I was so lost. "So it's in D.C.?"

"No. This one is not."

"It's called The Smithsonian?"

"No." Something about her tone was beginning to remind me of the time she'd scratched my car and hadn't wanted to tell me.

"So what is it called, Lucy."

"Why does it matter?"

"Lucy."

Silence. Something was definitely up.

"So if I Google Smithsonian . . ." I was about to.

"It's the Cooper-Hewitt Museum."

Well, she was right about one thing. "Yeah. I've never heard of that."

"Right." She sounded like a schoolteacher. "It's very small. Relatively. It only has one Van Gogh. But I need to see it."

I put her on speaker so I could pull up a browser and search for this museum. "Cooper-Hewitt you said?"

"It was originally named Cooper Union Museum for the Arts and—"

"Where is it located?"

"Oh, it's um, well . . ."

"It wouldn't be the Cooper-Hewitt Museum on the Upper East Side of Manhattan, would it? Are there two?"

"I don't think there are, no." Her voice trailed off, and I took her off speaker.

"Were you planning on telling me?"

"Noah."

"It's convenient that my name has the word *no* in it, huh?" I tried to keep the bitterness out of my tone, but there it was.

"We'd been getting along so well. I just thought this might be too soon."

"Too soon for what?"

"Well, if you must know, too soon for date night."

Shots fired. "I don't get you. You say you want my time. I offer my time to you, and it's too soon?" I gritted my teeth. "You were going to come here and avoid me? How is that not wasting time?"

"It's just more confusing when I'm with you."

"Yeah, well I'm finding this conversation confusing. Why don't you want to see me?"

"Isn't it obvious?"

"Not exactly." I paced toward the back of Adam's yard, but I felt eyes on me. They'd want to know why I'd raised my voice.

"I do want to see you. I want to see you so much it hurts."

My heart swelled at her admission. "I want to see you, too. What's the problem?"

"We're trying this *friends* thing, but I don't think I can see you without wanting more." She dropped to a near whisper. "I'll want to touch you. I'll want to kiss you. I'll want to find a hidden alcove and unzip your jeans. I'll want to slip my hands into your boxers and—"

My God. "And?"

"And what happens after that?"

I ignored her belligerent tone. "Then I slip your shirt up and unhook your bra. I run my tongue over your nipple, suck on you until you moan."

"That's not what I meant." Her voice sounded like sandpaper.

"Are you wearing pants or a skirt?"

"Jogging shorts."

A dozen memories of Lucy in shorts exploded in my mind. "Beautiful. I'd run my finger right up your thigh and slide your panties to the side."

"Noah." She was breathing shallow, a sound I loved to hear.

"I'd drop to my knees, worshiping you like you deserve. Your legs would open for me, wouldn't they?"

"Mmm-hmm."

"Can you touch yourself for me?"

"Hold on." I heard some muffled shuffling. I glanced around at the others, but the sun was setting, and they'd started to set the table or pile up grilled burgers or whatever they did. A door clicked shut on the other side. "We should stop this, Noah."

"Are you alone?"

"I'm in my room."

"Lay on your bed for me."

"I am."

"God, you're so beautiful. Do you know that?" My pants strained. What I wouldn't give to be home alone so I could join her, but I couldn't stop myself from talking her through this. "Unzip your pants, Lucy. Take them off. I want you totally bare. Okay?"

"Yes."

"I'm there with you. I'm on my knees beside you, and I'm running my fingers across your belly. Can you feel me?"

"Mmm. More, Noah."

"I spread your thighs open so I can kiss you right there on that pretty bud. Mmm you taste so good. Your finger is my tongue. Can you feel me?"

"Uh-huh." She groaned so beautifully.

"Do this for me, Lucy. Stroke farther down, find that spot where you're so wet for me. Are you wet?"

"I'm so wet. I want you so bad."

My cock was rock hard. I couldn't keep doing this.

With a glance at the others, I strode across the yard and slid open Adam's porch door. I held a finger up at Shane when he started to ask what was up. I forced my face into a scowl so he'd assume we were fighting, and then I climbed the stairs and ducked into a spare bedroom. Lucy moaned softly the whole time.

"I'm taking off my pants, Lucy." I grasped myself at the base, worried I might come on the spot.

"I want to see you."

Did I dare? It was basic Internet training not to send dick pics, but Lucy asked. I turned the camera to video and started recording while I stroked up and down, precum pooling at the tip. I opened our last text chain, attached the video and hit send. "Check your messages."

"Check yours."

A notification came up, and I slid it open. She'd recorded herself, shirt hitched up to her neck, bra unclasped, pants completely gone, and her hand was right on the spot I desperately wished I could touch.

"You're so fucking gorgeous, Lucy. I want to bury myself in you."

"God, look at you. I'm saving this video forever. I'm gonna get off right here from watching you."

I had her video on repeat as well. "Can you see me sliding into you?"

"Kiss me, Noah."

If only I could. "I'm nearly there, baby. Can you come with me?"

"My legs are wrapped around your back. Fuck me hard."

That was my Lucy. I stroked faster, wishing our fantasy could be reality. All at once, my balls tightened, and I was overwhelmed by an orgasm that ripped through me. "Oh, my God."

Lucy gasped on the other side, which was always a clue that she was there. "Noah."

Hearing her say my name like she'd say the name of God? That did not suck one little bit.

I suddenly realized where I was and what I'd done here. I waddled my ass over to the bathroom and found a roll of toilet paper. I needed to wash my hands, but first I wanted to check in on Lucy.

"Hey."

"I'm here."

"That was like old times, huh?"

"You just made my point, Noah. I can't even talk to you on the phone without it turning into something."

"So maybe we should steer clear of those private alcoves."

She laughed. "Maybe we should steer clear of each other for a while."

"No. Meet me when you're up here." I couldn't let this pass. "I want to show you around. It will all be above board. Promise."

"You can't promise that. We didn't make it through a phone call."

"Yeah, but see? It's out of our system now. Right?"

"If it worked like that, we wouldn't be having this conversation, would we?"

I smiled. She wasn't wrong. There was no universe in which I ever sated my desire for Lucy Griffin.

"We can try it. I can't exactly fornicate with you in the middle of Times Square. I'd very much like to introduce you to that horror."

Not that I could walk through Times Square without someone recognizing me. I'd make it work.

"Okay."

I double-blinked. Had I won? "Okay?"

"Yes. You can take me out Friday night. But it isn't date night. And there will be none of this. This was just pretend."

Whatever she wanted, as long as I got to spend time with her. "Sure. No date. Just you and me on Friday night. And I get to plan it all."

"Nothing romantic. Promise. Just friends."

"Promise."

The wheels were already spinning. How did I let New York City seduce the girl for me?

Lucy

Just talk on the phone, she'd said. *You can't get into trouble talking,* she'd said.

It wasn't like I could chastise my mom for her misguided advice without giving her a visual I'd rather not share.

I blushed remembering how hot that phone call had been. For the past few nights, my fantasies had grown more graphic, more filthy, more forbidden.

I was in so much trouble now.

The suitcase lay open on the bed, and even though I'd only be gone through Sunday, I'd already packed a week's worth of clothes.

Did I need to bring another book?

Did I need to buy a chastity belt?

Mom called from downstairs, and my heartbeat doubled. It was nearly time to go, and I wasn't ready.

I double-checked my messenger back for the fifth time to make sure I had a printout of our itinerary, plane tickets, hotel reservations.

Underwear, check.

Toothbrush, yes.

Phone charger! I ran over and unplugged the cord.

Why was I so nervous? The museum visit wouldn't take that much time, and the woman I'd spoken to on the phone had been lovely. I was looking forward to meeting her in person and seeing their collection.

And I'd seen Noah twice in the past month, not to mention we'd spoken on the phone. My stomach flipped over. Okay, *spoken* was a euphemism, and I had to admit that I hadn't been able to stop imagining what he might have planned for us. I hadn't thought about Noah in the future for so many years now, that I didn't recognize the feeling fluttering in my belly. Was it just nerves or something else? Something more?

I didn't like how my body craved him. I didn't like how he occupied my every waking thought.

"COME ON, MOMMY!" Owen had a set of lungs on him, and I could picture him balling his fists up to get that volume.

"On my way!"

I gave my suitcase one last glance, ran to my closet and tossed in another dress and a pair of slings. You never knew when you might go out dancing.

We carried everything out to the Uber and whisked to the airport. Those nerves swooped again. I'd avoided traveling for years. Owen had merely been a useful excuse to get out of business trips. I'd hear people talking about their plans to visit other cities or countries even, and I couldn't quite believe they wanted to go. I figured everyone was pretending to be that adventurous. I'd seen as much of the world as I wanted to from pictures. Why did I need to physically go to the Grand Canyon?

And the actual travel part of travel was such a nightmare. No sooner had we checked our bags than we had to unpack everything we'd put in our carry-ons, take off our shoes, and stagger along with a crowd through a very slow-moving line, examined like we all had nefarious plans.

On the plus side, Owen was mesmerized by everything. As soon as we'd made it through security, he ran into the first waiting area to watch a plane taking off out the window. I had to herd him on, but he walked with big steps and hummed his song extra loud. He reminded me so much of Noah, sometimes.

The thought knocked the wind out of my lungs.

A pain ripped through my intestines, and I doubled over, afraid I might vomit. Violently.

I dropped down on one knee for a minute to catch my breath. Owen nudged me. "What's wrong, Mommy?"

My mom grabbed him by the hand. "You need a minute, Lucy?"

I nodded until the knot in my side relaxed, then I stood, trying to laugh it off. "That was weird."

"I haven't seen you have a panic attack like that since you were a kid."

"Panic attack?" Is that what it was? "I've never had panic attacks."

"Oh, yes. You used to get so worked up." She rubbed my back. "This is a pretty big trip. It's normal to get overwhelmed."

"Well, I'm fine." I wasn't about to explain my existential crisis in the airport terminal. I started walking toward our gate. "Just not used to flying."

It was Owen who talked me through the takeoff. He held my hand and said, "It's okay. Don't be scared."

But I was. I was scared about being flung through the sky. I was worried about letting Noah entwine himself in my heart again. And an altogether more terrible fear, one that had been slumbering like a dragon, had only begun to wake. If I let Noah back into my life, I could no longer avoid telling him about his son, and then everything would change.

And I had no idea how Noah would react. There were a few messy possibilities, each progressively worse.

He might want to keep the status quo, keep this tentative friendship and try to see me whenever he could, but with no interest in meeting Owen or being his dad. This might be the easiest outcome, but once I'd told Noah, the status quo would become untenable. I'd never be able to continue a relationship with Noah if he felt that way. Not even friendship. As long as he was unaware, I didn't have to judge him. Honestly, I couldn't picture him taking this option, at least not for long. His issues with his own dad would weigh on him.

He might want to have a place in Owen's life without changing anything else. And that ought to be better, but it wasn't. I'd always assumed this would be the arrangement that would best suit Noah, but it was not good enough for my child. Owen deserved a dad who could be there for him. Not just *time to time*.

Of course, there was a better than zero chance Noah might cut and run, too freaked out about being a dad to keep seeing me. And that would hurt, but at least it would be a clean decision.

Most likely, he'd be so mad at me for keeping this secret that he'd refuse to ever see me again—at least at first. And I'd deserve that. I would so very much deserve that. I felt the pain of my decision every single day. But this was the reaction I most hoped for. I wanted him to be mad at me. I hoped he'd want Owen so much he'd hate me for keeping him away.

There was one last scenario, the one I couldn't even entertain as remotely likely, not with our history. Still, I sent up futile prayers that when Noah learned he had a son, he'd want to know him, would fall instantly in love, and rearrange his life so he could be present. This least likely Noah would also forgive me, and we'd find a way to be together. In the same house. Every day.

I had impossible dreams.

Owen snuggled against my arm, with Rabbit in the other. He was so small when he slept. I dragged a finger across his brow to move a lock of blond hair off to the side. Noah had wondered why I'd admitted to John that I'd been unfaithful. But even if a miracle pregnancy hadn't made it obvious, the arrival of a little blond cherub to a raven-haired mom and dad was a pretty huge clue. Owen had Noah's clear gray-blue eyes, but he'd gotten my lips. He was a pretty little thing. I'd have to remember to keep the guitars out of his hands.

The plane banked hard, and down below, city lights spread out forever. I nudged Owen so he could look out. He smashed his face to the window and said *Oooooh* so adorably sing-song that the people around us giggled.

Somewhere, in one of those buildings, Noah might be thinking about me. I was in his world now.

Chapter Sixteen

Noah

The hardest part of planning our date night—er, friend night—was limiting myself to a reasonable slate of activities. I wanted to show Lucy Times Square, but also take her to a show, walk across the Bow Bridge in Central Park, ride the subway, take the South Street ferry past the Statue of Liberty, and escort her to the top of the Empire State Building. If we had a month together, we could do all that and more. There were museums she'd love. Restaurants without end. And street food.

And I wanted to show her where I lived, where I rehearsed. I wanted her to meet Jo and Layla. She already knew Shane and Micah, but I wanted her to become friends with my friends.

I wanted her to want to stay.

It was a crazy stupid thing to want, and I fought to keep my expectations in check. But it had been over half a decade since I'd been able to dream about Lucy without feeling fifty kinds of shitty about it, and it was liberating to know she was free to pursue. Even before that, when she was mine, she still would never come up to visit me, so this was already more than

I could have hoped. Still, I couldn't help daydream that I could entice her to consider relocating so we could try this thing again in the same town.

I realized it was selfish to want her to come to me, but considering even then, I'd be on the road half the time, I knew she'd never go for it.

Obviously, I could resolve this by moving to D.C. to be closer to her, but then I'd have to quit the band. That seemed like a drastic action to take for a woman who might not want me in her life anymore regardless of physical distance.

She'd arrived in town the night before. She didn't tell me where she was staying, but I'd figured out it was Midtown based on limited information. She'd texted from the Uber and mentioned passing the Winter Garden theater. She said her mom was with her, and I wondered if she'd brought her as a ready excuse. "*Well, I'd love to spend the night, but I need to get back to Mom.*"

But when I'd suggested I could come pick her up and say hi to Mrs. Griffin, she'd asked where she could meet me instead. I was convinced she was gonna get herself lost, and the last thing I wanted was for her to feel frustrated or scared in the city.

I had come up with step one: Dinner.

Take a taxi to 1 Fulton St tomorrow at 6. Text me when you leave. Wear comfy shoes!

Now I sat in a restaurant with Shane and Layla on a break from rehearsal, trying to come up with something to do with Lucy after dinner. The biggest hurdle I faced were paparazzi. I had to make it through one night without Lucy's picture ending up on Page Six.

Fortunately, I wasn't *that* famous. Outside of a concert, if people weren't looking for me, they usually didn't find me.

Unfortunately, people had been looking for me ever since my girlfriend dumped me for a bigger name.

"It's the Samuel Tucker angle that makes the story interesting," Layla explained. "People are naturally curious."

I flagged a waitress and pointed to my empty beer glass. "Then they'll lose interest soon, right?"

She waggled her head noncommittally, neither yes or no. It turned out that Layla, with her fan site connections, had an uncanny knack for digging up the latest gossip about me. She'd gotten a taste of being under the microscope herself when her relationship with Shane, and subsequent speculation about her relationship with *me*, added grist to the rumor mill for the past couple of weeks. My little afterparty flirtation performance at the Boston festival had added fuel to that fire, and I'd already apologized profusely for whatever garbage people said about her online. But she'd handled it really well, shrugging it off like a pro.

"They might. It doesn't help that you're so pretty."

Shane looked up from his food. "Hey. I'm right here."

I cackled.

Layla rolled her eyes and leaned forward, toward me. "It also doesn't help that you're such a brat."

My turn to object. "I'm not a brat. I'm just—"

"—an asshole," Shane supplied.

He was lucky we were in a public restaurant or I might have punched him in the arm. "Takes one to know one."

"Boys," Layla scolded. "Look, the common wisdom is that you aren't taking the breakup with Crystal well. Your bad attitude at shows has lent credence to that rumor. I mean, you can't argue that lately you've been grumpy or surly." She half-smiled, and I could tell she was enjoying taking the piss out of me. "Or downright rude."

"And?" I didn't understand how nobody had noticed that I was always all these things. I gave fans my time because it was contractually obligated, but I only felt I owed them what they'd paid for—a great fucking show or a solid album. I still couldn't understand how a hug entered into the exchange. "If they want to blame my bad attitude on a broken heart, that's their prerogative."

Layla gave me an appraising look. "Fans love to chase after crazy theories, but they're often accurate or scarily close with their interpretations."

"Like when they thought you and I were dating?"

That earned a scowl. "They weren't wrong to notice that I had left that party with you. They couldn't have known that I was two minutes away from kneeing you in the balls."

Shane snorted. "He deserved it, too."

Layla started to bite into a fry but then waved it like a finger as she went on. "They might be wrong about Crystal, Noah. But they're only wrong about which girl you're grieving."

I didn't acknowledge her perceptive comment. Instead, I downed the entire glass of beer and then asked the question that had started this whole discussion. "So in your wisdom, Lucy's safely off the radar?"

"For now. If you keep a low profile, you should be able to manage without attracting any notice." She glanced at her phone. "I need to get back to work. And you—" she kissed Shane's cheek "—have rehearsal."

She patted my shoulder before she left. "Good luck tonight."

Shane and I headed back to the old garage we'd converted into a rehearsal space. I shoved my hands into my pockets, mulling over everything Layla had said and how to plan around any issues that might scare off Lucy.

I scanned the street for any of the odd people who'd sometimes hang around outside the garage. Sometimes fans visiting the city would go out of their way to try to meet us to get an autograph or a selfie. Those people never bothered me. But there were others who stood at a distance, taking pictures, watching us. Those people creeped me out, but normally I just ignored them. It was the possibility of introducing Lucy into my world that had me reassessing every possible interaction.

"Head out of your ass, Noah."

I shot a glance at my best friend. "Just thinking about what a weird life this is."

"It's the best." A month ago Shane wouldn't have had such a rosy opinion of the rocker lifestyle, but love had made him the eternal optimist.

"You've really lucked out with that girl."

He smiled. "I know. I can't believe I almost fucked that up."

He didn't see the irony that it was this whole lifestyle that had nearly fucked things up. "Layla's really adapted well to the spotlight."

"Yeah."

"What if she didn't, though?"

"Huh?" Shane slowed.

"What if she hated this life? What if she wanted you to leave it?"

He chuckled. "That's crazy. She's a music freak. She'll probably want to come meet us out on tour next week."

"But what if she didn't, Shane." I gave him a meaningful look. "Would you choose the band or her?"

His eyebrows drew together. "Are you asking this because she gave up her fan site for me? I didn't tell her to do that."

I gave up and let him rehash everything that had happened in the past couple of weeks, tuning him out as my mood darkened. How had Layla described me? Grumpy, surly, downright rude.

By the time I finally strapped my guitar on, I was questioning all my life choices. When Micah called for us to pick up where we'd left off, practicing one of his new songs, I snapped. "Don't we have better things to do than rehearse this song for the millionth time? It's done, and I'm sick of it."

Whenever we had some time off, Micah got a bug up his ass about the next album, and we spent every waking moment— okay, four hours a day—trying out different ideas. If we got anywhere close to perfect, we didn't get a break. Instead, he'd get us into a studio to spend entire days—actual twelve-hour days—laying down tracks until he was satisfied. Our albums were tight, much tighter than our live shows, because of his perfectionism. I couldn't have cared less about how polished the records were, but I actually loved tinkering with them while we were exploring. And coming up with those guitar solos I knew I'd get to play live challenged me and kept me content with the off time. Micah knew all that.

"I'll make a deal with you," he barked. "If you can pretend your mind is in the rehearsal this time, we'll move on."

Micah turned back toward the mic, no longer giving me the time of day. He didn't have to. I was on the bloody team.

Shane started a four count, and I let my hands take over the instrument, but my thoughts drifted back to my plans with Lucy. After I was done here, I'd get to see her tonight, and a thrill coursed through my veins. Micah eyed me, and I let loose on the solo, feeling the joy of both the music and the future, something I hadn't looked forward to in a very long time.

It was mere hours away now. Could I make her love my home enough to want to come back another time? Could I make her love me enough to want to stay?

Lucy

I wished I'd gotten Noah's suggestion to wear comfortable shoes before I'd walked three blocks across Manhattan. On the map, everything looked so close. How could it take so long to walk three blocks? Of course, people always complained that the National Mall was way bigger than they'd expected. Maybe we humans didn't have the capacity to understand how vast the world actually was.

I'd thought I knew how crowded a city could be, but it felt like the entire world had come to New York. Times Square had been a crush of tourists, hawkers, and a whole lot of filthy costumes. Pushing a stroller through that madness had nearly driven me to give up and spend the rest of the morning in the hotel, ordering room service. Mom insisted it would get easier once we got across town, and it had. But then I was assaulted by the smells. And I couldn't understand why anyone bothered to take a car when the roads looked more like parking lots.

"People come here on purpose?"

People lived here?

Noah lived here?

We made it to the MoMA somehow unscathed. I'd meant to drag Mom and Owen to see Van Gogh's *Starry Night,* make a quick tour, and then take an Uber to the Guggenheim for another whirlwind visit. Then we could grab lunch before I needed to meet a curator at the Cooper-Hewitt. But once in the MoMA, Owen wanted to get out and walk, so then we had to stop and check out every sculpture. We ended up losing two hours and decided to grab a bite there.

To get Owen to agree to the Friday morning art museums, I'd promised him we'd go to the zoo in Central Park on Saturday. I planned to squeeze in a peek into the Metropolitan Museum. I'd also told Owen we'd try to make it to the Museum of Natural History at some point, but I was beginning to think I may have over-planned for two days. It might require a second trip to take it all in.

And I hadn't even thought about the other sites we'd have to neglect.

In D.C. we'd just go across the Mall and into another museum or to the Capitol building or the White House. You could see most everything in a couple of days if you planned well. Here it took more effort to get from place to place. But knowing we'd have to grab a taxi to get to the next museum had encouraged us to stay longer and pay more attention. I wondered if people would get more out of the National Gallery if it were more isolated. It would be easy to get lost in one museum, and we still had so many more to see.

Maybe I was beginning to understand the appeal of New York a little bit. I was tired, but so energized by all the possibilities.

Mom went through the cafeteria line while I settled Owen in at a table. "Hey, buddy. Did you like this museum?"

"Oh, yeah!" His shoulders seesawed in his little dance. I pulled out a couple of *Star Wars* figurines buried in my purse and handed them to him so they could become a part of his choreography.

When Mom set down a couple of trays, I took a long drink of water. "I'm thinking we need to rethink our plans."

Mom groaned as she sat. "Maybe you should go on up to the Cooper-Hewitt alone. Owen and I can keep looking around here, or I could start back to the hotel. I understand there's a T-O-Y store."

It made me nervous to let them out of my sight in the middle of that apocalypse outside, but when we reemerged, the buildings and crowd looked considerably less intimidating. Maybe everyone had gone to day jobs. I knelt down in front of Owen's stroller and made sure Rabbit was tucked in beside him. He was singing, but he stopped to say, "Nana's gonna show me the Legos." He said it more like *Wegoosh*, but I got it.

"Tell her you can get one set." I shot a glance at Mom. His Duplo collection had its own room. "Maybe they'll have an X-wing fighter."

They set off in one direction, and then I hailed a cab, hoping I wouldn't get myself lost. The buildings fell away as Central Park loomed on the left, and I was transfixed at how it went on for blocks and blocks: another world I wouldn't be able to conquer on this trip. I was surprised at how sad that made me. After all, it was just a park.

The taxi let me off at the corner, and I checked the address to make sure I'd come to the right place. I'd looked at pictures online, so I thought I knew exactly what the building would look like. But the reality was so different. The enormous three-story estate somehow looked simultaneously like a mansion out of Gatsby or a high-end London hotel or an urban high school. In pictures, I'd seen ivy on the walls and a huge lawn that had given me the impression it sat deep in the country or on an expanse of private property. In reality, it sat across the street from Central Park on one side and a catholic church on the other.

I might have been wrong when I'd assumed that I didn't need to travel to see the world. It kept not looking how I was expecting it to.

I gathered my courage and entered through the gate onto the lawn I'd seen in pictures. If I hadn't been nervous before, I suddenly was now. I immediately wished I'd brought Owen. I'd never be able to describe this place to him. And when I went inside, that regret only grew. I'd bring him next time.

A wave of dizziness washed over me. What did I mean by next time?

After a little orientation, I found my way to the room that housed the Van Gogh, stopping along the way to check out all the cool displays. The layout of the building was so homey and comfortable. Some of the rooms looked like something out of a French palace. Others like a 1920s mansion. A staircase that seemed to come straight out of a movie set. The whole place was so fun, walking around was like a mini adventure. I'd definitely be bringing Owen here at some point. I couldn't believe I'd been at all nervous to visit. Now I didn't want to leave.

A young girl approached me as I examined the Van Gogh drawing. "Are you Lucy Griffin?"

I nodded.

She reached her hand out to shake as she said, "I'm Dajana Sipek. We spoke on the phone."

I made a mental note that she pronounced her name like *Diana* and shook her hand. After seeing the rest of the museum, I had to ask, "Why do you even have a Van Gogh here?"

"We have two."

"Wait, what?"

"Yeah. Would you like to see the textile?"

"Oh, my God. Yes."

She smiled. "It's great to have the high profile of being a part of the Smithsonian, but if I'm being honest, I'm going to be gutted to lose even one of our Van Gogh works."

"Well, it would just be a loan."

"Of course."

I followed her through a very cool atrium that held among other things literal bicycles. Not Dada bicycles. Just real bicycles. I was so charmed at the lack of irony. But when we stood before the Van Gogh, my knees nearly buckled. "I've never seen this before."

She grinned. "We keep a few secrets."

We spent the next hour chatting about our own art history backgrounds and wandering around the museum. I told her, "I love this environment so much."

She raised an eyebrow. "Well, we're always on the lookout for people who love art."

I laughed. I wasn't angling for a job offer. "Thank you, but I worked so hard to get where I am at the National Gallery, and I'm hoping to move up from assistant curator." Not to mention, moving to New York City was completely out of the question.

"Sometimes the most direct path requires a detour."

"That sounds like a fortune cookie."

"I'm just saying."

After filling out paperwork to start the loan process, I left the museum, letting Dajana know to expect my call in the following week so we could arrange the details. There were strict protocols around all transfers, and she'd need to get approvals, then arrange the requisite packing and shipping.

When I took my first steps outside, I was still in the haze of infatuation with the museum. I toured D.C. museums frequently, and they usually had new exhibits, so I didn't feel like I was missing much, but after visiting the MoMA and now the Cooper-Hewitt, I was aware there was a whole world out there to explore. I had renewed interest in making it to the Guggenheim and the Met before we went home.

For a split second, as I walked across the lawn to the exit, I felt adventurous and excited about the world, but then I walked through the gate and remembered I was in the middle of a foreign city. I had to fight to find a taxi, and traffic was insane. It took almost forty minutes to get back to Midtown. My fare was astronomical. I'd need to learn to use the subway. There was no possible way I could tolerate the city for long. It was out of the question I'd be able to live somewhere like this.

When I got back to the hotel, I found Mom and Owen snuggled up against the headboard, pillows fluffed behind them, watching the TV. Mom was fast asleep. Owen had a Lego set spread out in front of him.

I felt terrible that I was going to turn around and abandon him again. I sat on the bed beside him. "What do you want to do tomorrow, buddy? I don't think we can do both the zoo and the museum."

"Zoo." He put together a couple of pieces that clearly had nothing to do with the instructions. "Zoopty doop. Doopy zoop."

He didn't even glance up. I kissed his head and stripped down to get in the shower. I had about an hour before I had to go to some random address, and I had no idea what I'd find there other than Noah. And that was enough.

I took my time putting on makeup, even though I'd asked Noah to keep it light, friends only. Still, I went through my ridiculous amount of clothes, rejecting dresses because he'd said to wear comfy shoes. Comfy shoes meant my Keds. I worked up from there. Soft faded jeans that made my ass look amazing. I flipped through shirts. Why had I brought T-shirts? I found a cute black knit with a scoop neck. My cleavage looked incredible in that shirt.

Next my hair. Noah went crazy when I went to the trouble to style it just so. I worked some leave-in conditioner through it, then blew it dry, straightening it. Then I spritzed it and crunched it with my hands to volumize. The products smelled so good. I looked like a young Joan Jett when I'd finished. Noah had a total fetish for young Joan Jett. I had reason to know.

It might not be playing fair for friends-only, but I hadn't been out on the town in a long time. I wanted to look my best.

Finally, I sent the request for the Uber and woke my mom up. Owen didn't seem to notice I'd gotten all dolled up. I didn't want him to fuss that I was leaving, but he'd become so much more reliant on my mom lately I worried he was going to forget which of us had nursed him when he was a baby.

Well, he'd probably already forgotten that specifically.

Mom said, "Owen, baby, tell your mom who we saw today."

He stayed focused on his weird Lego creation but said, "Oh, yeah." Even the way he said that sounded like a little song with three notes. "Mommy, we saw Groot."

I laughed. "The real Groot?"

Mom colored in the rest. "They had a display at the toy store and some of the characters were out greeting the kids."

"Wow, that's exciting. Did you see Star Lord, too?"

Owen shook his head, but Mom said, "No, but . . ." She left a dramatic pause until I raised a curious brow. "I think I might have seen Brian Williams."

I chuckled. She'd probably imagined it. She had such a news crush on him. "Well, look at you all, running into famous people wherever you go." I supposed that happened more in New York than anywhere else in the world other than L.A. maybe. "If you see Lin-Manuel, tell him I said, 'Hi.' "

I gave Owen a kiss. "Nana will take you to get some dinner. You can have ice cream if you want. I'll be home tonight."

Then I was down the elevator and on the street, searching for a black Elantra. The driver verified the address, and we were off in the opposite direction than I'd gone earlier. I watched more streets pass, spying the occasional New York City landmark. And then all of a sudden in front of us, a bridge materialized. The Brooklyn Bridge. My heart sped up. This was a legendary bridge, and it blew my expectations out of the water. I'd seen it photographed and painted, but never in person. It was spectacular.

At the other side, the driver rounded a corner, and there in front of me I saw the loveliest view of all: Noah, standing on the sidewalk, hands in pockets, bouncing on his toes as he watched the street for me.

Chapter Seventeen

Noah

I never thought I'd see the day that Lucy Griffin would be in Brooklyn walking toward me, sunset orange tinting her skin. I wanted to reel her in for a kiss, but she'd insisted we keep the romance out of tonight, and I was weirdly okay with that. I'd had enough meaningless sex and fake romance over the years that I was happy to trade it all in to get back a little piece of my soul. I'd die happy if I could spend the rest of my life doing nothing more than drinking in Lucy as she looked at me the way she did right now.

Her smile spread across her face. Nobody had ever smiled at me with that level of joy unless they didn't actually know me. Total strangers out of their minds with fan lust didn't count. Lucy's smile meant I was doing something right.

I had to bite my lip to stop myself from gushing over how incredible she looked. She'd dressed for comfort, but that didn't mean she hadn't taken the time to show off all her amazing features. It took a ridiculous act of will power not to thrust my hands into her hair and drag her face to mine.

Instead, I shoved my hands in my pockets, and said, "You hungry?"

"Starving."

"Good. Because the first thing we're going to do is have some greasy burgers and split a black-and-white shake." She'd never been to a Shake Shack, so she cocked her head, and I explained. "Chocolate and vanilla."

I could have impressed her with the most upscale restaurant in Manhattan, but my goal wasn't shock and awe. My goal was to make her feel at home, to lull her into a sense of security. I wanted her to long to come back. I wanted her to want to stay.

We ordered our food and grabbed a booth. She checked her phone for a second but just as fast put it away and gave me her full attention. "So where are we exactly?"

"I guess this is technically part of Brooklyn Heights."

"And this is close to where you live?"

I scratched my chin, wondering how literal she meant that. It was the closest she'd ever been to my apartment. "It's in the same borough, but we're not within walking distance of my place really."

"Where is that?"

"It's called Park Slope. I live pretty close to Shane. Micah's not that far away either."

She shook her head. "I had no idea New York City was so huge. I'll never be able to see a fraction of it. My mind is totally blown."

I leaned my head back, cursing myself for not realizing that I should have come to meet her. Of course she was going to be intimidated by how endless this city was. I took a deep breath, determined to right this ship. "Do you know how you eat an elephant?"

She'd just taken a sip of the milkshake and merely shook her head with a confused look.

"One bite at a time."

That made the milkshake spew back out, and she grabbed a wad of napkins, muttering, "Shit shit shit."

Maybe I was the worst kind of cave dweller, but as I reached over and dabbed a pool of white off her lower lip, I got a semi chubby imagining my cum on her mouth. I bit the inside of my cheek, hoping a little pain would get my mind back in the friend zone. It was a good thing we were sitting. The last thing I wanted was for Lucy to know that, while I could appreciate her for as much as she'd give me, I'd never stop wanting to hear her scream my name as an orgasm ripped through her. I'd never stop wanting her.

Once the momentary crisis was over, she relaxed and asked, "Why were you talking about elephants?"

I'd have to demonstrate.

I waved at the empty plates before us. We'd both inhaled our burgers and fries. "Are you done eating?"

She slurped up the last of the shake and nodded. I stood and carried the trash to the bin. She followed, and I pointed over at the Brooklyn Bridge above us. "So you said New York was too big to see all of it. That's quite true. I've been here forever, and I tend to stick to my haunts. But we're going to take one bite out of the apple, and you can go home with a memory you'll cherish."

When she looked at me with those big eyes, I felt a hundred feet tall.

We headed up to the walkway, and she said, "No way," as she realized we were going to walk across. The sun hung low on the horizon, so the view of the city was particularly spectacular. She continued to say variations of *Oh, my God* or *Wow* until we were halfway across. Then she leaned over the rail and just stared at the Manhattan skyline.

I laid a hand on her back. I couldn't help myself. It was an experience I'd never imagined possible, yet here she was, with me, in my city.

"This feels so quintessential. Is this what it feels like to be a New Yorker?" In that moment, she seemed so open to anything, so I told her what it meant to me, knowing how insane it might sound.

"When I first came here, I didn't know what to expect. All I knew of New York was from TV which was mostly crime shows.

And, yes, New York is gritty and dangerous and all those things, but mostly it's about opportunity. This is going to sound cheesy as all hell, but New York feels like the essence of America."

She snorted at that, and I clenched my teeth. I hadn't expected her to mock my words. But she went a different way than I expected. "Noah, Washington D.C. is literally the essence of America. It's foundational."

Dissent I could deal with. I hadn't had a good argument with Lucy in ages. "It's just the seat of government, Lucy. But it's sterile. New York has a beating heart, and it's teeming with the American experience. Look around. This is the American experiment in a petri dish."

Her eyebrows rose. "Petri dish? Is that because you could catch a venereal disease from touching a lamppost?"

I fake laughed. "So funny. But you asked me if this was a New York experience and the answer is yes. Because every experience you have here is valid. Everyone is welcome."

Her crooked smile shot an arrow through my heart when she said, "I would love to see your New York, Noah."

My hand, with a mind of its own, reached up and pushed that incredible hair back, even though her hair didn't need any help. I just wanted to touch her. "I would love nothing more than to show you my city."

I had a feeling that we were no longer talking about a place on a map, and by the wicked look in her eye, I knew she was thinking the same as me. Thankfully, or sadly, we were perched on a very public bridge among countless passing tourists. I held out my hand and was relieved when she took it. We strolled slowly to the other side, and the whole time, I told her about the things I'd fallen in love with over the years.

"At first, I didn't want to be here. I missed you so damn much, but Shane was here, and music was the only job I was qualified to do. Then, Shane convinced me to explore and stake out those parts of the city that I can't live without. It's hard to explain unless—"

"The museums," she said. "I've only seen two museums, and I feel cheated that I won't have time to see them all."

I stopped. "I thought you had more art than you could ever explore on the Mall." She'd said that enough times.

The corner of her mouth sucked in between her teeth, and she gave me that look that said she either wanted to cop to everything I'd accused her of or punch me in the balls. I nearly covered my dick, but she laughed gently. "I may have been wrong about a thing or two."

"Like?" I wanted her to say she'd been wrong about me, but that seemed like a pipe dream.

"Like this bridge." She held up her hands toward the wonder of steel. "I didn't think I ever needed to see this for myself. I'd seen it in pictures and art. Why would I need to go all the way to New York to experience it." I didn't know if she realized it, but she laid a hand on my hip. "It makes me wonder what else I've been missing out on. Should I visit the Grand Canyon?"

I inched closer, hoping she wouldn't stop touching me. "I hate to tell you this, but the Grand Canyon isn't in New York."

Her fingers clenched my shirt. "I know, but what about the Empire State building?"

"That I can do for you."

Lucy

How do people deny themselves the pleasures they most want? Are there anonymous meetings for people who can't stop wanting a person? Are there self-help books to remind you why you need to?

Being this close to Noah was an exercise in self-restraint. He was, for the most part, respecting my boundaries. And when he wasn't, I couldn't bring myself to tell him he should. It was getting progressively harder not to beg him to take me home with him, to show me his apartment, his bed, to tell him I'd be his forever.

But I had someone else counting on me, and I was trying to figure out if or when I should tell Noah everything. It wouldn't be fair to let him think we'd moved back to our old relationship without confessing that truth. But confessing that truth might derail this delicate friendship. I just needed to figure out how much I could trust Noah before I could make a definitive decision to either be totally in or totally out. I couldn't do that while we were exchanging surreptitious touches under the pretense of arguing.

Noah directed me the rest of the way across the bridge and hailed a cab. As we whisked across town, I slid over closer to him. I had this whole fantasy about Noah in the back of a car because of that thwarted incident at the high school prom. Sadly, he'd sold his Skylark before moving to New York.

As I snuggled up against him in the back of the cab now, I sniffed at his T-shirt, breathing in memories and sex, but he put his arm around me and said, "I can't wait to show you everything."

When we got out, I was once again disoriented by the unfamiliarity of yet another place I'd never been. Noah nudged me and pointed up, and I recognized the very famous Empire State building. So two things were now familiar: this landmark and Noah. Somehow having him with me made all of this change exciting and fun rather than scary.

Inside, Noah bought the tickets, and we held hands as we waited for the elevator. In the back of my mind, I tried to remind myself that we should be keeping our distance, that any contact with Noah might lead us to scarring the children around us for life, but I couldn't let go of his hand. It was like a lifeline.

Finally, it was our turn, and as we rode up, Noah slid in behind me and pulled me back against him. I relaxed into him, focused on his arm wrapping around my front. We fit together like two halves of a whole, and I wanted the elevator to keep going up until we reached the clouds.

But the doors opened, and we followed a crowd up to the deck, another place I'd seen in movies and thought I could probably imagine it as well as reality. Again I was wrong.

Noah's hand stayed on the small of my back, more a reminder he was there than anything, and he let me lead us toward the railing. Maybe we *had* ridden into the sky. "It's like the stars are below us."

We drifted along, feigning interest in the view, but the wonder of all mankind couldn't compete with the miracle of this one man here with me tonight. Apparently, I wasn't the only one who found his presence more fascinating than the vast ocean of city lights before us.

A girl, maybe fifteen or sixteen, approached and said, "Excuse me. You're that guitarist from Theater of the Absurd, aren't you?" When he nodded, her eyes grew wide as saucers. "I thought so." She turned back to another group of teens and shot a saucy rebuke. "It is. I told you."

I was amused by how her demeanor had changed from nervous, to giddy, to argumentative over the course of a few sentences.

Then she sweetly smiled and said, "Do you mind if I take a picture with you?"

Her other friends drew closer, and now other people were watching. Camera phones rose up around us, and random strangers clicked pictures like Noah was the tourist draw. Only a couple more people asked him for selfies or autographs, but it reminded me that Noah wasn't mine alone. He wasn't who I thought he was all the time. Neither was he who these strangers thought he was. It rattled me a little to realize how easily I'd allowed myself to believe in the versions of ourselves we'd been before, when we were kids. We each had complicated edges now, and we no longer fit together like we had in the elevator. That had been an illusion.

When we'd exhausted all possible reasons for remaining aloft above the city, we descended to street level.

Noah asked, "Are you staying near Times Square?"

"Yeah."

"I can walk you there."

His arm slipped over my shoulder, and I leaned into him, walking intentionally slowly to drag this out. "This has been so nice."

"You say that like we won't see each other again. What are your plans tomorrow?"

"The Central Park Zoo in the morning. Museum of Natural History in the afternoon."

"Huh. I would have thought you'd be ping-ponging between the art museums."

He knew me too well, and I didn't have a good reason for straying from my own character, but there was one truth I could offer. "There's just so much to see."

"Would you mind if I tagged along? I'm not doing anything and I could act as tour guide again."

I should have seen this wrinkle coming. I took his hands in mine and faced him. Maybe it was time to come clean. It wasn't an ideal location, but I guessed we had a few blocks left. I took a deep breath. "Listen. There's something we need to talk about."

A man to my left said, "Noah!" and I turned toward his voice, at first assuming that one of Noah's friends had crossed paths with us, but then a flash of light blinded me, and he said, "Is this the new girlfriend? What's her name?"

Noah dropped my hands and lunged. The photographer turned tail and ran, but Noah chased after in hot pursuit, leaving me alone. I backed up behind some scaffolding. Why was there so much scaffolding everywhere? Even this temporary object had graffiti all over it. People passed by, bumping into me like I wasn't there, or staring at me like I was out of place.

I hadn't felt remotely nervous the entire time Noah had been at my side, but now I hugged my purse closer to my body, attentive to anyone who might mean to do me harm. Cars passed. A horn honked a few blocks over. In the distance, I could hear sirens. I had no idea where I was.

Then Noah came back around the corner. "Damn. I'm sorry. I couldn't catch him. I don't know who he was with."

"Does this happen all the time?"

"More and more lately." His jaw clenched. "I shouldn't have come up this way with you. These people have like a sixth sense for even minor celebrities."

"And they don't stalk you in Brooklyn?"

He snorted. "They stalk everywhere, but I guess they tend to cluster where they'll catch more fish, and we're just blocks from the theaters. If you keep your eyes open, you'll realize one day you're standing behind Patrick Stewart at an ATM."

"Has that happened to you?"

He shrugged. "He lives somewhere near me. Has no idea who I am, though. Why would he?"

"But the photographer did. Those kids did."

"The paparazzi are a different breed. You know Micah's girlfriend, Jo?"

I shook my head. "I've never met her."

"Well, she used to take pictures for a tabloid. That's actually how she met Micah, strangely enough." He smiled like that pleased him somehow. "Anyway, she once told me the job required an almost encyclopedic mind for even lesser celebrities, which is why she sucked at it. She hadn't even recognized Micah out on the street. But most of the paparazzi, she said, they make their money knowing who's who. That guy probably won't get much money from a picture of me though, so there's that."

"He'd sell a picture of us? But we weren't doing anything."

He scratched his forehead. "Yeah, but we were."

"We were just walking!" How would anyone be interested in that.

"We were holding hands. They can spin that story. He'll be frantically trying to figure out who you are in case you're like a princess or something. That would make the story better."

I laughed. "Well, sorry to disappoint him."

He sighed. "I'm really sorry. I don't think it will go anywhere, but it's something to be aware of. I have no control over that."

"And you still want to live here?"

"Yeah?"

We continued on, past one tall building after another. It was oppressive. And now that I was aware that there were people out there who wanted to violate us in ways I'd never worried about before, I couldn't stop furtively glancing around us, behind us, even above us, as if they stationed themselves like snipers to steal our images. It shouldn't have mattered. I was nobody. Nobody would care about me.

Finally we reached the hotel where Mom and I were staying, and I had to say good-night on the street. "Mom's probably asleep already."

"Are you tired? We could go get drinks. Or go dancing."

Dancing with Noah. That would be the image I fell asleep dreaming of. But the incident with the paparazzi had reminded me why this relationship could never work out. This was his world, and I'd never fit in.

He put his hands on my shoulders but stood a safe enough distance away that I didn't worry he'd push for a kiss. Of course I wanted him to. I knew he wanted to. The look was there in his eyes. I hadn't spent so many nights kissing Noah not to recognize the desire he surely saw in me. But he swallowed and said, "About tomorrow."

If I'd come up alone, there would have been no question that I'd spend the day with him. All day. And the night. If there wasn't a little one asleep upstairs expecting me to be there when he woke, I'd find very little to stop me from crossing the divide between us, a very imaginary divide, but one that might as well have been made of titanium.

But knowing Owen was there put the brakes on this runaway train, and I reconsidered telling Noah the truth when our son slept directly above us. I couldn't risk him asking to come up. I couldn't risk turning Owen's life upside down.

"I promised my mom—"

"No, of course. But listen. Could you maybe come out for dinner tomorrow night?" Before I could react he raced on. "Not a date. My friends like to get together whenever we're all in town, and I'd love for you to meet them. Jo is dying to get to know you."

It meant weaving our lives together even more when I needed to find a way to unmake this bond between us.

He leaned in a little closer with a mischievous grin. "You could bring your mom."

I laughed. "Well, I would not bring my mom." For one thing, I'd need her to watch Owen if I went. But should I agree to go? "Can I tell you tomorrow? I'd want to clear it with her first."

Of course I wanted to see him again. And maybe at some point, I could find the right moment to sit down and tell him everything. It was clear that we couldn't keep going on like this without him knowing the truth. Surrounded by his friends in a calm setting, maybe he'd absorb the news better.

"Yeah. Of course. Whatever you want. I just—" He ducked his head and ran his palm down the back of his neck, a move I found so irresistibly sexy, I nearly broke down and asked him if we could rent a room of our own. "Promise me you won't go back to shutting me out. Promise when you go home, we can still talk."

He must have read something from my silence on the walk back, but I nodded. I didn't want to lose him completely again. I just wondered if we could ever have a friendship that didn't come with the occasional benefits. The benefits would have been a really nice perk if I could content myself with those small tastes of Noah. But I hungered for him, and as long as we were doing this dance, I always would. It had been easier when we were living separate lives. The minute he showed up on my doorstep, it was like I'd taken my first drink after a lifetime of abstention. I couldn't stop.

But I nodded. He took my hand and squeezed it for a beat. "And don't worry about that photographer. Most of the time that happens and nothing comes of it. I mean, maybe it gets printed somewhere, but if you don't know about it, does it really matter?"

That was a good point. "I'll bear that in mind."

Not that I was all that worried. Noah would take the heat. I'd be the mystery woman. Let them run around trying to figure out my identity. I hadn't kept a social media presence in years. Not since Owen was born. I had nobody to share pictures of him with except Mom. They'd have to be super motivated to find any connection between me and Noah, and I doubted anyone would care that much.

Theater of the Absurd Fan Forum

Meeka wrote:
Did y'all see FanBlogger? They posted a few pictures of Noah taken in Midtown earlier tonight. Is it just me or does that girl look like the old girlfriend?

n00b wrote:
@GuyFawkes would know. She's the resident expert on Noah's ex-girlfriends. Does that mean the grieving period over Crystal bitch is finally over? Or is she just a friend? I haven't heard of him hooking up with anyone recently.

GuyFawkes wrote:
Oh, yeah. I recognize her. Pretty sure her name is Lucy. I did a little dumpster diving into Noah's deep Instagram feed and found some pictures from way back tagged as Lucy-Goosey. She's a lot younger there, but I'm sure it's the same girl. I clicked through on that account and it no longer exists. Maybe she's deleted it.

Morgana wrote:
Doesn't look like just friends to me. But then again, doesn't mean it isn't a wham bam weekend.

CrimsonClover wrote:
Okay, guys. I have arrived. Good detective work, but I'll take it from here. Her name is Lucy Griffin. I found her on a website that maintains records of high school students by cross referencing posts like the one @GuyFawkes found and doing some investigative snooping. I collected some images from old shows where she was seen hanging out with him really early on, and most of them are around D.C. which is close to where they went to school. Check these out.

GuyFawkes wrote:
So has she moved to NYC or just visiting.

CrimsonClover wrote:
It took me like five minutes to find her address in D.C. and I'm still verifying, but it looks like she was married but got a divorce several years ago. Not sure why she's suddenly reemerged here, but it's too soon to assume Noah's got a new girlfriend.

Morgana wrote:
Well, I guess that's good. But he still isn't in my bed.

Chapter Eighteen

Lucy

Word of advice: Design an itinerary for a day in New York, then cut it in half. If you're traveling with an almost four-year-old, cut it in half again. Maybe change out the museum for a playground. And add a nap. Long story short, by lunchtime, Owen was cranky and wanted to go back home. The hotel had been exciting the first night, but he told me Rabbit was lonely and missed Snuggle Bear. He'd been a trooper.

I suggested to my mom that we could try to change our flights, but she said one more day wouldn't hurt anything. And besides, she saw me checking my texts all day and finally asked me if I wanted to tell her what was going on with Noah. While Owen napped, I told her about the night before, about his invitation, and she said, "Go spend the evening with him. Meet his friends. Make some memories."

That's how I found myself emerging from an Uber in Brooklyn once again, this time in a residential neighborhood that reminded me somewhat of the street where my own town house sat. Somewhat. I climbed the steps, praying I had the right address and convinced I didn't when a major celebrity opened the front door. Noah had warned me about crossing paths with Patrick Stewart, but I hadn't dreamed of banging on rock star Adam Copeland's front door. Blushing hard, I tripped over my own tongue to apologize. "Oh. I must have the wrong place. I am *so* sorry."

I felt like a giant stalker. I glanced down the row of town houses in a display of confusion, but he said, "Lucy, right?"

"Yes?" How did he know my name? I checked my clothes for any clues. Was I wearing a name tag?

Inexplicably, Adam opened the door and waved me inside. Maybe he thought I'd come for a job, but then Noah appeared from somewhere deeper inside and hooted. "You made it!"

He'd said a get-together with friends. He'd never mentioned he was friends with massive rock stars. I froze mid-step, resisting the urge to slap my forehead. Of course Noah would be friends with legit rock stars. I kept trying to forget that was his identity, too. Maybe not to the extent of an Adam Copeland, but one day if things continued the way they were.

Out back, a number of others had gathered. I waved at Shane then scanned over until I found Micah. It eased my tension a bit to see familiar faces, though I hadn't spent any time with either in years.

Shane bounded up and pulled me into a hug. "It's so great to see you."

He'd grown up and filled out well. That geeky kid he'd once been still lurked around the edges, but he'd become quite handsome. I squeezed him back. "It's been way too long."

A girl with matching red hair sidled up beside him, and I was about to ask if he had a long-lost sister I didn't know about when he reached over and grabbed her hand. "Lucy, this is my girlfriend Layla."

I smiled, "Of course. Noah mentioned you."

Noah said, "Layla was just showing us some videos of one of her friends from back home." He didn't sound impressed. "Indiana," he added, as if that meant something.

Shane wrapped an arm around her. "Not just one of her friends. He's a musician. He had a song on the charts earlier this year."

"Wow," I said. "What's his name?" Not that I would have heard of anyone current.

"Dylan Black." She closed the video, like Noah had somehow shamed her, and I nudged him with my elbow. He could be such a snobby brat sometimes.

Micah joined us. "He's really good. He's been performing at that club I sometimes play over in TriBeCa. It's weird I've never run into him."

Shane laughed. "Micah when was the last time you actually played there?"

Micah scratched his head. "Well, maybe it has been a little while. But that's where Adam first came out to see me before he invited us out on tour. I have fond memories."

"We should go check him out." I got the feeling Shane's suggestion had an ulterior motive. It never hurts to keep the girlfriend happy.

Layla beamed. "He would really love that. He's been struggling a bit gaining an audience for some reason. Even with a song getting spins on AC radio."

"AC?" I asked.

"Adult contemporary," she explained. "He should be on rock stations. The song is finding the wrong fans."

Noah took my hand. "Layla's our secret weapon in the fan arena. She finds out everything."

"Was," said Layla, sheepishly. "I haven't been scouting out the fan sites for a couple of weeks." She turned to me. "I used to run a fan forum, but it got a little weird to maintain such a fan-centric site when I started dating Shane."

Noah smirked. "So you wouldn't have noticed if any of the gossip sites picked up the pictures of me and Lucy out last night?"

I laughed, a little nervous. "Nobody would care."

Layla narrowed her eyes. "Well, I *could* find out if you wanted me to revert to my old ways. I was never as good at ferreting out gossip as some of the other fans though. They were scary with the slightest piece of information."

"Really?" I found it fascinating. I'd never been interested in celebrity gossip. I'd never read fan forums. "Like what?"

"You should ask Eden or Jo about that." She gestured toward a patio table where a dark-haired woman bounced a baby on her lap. My brain connected pieces of information and I realized she was Eden Sinclair, Micah's sister. By process of elimination, that made the other woman Jo, Micah's girlfriend. I'd heard plenty about her from Noah. They were both stunning. I was curious to meet both of them, and as I appraised them, they each looked up and waved.

Jo stood and crossed the deck. "You must be the infamous Lucy. I'm Jo."

Eden waved from her seat, but I guessed the baby kept her from coming over. She hollered over. "I'm Eden. It's nice to finally meet you."

They'd heard of me? I blushed. "I'm glad to be here."

Layla said, "Lucy was asking about what kind of gossip fans could dig up."

Jo snort-laughed. "Everything. If it's on the Internet, they'll find it."

"It's the paparazzi you have to worry about," Eden called over. "Fans stay in their bubble."

"True." Layla nodded. "Though the paparazzi aren't quite as obsessive as fans."

Now my curiosity was engaged. "Would you be able to find out if anyone posted the pictures of me and Noah?"

"Give me a minute." Layla took out her phone, and her thumbs flew across the screen. She paused, then scrolled, then clicked. Then her eyes scanned, mouth twisted in a little button until she sighed. "Yeah someone posted them, but it looks like it's just a minor gossip site."

She turned the phone toward me, and I saw four pictures of me and Noah walking up a random sidewalk. A chill climbed my spine. "That is freaky. What does it say?"

"Just that Noah was out with a new girl." She winced. "Sorry, they make these guys sound like serial womanizers. It's part of the stereotype."

I shook my head. "It's fine. I'm not worried about any of that." I was, but I didn't want to think about it. "But no indication who I am?"

"No." Her eyes narrowed. "Not on this site."

My spidey senses tingled. She worded that too specifically. "But elsewhere?"

"Look. You're probably better off not knowing what's being said about you online. It can be a little unsettling at best. It can be really hurtful at worst. You are what stands between the invested fan and her fantasy of sleeping with Noah. Understand, these obsessions are harmless. Most of them know they'll never even breathe the same air as Noah, and they know if they did, they wouldn't end up his girlfriend. But the reality of a new girl in his life harshes the pretense they might. So they're motivated to know who you are."

"So you're telling me they know who I am." I wasn't sure how I felt about that.

Layla cast a glance at Noah, like she was checking with him before answering.

"Where are you seeing this?" he asked.

"I went to the Theater of the Absurd fan site. That's where I found the article with the pictures. The gossip site has no idea who Lucy is. The fans figured it out in about ten minutes."

"How?" This was blowing my mind.

She shrugged. "They already knew who you were."

Wow. "I don't understand this at all."

"Well." She paused again, and I could see her deciding whether to go on. She bit her upper lip. "It only takes one errant post to connect dots."

"What post?"

"I have no idea. I could keep digging if you wanted to know, but right now I'm speculating. They definitely know your name, that you live in D.C., and that you've got a kid."

The atmosphere around me collapsed, and I lost my balance, nearly falling onto the deck, but Noah's arms caught me just as he said, "What?"

Layla looked from me to him and back. "Oh, I thought. Oh, God. I—"

My weight either became too much or Noah lost the strength in his own arms, but I found myself on my butt. "They stalked me at home?"

Jo sat down beside me. "Just breathe. They probably just stalked your social media accounts."

I shook my head. "I don't share anything online."

"Would any of your family have posted pictures and tagged you?"

Jesus. "It's possible."

Layla sat on the other side of me, rubbing my leg. "Do you want me to contact the forum admin and ask her to shut down the thread?"

It was a little late for that, but still. It grossed me out knowing faceless strangers were digging through my life. "What would that accomplish?"

Eden knelt in front of me and tipped my chin up so she could look directly into my eyes. "It would make them realize they've crossed a line. And it would make you feel like you had some control."

I glanced up at Noah, afraid of what I'd see on his face. He was sucking on his upper lip, and I could make out the faint red splotches on his cheeks that he got when he was particularly angry. I said, "What should I do, Noah?"

He just said, "You have a *kid*?"

Noah

I'd split in two. My body stood on the patio while the girls surrounded Lucy. I wanted to push them all away so I could wrap my arms around her and tell her I was sorry. I'd brought this on her. I wanted to fix it. I wanted to hold her hand and tell her everything would be fine. I wanted to be the one to protect and comfort her.

But my mind was a damn war zone, and all my mouth could produce was the question that needed an answer before I could regain control of the rest of my faculties.

How could she have failed to tell me she had a kid?

Lucy nodded, eyes wide with a fear I hated. I wanted to make that fear go away, but I'd just stepped on a land mine, and my instincts were fight or flight.

"Why have you never told me that?"

I pressed my fingers to my temples, fighting to stay put, to hear the answer. Eden stood and walked back to the patio table so she wasn't between me and Lucy.

"Noah." Tears rolled down Lucy's cheeks, and I took a step toward her, but more shrapnel blasted me as I tried to reconstruct a whole past with this new piece of information.

Was this why she'd pushed me away all those years ago? Had she tried to fix things with her ex-husband because they had a kid together? I couldn't for the life of me remember her showing any signs of pregnancy in all the times I'd visited her. Did she go back to him and try to save their marriage with a baby? Or had there been someone else after me?

"How old is he? Or she?" My voice had raised an octave.

"He," she said, anguish written all over her expression.

The sane part of my brain was yelling at me to calm the fuck down, but she'd left a huge fucking detail out, and it struck me that she might have never intended to tell me because she'd never intended to let me back in her life.

"How old is he, Lucy?"

Micah laid a hand on my shoulder. "Hey, you want to come inside for a minute?"

I shook him off. I didn't want to be handled.

"No. I want an answer."

Micah wouldn't let it go. "It's not your place to demand an answer, Noah. Come inside and take a minute to get your shit together." His hand wrapped around my bicep, pinching me hard. "Now."

I forced my eyes away from Lucy and looked around at everyone staring at me. Shane turned away, clearly wanting to stay out of this. Adam gave me a quick nod, and if anyone knew what it was like to be blindsided by a sudden revelation, it was him. That decided me, and I let Micah pull me into the kitchen where I clenched a fist, cocked my arm back, and took aim at the wall, but I checked myself and stopped before I did any real damage. I didn't like identifying in any way with how my dad would have reacted, even if this was orders of magnitude more upsetting than his invented problems.

I spun back to face Micah, half wanting to put my fist in his face for tearing me away. "Why are you trying to keep me from talking to Lucy?"

He pointed at my hands. "You want to get control of yourself first, man. You don't have any right to know anything about Lucy. You need to understand that before you talk to her again."

"I don't have a right? I have every right."

"Why?"

I dragged my hands through my hair. "Because—" I didn't know. I'd always thought of her as *my* Lucy, but I couldn't say that out loud to Micah. Shane might understand, but not Micah. "It's kind of a big deal, don't you think?"

He nodded. "Yes. It is. But it's only news to you. She's known this for however long, and she had reasons for keeping it to herself. Her reasons are her own."

I breathed in and exhaled. My mind let go a little, but I couldn't quite get control of my emotions. "I mean, she was planning on telling me at some point, right?"

He shrugged. "When you get your shit together, maybe she'll explain it to you. But you need to decide right now that you don't control her timetable."

My head suddenly felt like it had filled with helium, and I lurched for the counter to have something to keep myself from collapsing. "Micah, what if—"

No, I couldn't even contemplate that.

Micah's hand on my back reminded me I wasn't alone. I looked at him and said, "We slept together once when she was married. But it was years ago."

What if . . .

My mouth tasted metallic. She wouldn't have kept something like that from me.

His expression lost that stoicism, and I could see he'd followed my train of thought. "I'm sorry, Noah. You still have to wait for her to tell you when she's ready to."

My anger resurfaced at how long Lucy had kept this a secret. "How do I not have a right to know?"

He gave me one more piece of advice that hit home. "Lucy will judge you forever for how you handle this right now. Take the long view, Noah."

God, I knew that. That was the only reason I was remotely tethered to self-constraint, but inside, the explosions continued to decimate my heart and soul, and a grief I couldn't even touch threatened to swamp me.

I'd thought the devil had taken everything he could from me, but what if Lucy had denied me a literal piece of myself?

I turned to the sink and threw up. Micah pinched the crook of my neck as if he could massage some stoicism into me. I took a long drink from the faucet and stared out the window.

Outside, Shane had taken a seat by Lucy, and all this reminded me so much of prom night after I'd ran off to pick a fight with someone who'd insulted Lucy. Instead of ending that night the way I'd planned, she'd gone back to the gym and hunkered down with Shane. I'd ended up going home alone, and despite a very dramatic gesture to apologize, it took me forever to get her to talk to me again. Well, a week, but it felt like forever.

Micah was right that she'd never forgive me if I couldn't behave like an adult. I didn't want her to go back home mad at me, but I couldn't get a handle on my emotions. I might not have a right to it, but I was furious anyway.

Lucy hadn't told me about her kid. In the past six weeks, she hadn't trusted me with that vital piece of information. I didn't know how old her son was. I didn't know if he was mine,

John's, or some random stranger's. I wasn't allowed to pry it out of her, and I was expected to be okay with that.

There were only two reasons I could think that she wouldn't have told me.

Maybe our relationship had never been serious to her, and when she'd said she wanted to be friends, I should have taken her at her word. All that flirting, all those promising touches, what had that meant to her if she wasn't planning on ever letting me back in?

Had I been deceiving myself that we'd ever have a future? Did she think I was that unreliable?

The other reason was that the kid was mine, and she didn't trust me enough to be a part of her life, to raise a child.

Surely, she wouldn't have withheld something that important from me.

But it was possible, wasn't it? Why wasn't I allowed to ask *that* question?

I paced in the tight apartment like a caged animal, fully aware that everyone outside was waiting to see whether I'd pull my shit together or burn the building down. I squeezed my fists so tight I heard my knuckles crack, and I held in the scream that wanted to rip from my bottom of my soul.

And the devil laughed at me as the age-old truth of my near-miss relationship with Lucy cycled back around: We never had enough time. She'd be gone tomorrow, and I didn't think I could deal with this fast enough to talk to her in a way that wouldn't wreck things permanently.

I did the only thing I could think to do in this situation: I walked out the front door and then kept walking.

Several blocks or miles away, my brain began to release its hold on me, and I considered the things I couldn't while she sat within a few feet of me.

What did it mean to me that she had a kid?

Would I want to raise someone else's kid?

What if he was my own? I'd never planned to be a dad. How could I be a dad when I hated my own father? When I'd hated Lucy's as much as my own?

I walked without direction or purpose until I found myself in Brooklyn Bridge Park overlooking the East River. The bridge in the distance reminded me of the night before, how easy things had been between us. And she'd known her secret then but hadn't shared it.

I found a bench and mulled through all the questions that had no answer, landing on the only one that mattered. Regardless of who the father was, did I want to raise a child with Lucy?

And if the answer to that was yes, would she even want me to?

The first was a question only I could answer. The second only she could.

Did I want to be anybody's father really? I'd had the worst role model on that score. Maybe only to be outdone by Lucy's shitty excuse for a father. They were so different in many ways, our dads, but they shared one thing in common: They'd never wanted us. Lucy's dad never bothered to stay home; my dad made sure I never could.

The effect my dad had on me was to make sure I could always survive on my own with just a guitar on my back. Nobody could kick me out because I was already gone.

But Lucy's dad made her mistrust the vagabond life altogether, and she was always searching for ways to burrow in and build fortresses around herself.

All this time, I'd been thinking we could find a way to work around my impossible schedule because I'd never factored anyone other than Lucy into the equation. I'd never pictured a kid in our lives.

A family with Lucy.

I took a huge breath and let it back out. All the things she'd said to me over the years about me not being there for her began to roost. She'd been telling me all along, hadn't she? She hated how I was always coming and going whenever it suited me, how she couldn't make a life with me if I couldn't make a home for her.

My God. I was no better than her dad.

And I'd just walked away again.

The tears fell hot and painful, like they'd come from a well that hadn't been tapped in years. My shoulders shook as I sought control, and I sat there and cried until I found myself alone and in desperate need of a box of tissues.

Staring out over the lower Manhattan skyline, the obvious answer came to me. I wanted Lucy in my life. Yes, I'd want a family with her. Of course I would.

The tears dried, though the anger at Lucy's deception still simmered. If I was grieving, I must have made it to bargaining because right then the only thing I needed was the whole truth, and I could only get that from Lucy. If I let her leave without having that conversation, then I'd probably lose my chance forever.

I forced myself back onto my feet, brain and body together at last, and I made a decision to take Micah's advice.

At the end of the day, I still wanted to prove to Lucy I could be whoever she needed me to be. I just hadn't expected her to need me to be this.

Chapter Nineteen

Lucy

"I should have known this might happen," I told Layla, blotting my cheeks with the tissue someone had handed me.

"I should've thought before I said anything." She frowned. "All of us here have nearly had our relationships wrecked by irresponsible gossip, and I can't believe I'm the one who spread it this time."

"But you didn't mean any harm. This was my own stupidity." I focused on a knot in the wood on the deck, trying to grapple with what had just happened. "I thought I had more time."

I expected someone to remind me I'd had plenty of time. And they'd be right. I'd had years to come clean, and I'd always known that Noah would hate me when this day finally came.

"I'm sure he'll be back." Shane hadn't left my side even after Noah up and fled. I would have expected Shane to take Noah's side, but I was grateful he stayed beside me and rubbed my back. "You know Noah. He's Mount Vesuvius, but he'll have an entire argument in his own head and come back."

That wouldn't really resolve anything. If I'd told Noah myself tonight like I'd planned, it might have blunted the impact, but timing wasn't really the problem. Everyone here assumed I was worried about Noah's anger, but if anything, I felt relief. Relief that the burden of this secret was finally lifted. Relief that Noah hadn't reacted with complete indifference.

That relief didn't touch the guilt that grew to fill the newly vacated emotional reserves. And new fears arose as I waited anxiously for Noah to return and resolve the questions that grew in my mind.

He might never come back, of course. It wouldn't take much for him to realize he could be Owen's biological father. Would he even want that?

I always figured he'd want to be a part of his son's life, but only passing through. Noah could promise more and actually mean it, but if he failed to live up to his intentions, he'd leave my son confused and disappointed. If Noah did meet Owen, I never doubted that Owen would love his dad. How could he not? They were so much alike already. But I couldn't watch my happy boy suffer any sorrow due to a dad he'd grow to idolize who would drift in and out of his life.

A worst-case scenario I didn't want to even acknowledge was a Noah who fought to gain custody or who'd force me to share Owen with him, dragging him back and forth across state lines and tearing him to pieces.

I'd almost rather Noah have no interest at all in getting to know him. In that case, I'd rather he just keep walking.

After thirty minutes had passed, I realized that everyone was in a state of limbo, unsure how to carry on while I sat on the porch, dabbing tears from my cheeks with a severely overused tissue. I was considering calling an Uber to get out of their hair when the front door opened, and then a very red-eyed Noah slipped out onto the back porch. His hangdog expression gave nothing away except that he'd calmed down enough to stop threatening to destroy inanimate objects.

When he held out his hand and said, "Will you come with me?" I hiccuped in response.

Micah took a step toward us. I appreciated that he'd intervened before, but this wasn't his fight.

I took Noah's hand and scrambled up off the deck, stomach knotting in anticipation and fear of the unknown.

"Can we borrow your car service?" Noah asked Micah.

Micah texted something, and almost as soon as I'd gathered my purse and joined Noah on the front stoop, a town car pulled up. Noah opened the door and ushered me in. He gave the driver an address and then leaned against the door on the opposite side of the back seat, looking at me like I'd become a total stranger. He didn't say a single word the entire ride, not even to tell me where we were going, though I suspected it.

We only went a few miles. Where we got out wasn't that much different from where we'd come from. More town houses. More sidewalks with trees looking out of place. More cars passing on the street. Never-ending city.

"Is this where you live?" I asked to break the silence.

"This way," was his only response.

I followed him to a corner of a slightly busier street but noticed that across the way was the entrance to a park. "What's that?"

"Prospect Park."

"Is it big?"

"Pretty big. It's like the Central Park of Brooklyn."

"What can you do there?"

He reached in his pockets and retrieved a key. "Boating or horseback riding or ice skating. There's also a zoo, a botanical garden, a lake, and a carousel. A museum."

"A museum? The Brooklyn Museum?"

"Yeah."

The small talk calmed my nerves a little. He couldn't be completely pissed if he was talking to me, right? Or maybe it was a false sense of security, and he didn't want to scream at me in front of his friends or in public. My heartbeat pulsed in my fingertips, and I just wanted to ask him to stop and tell me what he was thinking.

He touched my elbow and pointed me toward a building rather taller than the town houses we'd passed, maybe ten stories high. A doorman held the door open and said, "Good evening, Mr. Kennedy."

As we entered an incredible lobby, I commented on the obvious. "You have a doorman."

"Yup."

"Adam didn't have a doorman."

"Are you calling me fancy?" He hit the up button on the elevator. "I like the extra security."

It surprised me. I realized that whenever I'd pictured him up here, I'd imagined something like the places where he'd first lived before the band had started having radio success. He'd sent me pictures of a squalid one-bedroom apartment he'd shared with Shane, futons on the floor, Chinese take-out containers also on the floor, clothes everywhere. I'd never updated my imagination with his newfound wealth. Perhaps I needed to upgrade my image of Noah as well.

As we rode the elevator, I studied him, looking for signs of the temper he'd always hated about his own dad, but mostly he looked sad. The evidence on his cheeks that he'd been crying gutted me, but his calm now made me suspect he'd come to some sort of a resolution. I steeled myself for the worst.

He could have ended things at Adam's. There was no need to drag me to his home to tell me to get out of his life, so I hoped against hope he just needed a safe place to talk things out.

And that scared me almost as much as anything else.

We exited onto a small landing, and he nodded to a door a little to the right. "That's me."

He hesitated, either having second thoughts or waiting to see if I might. Then he went straight to the door and unlocked it. Despite my nerves, I was so curious about how he'd been living for the past few years, I went right in, desperate to rewrite my old assumptions of Noah with every new person or place he introduced me to.

We entered a foyer with a kitchen to the right and another room beyond. I glanced into the kitchen and took in the top-of-the-line appliances and the table and chairs at the far end. In the living room area, a pair of double doors gave another view of his eat-in nook. The decor was colorful and cozy, and his home was neat and orderly, but other than a framed picture of one of their album covers, nothing struck me as all that personal. I didn't see a whole lot of Noah in here.

A hallway promised more, and once I'd breached his fortress, I needed to have a full mental map of his world. "Take me on a tour?"

"I've been waiting for you to say that for years."

I laughed. "Of your apartment?"

He showed me the office space, a small spare bedroom, and finally his own bedroom. I didn't spend too much time wondering who else might have shared that king size bed. I tried not to picture myself sharing it. Right now, we had more pressing needs.

I headed back to the living room and sat on his sectional, across from a fireplace and a large-screen TV. His apartment felt safe and homey. It was everything I might have wanted, except that it was located over two hundred miles from my home. Windows across one wall were shrouded in gauzy curtains, and I imagined the view would be worth checking out.

Maybe he paid a service to keep it tidy, or maybe he didn't spend much time here. Or perhaps, he'd grown up and become responsible. I could no longer deny the possibility that Noah had created some stability in his life.

The time had come to let him into mine. We needed to talk.

"My son will be four in December."

He dropped onto the turn of the sectional. I watched his mind at work, doing the math. It wouldn't take long.

"You left your husband four years ago."

"He left me. Closer to three years ago."

"He left you with a child?"

"Yes."

"Didn't I see you in March that year?"

I nodded.

He leaned back and exhaled.

"Did you know you were pregnant when you told me to stop contacting you?"

"No. I didn't know."

"Did you tell your husband about us before you knew?"

"No."

"But you did after?"

I swallowed. "He and I had been fighting. We hadn't been together like that for months. We weren't even sleeping in the same bed."

He stood up and paced over to the window. His hands opened and closed, so I just held my breath and waited. I couldn't blame him for feeling betrayed and angry, but I couldn't change the past.

When he turned back, he just said, "Why?"

"Why?"

"Why didn't you contact me?"

That was the question I'd always known I'd have to answer one day, and I had no right to cop out with a non-answer, even though it *was* complicated.

"You know what kind of family I've always wanted." I closed my eyes. "And I was afraid that if I contacted you, you'd feel responsible—"

"I was responsible, Lucy. I would have wanted to know this."

I swallowed and pressed on. "I worried you'd feel responsible and try to be a part of his life, only to disappear again."

He shut his eyes. "You thought I'd be like your dad, didn't you?"

"I—" I wanted to lie and tell him I never did, but his jaw tensed, and I gritted my own teeth to have an honest conversation. "You already were."

His face crumpled a moment before he dropped his head into his hands. "I never meant to do that to you."

"I know. It was the nature of your career and this life you chose. When I sat down and thought about calling you, you'd left the country on a tour in Europe, and I really didn't want you to make a hasty decision you'd later regret. So I waited for you to come home, and as time passed, it became really obvious to me that to be with you would always mean being alone. It's always hurt more to have you for days and then lose you for months."

He lifted his head, and his eyes had rimmed with tears again. "You still could have told me."

"Yes, but it's a bell that can't be unrung, you know? And I needed to think of my son, Noah. Once I told you, I couldn't take that knowledge away from you ever again. What if you decided to come into his life only to abandon him for months or years at a time? And what if you left the band only to resent me for it because it wasn't the life you would have chosen. I thought everyone would be better off this way."

I could hear how tinny it all sounded when the man all my decisions had impacted stared back at me with wide-eyed disbelief.

"You don't think I would have wanted that choice? You don't think I'd have wanted to share the burden with you?"

"Owen was never a burden to me."

He jerked back like I'd slapped him. "Owen? My son's name is Owen?"

The guilt overwhelmed me at the look on his face, and a tear rolled down my cheek. "I'm so sorry, Noah."

He shook his head. "He's three now?"

"Yes."

"How can I know what your life has been like when you've never told me?"

His tone had grown more sad than angry, and I was a bit sorry for the change. I'd rather he yell at me than look so hurt. "Do you have pictures?"

This was really happening. I couldn't tell him no.

I took out my phone and shakily scrolled through the gallery until I found the last picture I'd taken. "Here's one."

He was on the sofa beside me in a second, tentatively reaching for the phone. The air expelled from his lungs like he'd been punched. "Oh."

"Oh? What does that mean?"

"He's really real. I mean, I didn't think he wasn't, but he'd been an idea. He's really—"

"Yeah."

"He's blond."

I laughed. "That he is. And he has your eyes."

He went to touch the picture and it moved to the next, another shot of Owen, eyes wide open in awe. I thought it might have been from the polar bear exhibit.

"He looks really happy."

"He's such a happy kid. He reminds me so much of you."

"Me?"

"Yeah. He's always singing and dancing. He's so interested in everything. He was excited to see New York."

"He's here?"

"Well, yeah. Why did you think I wanted to go to the zoo?"

He let out a deep sigh. "That makes so much sense now. And why your mom is here."

"Yeah. She's watching him right now."

He leaned forward, elbows on knees, and laid his forehead against his knuckles. He was doing an amazing job of wrapping his head around his new reality. I couldn't have hoped for more really. I knew we weren't out of the woods yet. I knew he was going to be mad at me again and again for keeping such a vital secret. And I also knew that while he was eager to hear about Owen today, there was still a strong possibility his interest would fade in time.

So when he asked, "Can I meet him?" I was caught completely off guard.

"When?"

"Today? Tomorrow?"

"It's too soon. I don't want to rush this."

"You don't have to tell him anything. I just want to see him, talk to him. Please."

It was the way his voice broke on that last word that decided me. "You can join us for breakfast tomorrow. I'm warning you: He might not want to talk to you at all. Or he might inter-rogate you. Do you have anything *Star Wars* related?"

"It's like you don't even know me." He got up and went into another room. When he came back he held a model of R2-D2. He flipped a switch and lights came on. "Watch this." He set it down on the coffee table and it started rolling forward. It moved like a Roomba, finding the edge then backing up, run-ning into a coaster, then spinning around.

"I think this might be a little much. I was thinking of may-be an action figure."

"Who's his favorite?"

"Right now, it's BB-8, but he has one of those."

He reached over and took my hand. "Thank you, Lucy."

It was the last thing I'd expected from him, and I gave him all I could. "I may have been wrong, Noah. I want you to know that everything I do, I do it for that little boy right there. I hope you will understand that. I hope you'll forgive me one day."

"Micah cautioned me that I have no place being angry, and it's so much for me to process that I'm actually just numb right now. I'm bereft that I've missed three years of my son's life, Lucy. I can't deny that. But you're probably right. If I'd contin-ued to tour the way we have for the past three years, I would have only seen him in bursts. But he'd know me." He exhaled hard. "I want to know him."

"Then tomorrow?"

"Tomorrow."

Noah

Thank God for Micah. If I'd followed my lizard brain in-stincts, I would have driven Lucy away, and she probably never would have trusted me with a truth she'd been carrying around with her for so many years. It cut deep that she hadn't trusted me enough to tell me, but as I lay in bed, unable to sleep due to anticipation and nerves, I began to think about the future and what Lucy had most feared from me. And I realized she was one hundred percent right.

I couldn't be a father to a child who lived in another town.

And I couldn't be a dad when I spent half my life on the road.

Either something would need to change, or I needed to meet my son, then bow out of Lucy's life forever. I would meet him, though. I wouldn't go another day without looking the boy in the eyes and getting a sense of what kind of person we'd created. I needed to see him more than anything I'd ever needed in my life.

So I tossed and turned, imagining things I might say to him, ways to make sure he wouldn't shut me out.

I had a son.

When I got up, both Shane and Micah had left me text messages checking in. I texted Shane back, but I called Micah. I owed him a debt of gratitude for his intervention. Shane was my best friend, but he'd let me crash and burn rather than risk my legendary wrath. Micah had always been immune to my temper tantrums.

He gave me one bit of advice before I hung up. "This is the first time your son is meeting you, too, Noah. He may not know it, but this will be an important day for both of you. Be cool."

"Be cool. Got it." I was far from cool. I went through my *Star Wars* collectibles, considering which would most please a three-year-old before I stopped and realized I was trying to figure out how to bribe the kid to like me.

Eventually, I just showered and shaved, put on a nice pair of slacks I never wore, changed out of them for a pair of jeans because I didn't want to pretend to be someone I wasn't for my son, then compromised and chose a button-up shirt. I debated styling my hair and putting on cologne before I started laughing at myself. This wasn't a date. It was just the most important day of my life.

I called the Uber a little earlier than necessary, so I arrived at the diner first. I paced the sidewalk, watching every person who turned the corner, my heartbeat accelerating at each possibility that this would be the moment I'd lay eyes on my son.

After a while, I walked down to the far corner so I could see if they were on the way, and when I turned back around, they were coming toward me from the other direction. I waved. Lucy waved. Her mom gave me a smile.

Owen was busy pointing at something across the street. I met them in front of the diner.

Lucy said, "Owen, remember I told you we were going to meet with a friend of Mommy's for breakfast?"

He nodded and glanced up at me. I knelt down in front of him and took him in. He did have my coloring, but he had so much of Lucy. Her mouth, the shape of her jaw, and when his face transformed into a curious smile, I could see that he had her mannerisms. Was that because of genetics, or would he have had mine if he'd spent any time with me?

I held out a hand in greeting. "Hello, Owen. I'm Noah. I'm so happy to meet you."

He tilted his head, eyes narrowed. "Your name is mine backward."

"What?" I threw a look up at Lucy, and I could tell by the shock on her face she'd never said that to him before.

"Owen. Noah." He wasn't completely wrong.

"I think that's really cool," I said. "It's like we're the same, but different."

He laughed. "How can you be the same AND different?"

"That's a good question. How are BB-8 and R2-D2 the same but different?"

His eyes got wide. "You know about BB-8?"

I laughed, super tempted to ruffle his hair. He was flat out adorable. I had an adorable kid. I wished I'd brought my BB-8 remote control toy now. Maybe next time. *Please let there be a next time.*

Lucy said, "Come on, you guys. We can talk about *Star Wars* while we eat."

I followed a little behind so I could pull myself together. I had to blink a few times to make sure I wasn't about to well up with tears. How cool would I be to cry at breakfast?

While Lucy knelt to strap a booster seat to a chair, her mom lay her chin on her fist and focused all that parental attention on me that I'd always found so unnerving in high school. "It's good to see you again, Noah."

"You too, Mrs. Griffin."

"Please. I think you can call me Sara now."

That was never going to happen. "I—"

"Or how about Mom?"

"Mom." Why not? It was a day of sudden parentage. "This is all so overwhelming."

She lay a hand on mine. "You're doing great. You're here. That's a start."

I didn't like the implication that I hadn't been there due to some failure on my part, but I let it go. I could have taken a different path yesterday, and we all knew that. I was so glad I'd chosen this one.

Lucy sat down in a dramatic show of exhaustion and began scanning the menu. She said, "You want pancakes, buddy?"

"Yup. Pancake, bancake, gancake." He giggled at the funny words he'd made up. "I want bacon, Mommy. And juice." He said juice like *jyoosh*. It was super cute, and I exchanged an amused look with Lucy.

We all ordered, and I turned to Owen, high on our initial successful bonding over *Star Wars* and said, "What did you like about New York?"

He started fussing with the strap around his waist, and Lucy turned to help him get it right, saying, "You liked the zoo, didn't you?"

He nodded, then rubbed his eyes. He was seriously fidgety. It reminded me of me. That was the first whoosh of mind-blowing realization. He was mine. He was like me. He said, "I like the buildings."

It sounded like *beeoudings*. I was so enamored with his idiosyncratic way of speaking. I knew kids took time to learn to pronounce words, and my mom had told me all my special mistakes, but the way she'd teased me about them had made me hate them, hate myself for the way I'd been different, for how

I'd been slower and stupider than everyone else. But Owen was perfect.

When the food arrived, the uncanny sense of seeing myself in someone else only redoubled as he danced his bacon on the plate, humming a little made-up song before taking a violent bite. I noticed he had a pile of strawberries he was ignoring and wondered if I could trick him into eating them the way my dad had when I was a kid, by stealing from my plate. Nothing had made me gobble my food like my old man wanting it.

I slid a hand over, pretending like I was about to take one, and all at once, my ears were bleeding with a sound almost inaudibly high-pitched. Diners at other tables turned around to see what was going on, and I realized Owen was making the sound.

Lucy wrapped her arms around his head and pulled him to her chest. "Shhhh. What happened?"

Owen heaved a sob. "My strawberries!"

She looked over at me, and a wrinkle creased her forehead. Did she think I was going to bail because her kid had thrown a tantrum over strawberries? I smiled back. More proof this was my kid.

"Look," I said, and Owen slid his gaze my way from the corner of his eye, very reluctantly obeying. I probably only had the adult card in my favor at this moment, but I'd use it. I picked up a strawberry from my plate and moved it over to his. "Do you want mine?"

He slowly sat upright and gave me the most suspicious look, then turned to Lucy, then back and very cautiously nodded with a dramatic shudder-sniffle.

All the adults breathed in and out at the same time. Crisis averted.

"So you like strawberries, huh?"

Lucy said, "I should have warned you. He saves his favorite things for last."

"That's really smart." I caught eyes with her. "Sometimes my favorite things come later."

Breakfast ended too fast, and Lucy said they had to be heading to the airport. "I could come with you," I said before I knew I'd had the thought.

Her eyes lit up for a second, but she blinked and hid the emotion I knew she'd felt. "And do what?"

That was a valid question. "I could come spend some time with you. You're always asking me for time."

She shook her head. "I don't know. How much time do you have to give?"

I knew she was asking when I'd have to go on tour again, and the answer was fatal. We left again in a couple of days. I'd have to be back up here by Tuesday. We'd be gone for another couple of weeks. It was always like that. And when we got back from that spate of gigs, we had to go back into the studio and record a few more songs. And in the fall, our agent would have us opening for a bigger band on some national arena tour, maybe even Europe.

And I found, I didn't want to go. I didn't want any of it.

I'd already missed so much time, so many years with Lucy. I'd missed knowing my own son. I wanted to make it all up. I wanted nights in Lucy's bed and mornings at a table with my own family, not an empty breakfast nook and the occasional hookup. I wanted this right here.

"If I said, as much time as you want?"

She didn't look like she believed me. "You're going to what? Quit the band? Come be an unemployed house husband?"

"Why not?"

"That is a recipe for disaster, and you know it."

"Isn't that what you've always wanted?"

"That was a fantasy, Noah. You've got your job. And now that I've seen the life you've built here, your home, your friends, I don't think it would be fair to make you give it all up for me."

"I would, though. For you. For Owen."

She side-eyed me. "You can't possibly commit to that after thirty minutes together."

I gave her my most earnest expression. "I can commit to you, to both of you. This hasn't been enough time, Lucy. I want more of this."

"Eating breakfast in a restaurant with a kid isn't real life, Noah."

"I know that. I want to come be a part of your real life."

"You'd be unhappy. It would be what you warned me about before, quantity time. I don't want you to resent me."

Why was she fighting me? I was offering her what she'd always wanted.

"Please, Lucy. How can we make this work?" I looked over at my son who was in the process of attempting to escape the confines of his seat with vigor. "How can I become a part of his life?"

"I don't know."

"That's not good enough."

She rubbed her temples, and I could see the toll this was taking on her. She'd known all along that there was no pat answer, no easy solution. One of us would have to sacrifice, one of us would need to make a drastic change. I could quit the band or go on hiatus, but I had people counting on me.

"Can I come for tonight and tomorrow at least?"

She glanced at her mom then back to me. "I have to work tomorrow."

"Please?"

Her eyes closed, and I saw the moment the fight went out of her body. "Where will you stay?"

I grinned. Victory was at hand. "I'll get a room."

"Don't expect anything, okay? Nothing has changed between us. We're friends."

I laughed. "So much has changed, Lucy. So much."

Once we'd paid the bill, we exited the diner, making plans for me to get a flight that night, following her. I knelt again to speak to Owen when, out of nowhere, I heard the unmistakable sound of the bursting clicks of a camera. I stood and spun toward the photographer who was already skipping backward, still shooting pictures. I considered chasing him down, but then I remembered I had an audience. At least that aspect of my life might come to an end if I dropped out.

The idea had taken root, and I had to at least consider it.

Chapter Twenty

Lucy

Why had I given in?

A voice whispered: *Because you wanted to.*

I'd never anticipated Noah casually offering to throw away everything he'd worked for to be a part of my life. Never.

And the regrets that kept me up at night returned in full force to chastise me for what might have been if I'd told him sooner. But there was no way of knowing how Noah would have reacted four years ago. Past Noah belonged to a band that was so hungry for a taste of success, they toured constantly. He used to come visit on a whim, but once I'd gotten married, he only came through when the band did, and the last time I saw him, neither of us knew that within a year, they'd be on a meteoric rise, that Micah would end up in a spread in the *Rock Paper*, that they'd have a radio hit, their first. Nobody knew Noah would be asked to be the face of some marketing campaign.

Past Noah wasn't ready for a family.

I wasn't sure if present Noah was ready, and I didn't want to be the one to insist he should be. But did I want him to? So badly.

I dreamed of it. I fantasized about it. I created alternate universes in my mind where I could clone him, keep him, but also set him free. I was a paradox. I was a mess.

But for the first time in years, hope blossomed in my chest when I got a text from him letting me know he'd be arriving at my front door in less than an hour. His plane had landed, and he was here. Only for a night and a day, but I was learning to take my Noah where I could. He'd be coming here just to see us. He'd be coming here in the full knowledge of who Owen was to him. This was more than I'd allowed myself to dream.

The doorbell rang, and I told Owen, "You can stay up a little later tonight, but go get ready for bed now."

He ran up the stairs while I opened the front door. Noah had never been inside my home, and he looked around the same way I had in his, like he wanted to see inside my soul. His eyes ran along photos on the wall, professional pictures of Owen as a baby, artistic black-and-white shots of crinkly feet, one gloriously beautiful picture of him laughing amid soap bubbles when he was nearly two, another of him as an infant in my arms.

"Come into the living room. Owen will be down in a minute."

My mom sat on the loveseat. I'd told her she could go out, but she gave me a knowing look. "You might need me here," was all she would say. I didn't know what she could possibly mean, unless she worried Noah was going to lose his temper and lay into me. It's what my dad would have done.

Noah looked at the open seats and chose one on the long sofa nearest my mom. I sat beside him, but at a distance. Little feet pounded down the stairs. I could never understand how a thirty-pound kid could sound like an elephant.

When he ran into the living room, he yelled, "NOAH'S HERE!" Then he turned on his heels and ran right back upstairs.

"Uh. Okay." Noah scratched his chin. "What just happened?"

A second later, the herd of bison slammed back down the stairs, and Owen raced in and jumped on the sofa, standing on his knees, between me and Noah with his badly misshapen Lego X-wing fighter. "Look! It's Po!"

Noah took the toy and flew it around, saying, "Pew pew." He zoomed the plane back into Owen's hands. "I have one of these, too, but Luke is flying mine."

"Can you show me?"

"Oh, no. I can't. It's not here."

"Can you go get it?" Owen didn't even glance at Noah, just kept flying the plane.

Noah looked dismayed. "Next time, I will. Okay?"

Owen shrugged. "Can you read to me?"

My heart melted at that. I said, "Owen, do you want to show Noah your room?"

Owen jumped up and held out his hand. He pulled at Noah who faked a groan, like getting up was a monumental task. He let himself be led upstairs, and I tiptoed after, spying around the corner as Owen pointed at his things, held up Rabbit, grabbed a book off the shelf, opened his toy chest. He wanted Noah to see everything he owned. Other than my mom and me, no other adult had ever breached his fortress, and I thought that maybe he was excited to have another boy to appreciate his many objects.

I could tell Noah was starting to panic, unsure how to corral this tiny whirlwind, so I whispered around the corner. "Owen, I think it's time to get in bed."

He slumped, then dragged his feet across the floor in a show of reluctant obedience.

Noah said, "I can't read to you if you aren't in bed."

That did the trick. Owen hopped up and let Noah pull his covers over him. My heart was going to break at the tenderness of the scene. I was about to go fetch my phone to get a picture when I sensed my mom edging in behind me. She shoved the phone at me, and I took it gratefully. Once I'd shot a dozen pictures, I leaned my head against the door jamb and watched as Noah read from *Where the Wild Things Are*. Owen's lips moved with the parts he'd heard so many times he could almost read along. He yawned and snuggled down a little farther into his covers, and then . . . he took Noah's hand in his and closed his eyes.

Like a pro who'd been reading to kids his whole life, Noah read quieter until he turned the last page and then managed to stand up without bouncing the mattress. He took one dramatic step away, watching Owen for signs of stirring. When he'd made it to the edge of the room, Owen let out an enormous breath. I flipped out the light.

"Good job," I whispered.

He leaned back against the wall with a quiet sigh. "That was the most wholesome thing I've ever done in my life."

We carefully descended the stairs to find my mom waiting in the vestibule with her arms crossed. It was like some weird reverse image from our youth, and I felt for a minute like we'd gotten caught sneaking back in. Instead, she said, "You two should go out while you can."

"Go where?" This wasn't New York. I couldn't show Noah anything he hadn't already seen. Not to mention it was Sunday night.

"Take a walk. Go get a drink. I don't care. Unless you want to spend your evening watching TV with me, find somewhere to go."

She knew I was trying to maintain a space between us, but she was incorrigible. She'd effectively made it impossible to spend the evening staring at Noah across the kitchen table. Maybe she hoped she could manipulate us into bridging the chasm that had opened between us.

I grabbed my bag and said, "Let's go."

Out on the sidewalk, Noah took my hand as we headed in no particular direction. He said, "I see what you've done to protect Owen, and I want you to know that I do respect it. Objectively, I understand the choices you've made."

"But?"

"But it really sucks for me."

I started to apologize again, but he cut me off.

"The thing is, you were right. I don't know how things might have been, but Owen is such a happy kid, and so obviously whatever choices you've made have been good for him. It might have been the same no matter what, but I can't argue with results." He stopped and looked up toward the moon, though I doubt he was seeing it. "I just wish I could have been a part of it somehow. Even if it had only been as Noah, the friend who knows about *Star Wars*."

How had that possibility never occurred to me before? "You'd be willing to do that? Just hang back and be in his life as a random person? Not his dad?"

An expression I'd never seen before passed over his features. It was like he was seeing me for the first time, like he didn't know who I was. "Of course. You ought to know better than anyone that the title of 'dad' doesn't mean much to me. I would have traded my own father for a total stranger who knew how to parent properly. I've never had anyone to show me how, but I suspect you could."

"Noah, the friend." It was such a simple solution.

"If that's what it takes to get to know him. Lucy, I missed everything about him up until now. Don't make me miss anything else."

All the fears I'd carried over the past few years lifted from my shoulders. "That might be the best thing for now."

"Is it weird I want to show him things, influence him or maybe indoctrinate him to be more like me?"

"That's kind of what parenting is. Molding little people into shape." I sighed. "But you also have to be willing to accept them when they don't turn out like you."

"Yeah." He sighed. "I know all about that from experience. But mainly, I was thinking how I want to make sure he listens to the right music."

I laughed. "From *my* experience, I'm going to guess he'll disappoint you there as well."

He smiled, but the expression faded, and he got a faraway look in his eyes. "I don't like secrets, Lucy."

My shoulders tensed, and I understood that he was talking about the secrets I'd kept from him. "I know. I'm sorry, Noah. I really am."

He ran a finger across my forehead. "But I can see now how they can protect people. How you've protected Owen. How doing things this way could give us time to transition."

It was a start. I didn't expect him to have adjusted so quickly, and I regretted for the millionth time that I hadn't trusted him sooner, even though there was no guarantee he would have been ready for this before now.

"Maybe one day—" I started.

"I hope so."

His hand slid down, threading my hair, until he was tickling my neck, and he leaned forward and kissed me. I hadn't been expecting it, so it knocked the air from my lungs. I pushed him away so I could recalibrate.

"I thought we'd just talked about Noah, the friend."

He smiled. "We also talked about keeping secrets. And if we're not telling him I'm his dad, we don't have to tell him I'm in love with his mom."

"You will be the death of me."

He just raised an eyebrow. "Little deaths?"

"Incorrigible."

"Your mom kicked us out. We should honor her wishes and use the time wisely."

"What did you have in mind?"

Noah

What I had in mind was Lucy.

The whole time she'd been pushing me away this past weekend, talking of friendship, I'd sincerely believed she didn't want to be with me, despite the little touches, despite the constant wistful looks. But with the revelation of her secret came a new understanding. She wanted me, however she could get me, but she'd been factoring Owen into the equation. So I took myself out of that dynamic. I hoped that the result would be the Lucy I'd known years earlier.

That Lucy wouldn't have turned me down quite so easily.

That Lucy couldn't push me away.

After she was married, we had a good reason to keep our friendship strictly platonic, but even that had failed eventually.

My intentions were not entirely dishonorable. I would never do anything Lucy didn't want, but I happened to know what she wanted was me.

I said, "Will you come with me?"

She said, "Anywhere."

And that decided me. I turned us around and began walking the direction I'd come earlier in the evening, when I'd been a bag of nerves hoping for some magic that had never quite taken for us before.

Except once. Magic had struck when we'd made Owen. I marveled at how miraculous that was. One night together, and we'd made a kid.

Incredible.

The anger at Lucy for keeping him from me would punch me in the guts when I wasn't ready for it, and I kept attempting to use some Aikido and redirect it out to some faceless villain. But I didn't know Aikido, and Lucy had been the one who'd lied. Every time, I worked my way through my emotions again because I knew this was worth it.

I thought back to my own dad, how he could have treated me with patience, understanding, and respect, and maybe I wouldn't have turned into someone who Lucy couldn't trust to be there for her. I thought about what he'd missed out on in his own life because he couldn't channel his anger. Maybe he never cared that he'd lost a son.

But I did.

It was my intention to be a positive influence on Owen, and the best way to start was to ask Lucy all the questions that had piled up of the past twenty-four hours.

"Why did you name him Owen?"

She shot me a confessional look. "Can you believe he guessed it right away? I wanted to honor you somehow, and so I tucked your name into his."

That pleased me. "If you'd had a daughter that would have been tricky."

"Noelle."

"Oh." I couldn't believe she'd thought of that. I wondered what names I might have wanted if I'd been involved. I liked Owen though. It fit the little guy.

Next time—and I hoped there'd be a next time—I wanted to be a part of all of it. I wanted to watch Lucy's belly swell and argue over why we couldn't name a boy Bowie or a girl Joplin. We'd build a nursery and paint the ceiling with stars.

I breathed in and out again, stepping out of the way of my unwanted anger to let it flow into the heavens. The past was the past. I couldn't get back what I'd lost with Owen, so I focused on now.

"What does he like to do?"

"Swing. Build things. Typical kid stuff. He likes dinosaurs and trucks. You know about his love of *Star Wars* though he hasn't really seen much of it. It's more that the marketing is hard to avoid. It's the same reason he likes superheroes. They're ubiquitous."

"What about music?"

"Wheels on the Bus? I sometimes put on some classical or jazz at night for him to sleep to, and he likes it. He knows pop music some, but his taste is pretty suspect."

"Like what?" Was I fishing for her to name one of our songs? Surely he wasn't exposed to rock music yet.

"Boy bands are a hit."

I grabbed my heart. "Say it ain't so."

"It's so. I'm so sorry."

"I could remedy that."

She laughed. "I'm sure you will."

That other feeling hit me. The one that felt like freefalling on a rollercoaster. The one that twisted my face into a weird smile. It kept hitting me in waves whenever I realized: I was a dad. I was going to have a role in my son's life.

I might have agreed to keep it a secret from him for now, but I could dream of a future where her *maybe one day* could be realized.

"So for the past few years, it's just been the two of you?"

"And my mom."

"Weren't you lonely?"

"I dated some. I just never found anyone I'd be willing to bring back to meet my kid."

"I was the first?"

"You have a place of honor, don't you?" She paused. "I was killing time going on dates, Noah. I never would have brought anyone else home. Nobody else would have replaced you."

"I tried to replace you. I tried for years, but I gave that up and settled for killing time." I sighed. "Nobody was you. And I only ever wanted you."

"I never thought this could be possible."

I wanted her so desperately in that moment. I didn't care that we were still half a block from the hotel. I walked into her, forcing her to waltz backward with me until her ass hit the wall of the closest building. My hands were on her shoulders, sliding up her neck to perfectly fit against her cheeks, and I kissed her. Not like a moment before which had been a surprise attack to knock her off guard, but slow, deliberate, giving her all the time in the world to tell me no.

She didn't tell me no.

Our lips brushed, reminding me so much of the night weeks before outside the concert venue, when those two girls had interrupted. With nobody to interrupt us now, I slipped a hand inside her shirt and drew her into me. The first soft moan she emitted pushed me from aroused to steel rod hard, and I pressed into her so she'd feel it too, so she'd know I wasn't playing around tonight.

"Noah."

This was where she'd tell me to back off, to remind me we weren't doing this. I relaxed my grip on her, ready to do as she asked.

What she asked was, "Where are you staying?"

Thankfully we'd been heading there this whole time. I gestured toward the awning up the sidewalk. "We're here."

"Was this your plan?"

I unfastened her top button and lay a kiss on the small hollow of her throat, trailing my tongue along her collarbone. "No. I was planning on staying right here."

She swatted me, then she grabbed the collar of my shirt and pulled me back to her, and I thought for a second she was going to have me right out there in public. "Show me your room."

We were like teenagers again, rushing down the street together, so intent on our destination, we didn't stop to make a plan. We were halfway up the elevator, her ankle wrapped around my calf, my hands gripping her waist, when I remembered. "I don't have any condoms."

She broke the kiss and gave me a long appraising look, but she didn't ask, so I answered the question. "I've been tested. I got tested right after I saw you, right after I caught my last girlfriend cheating on me." I didn't want to be talking about this.

The elevator slowed, and the doors opened. I fished out my key and directed her down the hall toward my room. I'd taken whatever room they'd had available. It was the closest hotel to Lucy's place, and I hadn't expected to be here with her.

We went inside and I sat on the end of the bed. I worried she might change her mind and leave, but she stepped closer to me, then put one knee on the mattress and threw the other knee over me, straddling me, sitting right over my cock, and she tilted her hips just so.

She unbuttoned my shirt. "I don't care about your ex-girlfriends, Noah. I don't want to know about them. That was your life. I had no part in that life. But tell me you're clean. Tell me you're safe."

I held her waist, encouraging the rhythm she'd started to set, hardening in my pants uncomfortably. "I'm clean. Are you taking birth control?"

She shook her head. "I'm not. We should stop."

She kissed me, and I realized that the only thing that had kept us from this exact situation sooner had been lack of opportunity. Except when she was in my apartment altering my life with her confession.

I flipped her off me and onto her back, crawling over her, pushing her arms up over her head, taking control of her, loving the guttural groans that elicited. "Do you want me to stop, Lucy?"

There were other ways to release this painful tension. I unbuttoned her jeans and slid the zipper down. She said, "Please, Noah," and I knew her well enough to know she wasn't begging me to stop. I kissed her neck, then let go of her wrists so I could push her shirt up and lick the skin below her bra. She was a disaster of disarray, and I didn't know where to begin. She sat up on her elbows and reached one hand back to unhook her bra. While she removed her shirt, I did the same. It had been years since we'd laid eyes on each other, and I paused to look at the newer version of Lucy. She'd gotten softer over the years. When her bra came off, I found her body intoxicating. "You're gorgeous."

I leaned in to suck on a nipple while my hand slipped under the edge of her panties. If I could give her this, I wouldn't ask for more. Just to see the look on her face when I made her feel so good.

My fingers skimmed over the swollen heat of her and found slick wetness that I dragged back, watching her fall apart. I whispered, "I love you," as I stroked her slowly, circling and then dipping back into the source of that elixir I so wanted to taste.

"Don't move." I slid down and tugged off her shoes, then peeled her jeans off. Her panties remained, which was a delightful erotic fantasy for me, like gift wrap to discover the present that it was hiding. I didn't pull those off. Instead. I knocked her knees so she'd give me access and pushed the curtain to the side.

"Noah, please," she groaned.

I leaned in and ran my tongue from the top down to her wetness.

She sucked in her breath, and I loved that I was bringing her that pleasure. I lay my lips on that hard nub that she'd once explained to me was like her mini cock. I tried not to laugh remembering that. Instead, I stroked her with my tongue. She'd taught me how much more intense this was for her when I slid a finger—or a vibrator—inside her. I didn't have any toys, and for the thousandth time, I wished I could fuck her and suck her at the same time. I thanked God I had fingers to reach that place that brought her closer to nirvana. I used my thumb to massage that space in between, and it only took a few minutes before she bucked and said, "Oh sweet Jesus, Noah. I haven't managed to do that for myself in the past several years."

I smiled. "I'm better than a machine?"

"Remains to be seen. Take your pants off."

I lived to serve. I stepped back and removed the rest of my clothes, then stood before her, praying she still liked what she saw.

Chapter Twenty-one

Lucy

Oh, sweet Jesus Christ, why had I asked him to strip?

I could have reciprocated with a quickie hand job and called it a night. I was that close to getting away without rounding the bases, as we used to say. But there was a reason Noah was a repeat offender on the lists of hot eligible bachelors in rock.

Okay so I may have looked at those articles. Guilty as charged. I didn't think it was that contemptible considering he'd fathered my child. That may have been a rationalization, but this boy was always the most beautiful person I'd ever laid eyes on. And he was even hotter in the flesh.

There'd never been any question of my attraction to Noah, and I knew I'd pay for tonight in a thousand ways. But I didn't care at the moment. That was a problem for another day. Right now, I needed him like the desert needed water. I couldn't be this near him without wanting our bodies to be as close as humanly possible. I only regretted we couldn't get even closer. I'd climb inside him if I could.

But we didn't have a condom, and so I sought some will-power and held out a hand to get him to lay beside me so I could at least give him the relief he'd given me. At least once he'd gotten off, we'd be out of the danger zone. Temporarily.

That was the plan anyway.

The problem with that plan was that touching Noah wasn't something rational I could manage, and when his cock hardened in my hand, when his breathing grew ragged, and he rocked his hips, my hunger for him grew. I'd never be completely satisfied. I'd never stop wanting to feel him against me, in me.

He turned toward me and sought my mouth as I stroked him, completely aroused now by his arousal. I was about to gather the will power to push him over, to crawl down his body and slide my lips around him when he whispered, "We could make another baby, Lucy."

"Noah." I tensed at his sudden spontaneity. "That's not a decision you make because you don't happen to have condoms handy."

He raised up on one elbow. "Not necessarily tonight." I relaxed again until he added, "But then again, why not?"

It was impossible to have this conversation while we were both lying naked together for the first time in years and his cock pressed into my side. "Is this the sex talking, Noah?"

"You think I'm motivated by sex?"

I waved at his erection. "A little bit."

When he climbed out of the bed and picked up his pants, I saw he meant to dress, and I couldn't begin to process what had gotten into him. "What are you doing?"

He pulled his pants on. "First, I'm going to go buy some condoms. Then, I will be back to discuss rationally whether or not we are going to use them." His shirt went over his head, and he patted his back pocket, verifying he had his wallet. "Stay here."

He left me alone, horny, and confused. I threw on my shirt and underwear so I wouldn't feel quite so sleazy as I waited and pondered the ramifications of what he'd said.

Did I want to build a family with Noah? Of course I did. Did I want to fuck him with or without a condom? That too.

But we hadn't ever discussed it before, and I didn't want to rush into another huge life change without thoughtful planning this time. We couldn't career from one day to another the way we had. We couldn't live in each other's lives like time travelers who only shared stolen moments.

After an eternity, the door swung open, and Noah tossed a box of condoms on the bed.

"Optimistic as ever, I see."

"If I'd been optimistic, I would have had these here to begin with."

I giggled at the image of Noah Kennedy, tent pitched in his pants, sex hair like crazy, racing around a luxury hotel lobby asking for condoms. It fit actually. And it reminded me again of how wild we'd once been. Though, in the past, neither of us would have been responsible enough to stop to get the condoms. Exhibit A: our child.

He sat beside me and drew my bare legs over his clad thighs, rubbing my skin gently, but not seductively. "I meant what I said, Lucy. We could have more kids together."

"Wouldn't that only complicate things? Our situation wouldn't change."

"This is the only situation I want. Nothing else matters."

"It's just kind of sudden, don't you think?"

He snorted. "No. *That* it is not. I lost you once when you got married. Then I lost you again when you banned me from your life. And in all that time, I told myself that if I ever had a chance with you again, I wouldn't let you go. I will do whatever it takes."

"And tomorrow?"

"Tomorrow? I'll feel the same way."

I touched his cheek. "When you head back home, when you're back on tour. What then?"

"Who said I'm going home? I told you: This is what I want."

I sat all the way up. "You're serious?"

He nodded.

"What will you tell Micah?"

"I'll tell him I'm going on hiatus."

"And when he fires you?"

"Then I'll be free to be wherever you need me."

That was all I'd ever wanted from him. So why did it make me so uneasy?

But then his hands slid up my thighs until his fingers hooked the edges of my panties, and he said, "Now, I believe we were in the middle of a different conversation."

I placed my hand on his. "What will you do?"

He shrugged. "We'll figure it out. But to start with, you."

He wrapped his hands around my legs and yanked me so I fell onto my back. He stripped off his shirt, and I no longer wanted to have this conversation. I just wanted to be with him. Now. Forever would wait.

Noah

I peeled my jeans back off and lay beside her. She had too damn many clothes on. "I thought we'd already taken this off," I said as I tugged at the hem of her shirt.

Worry lines creased her forehead, and I knew she was still processing what we'd been talking about. I didn't know how to convince her I'd meant every word. I lay a kiss on her neck and whispered, "I hate touring."

She snorted. "What?"

"I hate it. I hate the hotels. I hate the bus." I shifted so I could focus on her nipples. God, I loved the feel of her on my tongue.

"Why do you do it?"

"It's part of being in the band. I'd give anything if I could just make music without all the rest of it."

"I never knew that."

"I do love performing. And I'm no good at anything else."

Her fingers gently caressed my hip. "I'd disagree."

Just that small touch and I was instantly hard again. "We don't have to rush to any huge decisions today."

She stiffened. "About the band?"

"Fuck the band." I laughed and waved a hand at our state of undress. "No, I mean about this."

I reached for the condoms, but she stayed my hand. "You'd stay by my side?"

"Always."

"What will you do?"

I didn't want to think about that right then. "We'll figure it out."

"Are you sure about this? You've just found out you have one kid. Would you be ready for another so soon?"

"Without a doubt."

She looked into my soul, like she could glimpse the future there. "I want to trust you."

"You're all I've ever wanted, Lucy. Now that I know there's more, I want a family. I want to be there for every part of it."

She found me again, touching me in ways that were going to make the condom unnecessary. When I knocked her onto her back and rolled over, above her, she said, "It's likely I won't get pregnant anyway."

"Then we'll have fun trying." I waggled my eyebrows at her, aiming for playful, but instead a tear spilled from the corner of her eye, along her temple. "What is it?"

She sighed. "I can't believe I'm here with you."

"I feel the same."

"All this time."

I brushed her hair from her face, erasing the tear with my thumb. "Don't. We're here now."

"I've always loved you, Noah. Whatever else I've thought I needed, I never stopped loving you."

"I know."

She dragged my face toward her, kissing me like it would be the last time. "Now would you fuck me?"

I smiled. "Such a filthy mouth you have."

She said, "Please," and I slid into her, to the hilt. And holy fuck it felt so good I nearly came from that first thrust. I stayed that way, just feeling the connection, her warmth, her wetness. I leaned in and captured her mouth with mine, brushing her lips with my tongue, savoring this perfect moment. Finding myself in her.

"You're my soul, Lucy."

"You're mine."

I dropped my head onto her collarbone, fists clenching the bedsheets. It was so good. Had it always been this good between us?

She hitched an ankle behind my knee, and it unleashed some brutal instinct to take her, to make her mine. I pushed her hands up above her head, claiming her, pinning her in place. She groaned my name, and I couldn't restrain myself. Again and again, in and out, endorphins rushing through my body, leaving me frenzied and wanting more, chasing the pleasure I knew would be gone even as it came.

I wanted her to feel it too. I lifted my hips and found her with my thumb, relishing how her back arched, how her nipples contracted, how her mouth fell open, and she gave in to me. I watched for the signs that she always gave me, the moment she let it all go, and when she tightened around me with a gasp, I couldn't hold it back anymore. I released my desire into her. I thought I might actually die from the excruciating pleasure.

As I dropped beside her, sweating like I'd played an hour-long set onstage, I whispered, "I love you," and pulled her to me. We fell asleep like that, and it was possibly the best moment in my entire life.

Chapter Twenty-two

Lucy

Perhaps fairy tales do come true.

I woke up sometime during the night, snuggled against Noah, wondering if everything had really just happened. Had he meant any of it? Had I been a fool again? But after I got up, got dressed, and told him that I needed to go home to be there in the morning for Owen and to go to work, he asked, "Can I come over for breakfast?"

And so early on Monday morning, Noah, Owen, my mom, and I sat around the kitchen table, like a proper family, passing around the jam and butter, and making plans.

When I told Owen to go get dressed for school, he fussed as always, but Noah said, "Do you think I could take you there with your mom?" and Owen ran to get ready.

Noah watched him go with a sweet smile curling his lips, "It's probably too soon to ask to hang out with him, huh?"

My mom gave me that look. It said, *I told you so.*

We walked together, the three of us. Owen refused to ride in his stroller, wanting to be a big boy. He held both of our hands, chatting up to Noah about some nonsense about a movie that he needed to express.

"The big monster is scarier."

Noah exchanged a glance with me but parried easily. "So you like the blue one more?"

"No, silly." Owen giggled. "The big monster *is* the blue one."

"Which one do you like?"

"The funny one."

"The funny monster, of course."

When we entered the school together, some of the moms turned and stared, eyes wide. I wasn't sure if they were appreciating how hot Noah was or if they recognized him. I ignored them and went into the office to see about getting Noah added to the people approved to pick Owen up or drop him off. When I wrote down his name, the secretary said, "Isn't he that guitarist?"

"Oh, you're familiar with his music?"

She snort-laughed. "No. I'm familiar with my daughter's crushes."

I painted a grin on my face. "Well, he might be back here later. Please help him get familiar with the set up. Thanks."

Noah walked me to the museum and kissed my cheek, and it was nice, like we were a married couple, and that thought gave me butterflies. Married to Noah. It hadn't seemed remotely possible, and now, maybe we could have the life I'd tried to make with someone else, the settled stable life, the safe life.

"What will you do today?"

He scratched his chin. "I was thinking, I might just walk around a bit, check out the neighborhood. It might be a good idea for me to find my own place at first, don't you think?"

I hadn't thought. "Yeah."

"Then I'll call Micah in a bit, when I'm sure he'll be up and in a decent mood."

"How will he take it?"

Noah shrugged. "I don't really care."

"Can you meet me for lunch?"

"That would be perfect."

He gave me another kiss, then turned and began walking back the way we'd come, looking gorgeous and entirely out of place, and I felt uneasy again, but I shook it off as a reasonable anxiety for an uncertain future.

I'd never expected to win, and so I'd never anticipated the mixed feelings this victory brought with it.

It was like I'd gone on an expedition and bagged a wild animal. Now that I'd brought Noah home, what did I do with him? There were no manuals on the care and training of rock stars in domesticity. What was he going to do here?

I believed he believed this was going to work, but whenever I'd made these plans in my head, it had been so removed from reality, I'd gone ahead and transformed Noah into some version of me, someone with a desk job or some other occupation that worked with my fictional life plan. Someone who'd be content in a cage.

I forgot leopards can't change their spots.

After all, my dad always came home full of promises, full of plans for the next big thing. My mom always fell for it, and I suspected I finally understood why. Because she wanted to.

But Dad had finally cut us a break and left us alone for good. I hoped I wasn't repeating her mistakes. I hoped I wasn't expecting Noah to achieve the impossible.

Priya caught me as I was coming in and forced me to get out of my head. "Lucy, come talk to me about your trip."

"Right." The Van Gogh. I tensed. "Sure, I'll be right there."

I'd considered what Dajana had told me at the museum, and while I knew the drawing would be a valuable addition to our collection, it would be such a substantial loss to theirs, and I couldn't help take that into consideration. Priya would not see it that way.

I took a few minutes to take my things to my office and breathe away my own anxiety.

Maybe nobody's truly content in a cage.

Noah

The initial relief of my decision to take a break from the band was quickly replaced by a new set of problems.

Where would I live? Should I get a town house near Lucy? Or maybe some kind of efficiency with the hope that it was a temporary step before moving in with her some day? Would she want to find a new place together eventually?

How would I support myself once the money I'd saved had run out? On the surface, I appeared to be doing fairly well, but most of my money went into my apartment. I paid a premium to have the security that kept fans from showing up on my doorstep. What was left covered modest expenses or went into savings.

What kind of job could I do around here? I could try to join a local band or play pickup shows. It probably wouldn't pay that much, but as long as I could perform, wouldn't that be enough?

Maybe music could become a hobby while I worked . . . somewhere real. Where though? I had no skills.

Maybe I could switch to acoustic and start a solo career like Micah had done. Granted, I wasn't the songwriter he was, but cover artists made a living.

I could probably teach guitar.

I tried to think of a situation where I could keep one foot in the band long distance, but even recording our albums or rehearsing required me to be in New York. Maybe I could convince them all to move here. I laughed at that idea. Shane might be willing to come back if he hadn't just started dating Layla, or if she hadn't just started working at a rock magazine headquartered in Midtown.

The only solution I had was to take a break from the band and then just never go back.

I could live off savings while I got my GED.

Maybe I could turn to modeling. I'd had a fairly lucrative watch gig a year ago, and there'd been a cologne company talking to our manager. But would they want me for my looks alone if I wasn't in the band? Who was I by myself?

I'd walked up and down every street near Lucy's until I ran out of excuses for calling. With my heart racing, I opened my contacts and hit Call.

"Noah! Where are you?"

"I'm in D.C." I laughed with pretend breeziness. "I took your advice, and everything is great, really great. I met my son—Owen—yesterday, and I begged Lucy to let me come down and spend more time with them."

"Hey, that's great. I was worried about you. Thanks for checking in. Are you coming back tonight or tomorrow morning?"

"Yeah, so that what I'm calling about."

"Uh-huh?"

"I kind of promised Lucy I'd stay here for a bit."

"A bit? What's a bit?"

"Well—"

"Noah, we're leaving tomorrow. We're contracted for twenty gigs. You know this."

"Right, but—"

"But nothing. We have an agreement. You signed it. You can't bail on a tour the day before we leave."

"You don't understand. I've promised Lucy—"

"You promised us, Noah."

"What if I needed to go into rehab?" This had sounded like a reasonable argument until it came out of my mouth.

Micah paused, then asked, "Do you?"

"No, but . . . It's just as urgent."

"Insurance covers your absence if you go into rehab."

"I can't leave right now. Lucy will never forgive me."

"What do you want me to do, Noah? Cancel the tour? You want to fork up the money to cover the losses?"

My heart tightened. There was a steep penalty for defaulting on shows. I never expected Micah would be so ruthless about this. "You know I can't."

"And I can't go out without a lead guitarist."

I didn't have any answers.

"Dammit, Noah. If you'd given us any advance warning, we might have been able to find someone to fill in."

"If someone fills in for me, would you release me?"

"I don't know. Honestly, I never thought it would come to this."

"I wouldn't ask it if it weren't so important."

"Find someone to take your spot, or be on the bus tomorrow. It's only for three weeks. Lucy kept a secret from you for four years. I think she owes you a little leeway."

I laughed. "Are you the same person who told me to do this right?"

"I didn't mean for you to fuck us all. Jesus. Can we talk about it on the bus?"

He had me in a vise grip. I could try to find someone to step in for me for a night here or there, but I'd never find coverage for the whole three-week tour at this late a date.

"Fuck." I exhaled, already trying to picture the conversation I was going to have to have with Lucy. "Fine. I'll see you tomorrow."

I checked the time.

She'd be expecting me for lunch, so I started the long walk back to the museum. I passed by the daycare, tempted to peek in on Owen, but knowing how Lucy felt about absentee dads, I didn't want to complicate things further by bonding with my son when there was a pretty good chance she was going to throw me out of his life.

I shook my head.

"Damn."

Lucy

My morning had gone about as poorly as I'd expected.

When I'd told Priya, "I don't think the Cooper-Hewitt will be happy to loan the Van Gogh to us," she'd said, "It was your job to convince them otherwise."

I sighed. "They only have the two."

She raised an eyebrow. "They have two?"

"We have six."

"We're the *National* Gallery, Lucy."

"Right." I didn't have a good response to that.

"I should have sent Farid." She turned and left, probably to talk to someone over my head about my responsibilities.

I wanted to care, but I suddenly found that I just didn't. Life was bigger than this. So much bigger. I hadn't even known how big it could be, hiding out here among still life representations of the world.

My life had been as two-dimensional as that Van Gogh, and I'd let myself stagnate because I hadn't had faith in the three-dimensional world. I hadn't had faith that I could attract a work of art like Noah into my personal collection.

Despite Priya's disapproval, I floated on air back to my office with the knowledge that I'd be meeting Noah for lunch, and Priya couldn't take that away from me.

Why had I waited so long to take a chance on Noah? I'd been protecting myself against an imaginary injury. But given the opportunity, Noah had proved that he was worth the risk, and finally the pieces were falling into place against all odds. It might be bumpy at first, but we'd work it out.

So why did I still have qualms?

There was a knock on my door, and I looked up to see Noah. God, he was truly beautiful. No painting or sculpture in the entire museum could hold a candle to him. Not now and not ever. The artists of yore would have looked on him and decided that there was nothing they could do but hope to capture his beauty on a canvas or in marble. I crossed my office to meet him, recalling every second of the night before.

"Well, hello."

Maybe we could sneak off and order room service in his hotel. Then I could pass the rest of the day dreaming about the moment when we might steal away again. My mom would happily watch Owen after he'd gone to bed. I was already imagining the day Noah would live with us, and we wouldn't have to sneak at all.

He leaned forward for a kiss. I'd expected a quick how-do-you-do, but he lingered in a way that held meaning, deeper significance. Yeah, room service lunch was definitely looking like an option.

But when he pulled away, he rubbed the back of his neck the way he did, and my gut clenched. I tilted my head and drank in the signs I'd missed before, the tight worry in his clenched jaw, the crease in his forehead. "What's up? Did something happen?"

His laugh was short, punctuated, like a surprise. "You always knew me better than anyone else."

"So? Is someone hurt?"

He took my hand and said, "Where can we go talk?"

And then I knew. I knew it like I always knew it was going to rain. Like I always knew he was going to leave. "You're not staying."

He inhaled and let the air out extra slow, biding time, bracing for impact. "I'm staying, it's just—"

"Not now."

I should have known it. Yesterday morning, I'd been prepared for this, but that was before he'd charmed me, before he'd made promises he could never keep. Before I'd dared to hope for something more.

His eyes closed, then reopened, and he focused on me. "It's the contract. I'll figure it out, but I can't—"

"You're going out on tour. When?"

"Tomorrow."

I shook my head at myself, at fate, at the imbalance of time. I never got more of Noah than the music ever would. "For how long?"

"Three weeks, unless I find someone to replace me."

"Replace Noah Kennedy." I had to laugh. "Like that's so easy." I turned back in to my office. "If I could have done that, believe me, I would have done it years ago."

"It's only three weeks."

"And you'll be back after that?"

"Yes." He said it so fast, he must have thought it was the right answer.

"For how long then?"

"I just need to find someone to take my place."

His face was a portrait of pain, and I believed he wanted to stay, but that was the trouble with the life he'd chosen. Despite his best intentions, things would never go my way, and I'd always be reliving this moment, this disappointment. He'd never manage to be where I needed him. This was the exact heartache I'd wanted to spare our son.

"And what do I tell Owen?"

"Nothing. He doesn't even know who I am." His voice rose with anger. "He has not the first fucking clue who I am."

I should have kept it that way, apparently. "And obviously that's a good thing."

"Is it? Do you really believe that it's better for him to go through his life with no idea who I am to him?"

"If you're going to pick up and leave whenever Micah crooks his finger, then yes. You see how Owen's taken to you already. I can't do this to him."

His shoulders sagged. "It's only three weeks, Lucy. I'll be back."

"You've said that before."

He stared up at the ceiling. "I was coming back the last time. You told me not to."

"And I was right. The band always takes precedence. So go. Go be with your precious music, get your rocks off onstage. I'll be right here, raising our child. But don't think you can come and go as you please. I don't want a fraction of you."

"Lucy."

"Just go. You don't want to miss your flight."

And he did. He left and took all the oxygen in the room with him.

I stared at the empty doorway until it was clear he wouldn't turn around and change his mind. And I remembered watching my dad drive away while my mom sat on the front porch steps, silently crying, wondering why she wasn't enough.

I was done with this bullshit. I blocked Noah's number then sent off an email to the Cooper-Hewitt to push Dajana for the Van Gogh. I could at least salvage my job.

Chapter Twenty-three

Noah

I had no idea what city I was in. I was onstage in the middle of "Close Enough." Girls crammed against the stage, calling my name. I was playing like shit. Micah kept shooting me dirty looks. He'd accused me earlier of sabotaging the band, trying to get fired, but that wasn't accurate. I didn't care if I got fired, but I'd never intentionally fuck up my set.

Since I wasn't talking to Micah, I hadn't told him that. I hadn't told him that I was distracted by the fact that my fucking soul was destroyed. I hadn't told him that he was traveling with a shell of a man who couldn't even find his way to the music.

And without the music, I was in hell.

I guessed this was what happened when the devil finally came to collect his due. He'd just dangle before you the life you might have had, like an ironic twist—if only you hadn't chased the wrong dream. If you hadn't sold your soul for smoke and ash. Then once you had one taste of heaven, he'd send you right back to the so-called success your soul had bought. And that was your hell for eternity.

The song came to an end, and none of the girls at my feet seemed to notice or care that I'd missed half my notes. All that mattered were the pictures they captured to share with their followers. I glowered at a girl with black hair who reminded me so much of Lucy from years ago. She blew me a kiss, and I stalked away from the edge of the stage toward Shane while Micah made some stupid banter.

Shane raised an eyebrow at me, signaling for me to pull my shit together, but I wasn't talking to him either. His fucking girlfriend was taking a train to meet us at our next gig, and he was sunshine and rainbows. I was just done.

Somehow I got through the rest of the show and dropped my guitar into the stand.

I scrolled to my text messages to verify Lucy hadn't replied. I hit Call to let it go to her voicemail. I figured she'd blocked me and wouldn't even see a notification I'd called, so I didn't bother planning out my words. "Come on, Lucy. Call me back. I don't even want to be here." My voice cracked. "I'm dying without you."

A giggle behind me made me spin to find that dark-haired girl watching me. She slunk over with a Cheshire grin. I shook my head. "Not gonna happen."

I pushed through the fans who'd found their way into the hall around the green room, ignoring requests for autographs and selfies. I heard someone say, "I always heard he's an asshole."

Good. Let them lose their fascination. Then they'd all be happy when I left the band for good.

A hand connected with my shoulder, and my back hit the wall. "What the fuck, Noah?"

I shoved Micah off me, but he pushed me back again. "It's three fucking weeks. Why are you being such an emo baby?"

I slapped his hand away. "I fucking told you. I told you if I came out on tour it would fuck everything up."

"You're always so goddamn melodramatic, Noah."

"I am not exaggerating. She won't even take my calls."

He rolled his eyes. "She'll get over it, man."

I wanted to punch him. Maybe if I did, they'd have to send me home. Instead, I elbowed around him and stomped outside.

Fans were still milling around. Someone approached me, and I barked, "No," before climbing on the bus. I had no idea if we had a hotel or if we were traveling by night. It didn't matter. I could hole up here.

When I woke up, the bus was moving, and I could hear the guys talking up front. I sat up and listened.

Shane was saying, "They've been like this since high school. It's always fucking and fighting with them."

"But will he straighten this out?" Micah.

"It would be better to find a competent session guitarist than deal with all this fucking attitude." Rick had some nerve to throw me under the bus.

I emerged from the back. "It's not always fucking and fighting, Shane. I thought you of all people would remember that everything was great until I took off with you to chase this so-called dream." I faced Micah. "And no, I won't straighten this out. I had something I'd been searching for my whole life, right there, right in my hand, and you pulled rank on me. So I'm here, but my life is fucked now." I looked at Rick. "If you can find someone to replace me, by all means."

We traveled in stony silence until we made it to Toronto. I hadn't realized we'd been in Canada or when we'd crossed the border. I must have handed my passport to someone, but it was all a blur.

The bus pulled into a parking lot at some random hotel, and we spilled out. Shane said, "She's here," and we headed to the registration desk where Layla and some other guy met us. As mad as I'd been at everyone, at Shane in particular, I felt an immediate pang of secondary jealousy for him. Even I could tell the guy with Layla was an upgrade in the looks department. Shane wouldn't deal well with that.

So it shocked me when he crossed the lobby, hand out, ready to shake. "Hey!" He turned to me and said, "Noah, this is Dylan! Remember? We told you about him."

I had a vague recollection of them talking about the show they'd gone to see in TriBeCa, how they'd been impressed with his performance, but I'd shut it out. I hated everyone.

Dylan strode toward me. "Oh, man. Noah Kennedy? You are like an idol to me."

I laughed bitterly. "Well, that's a pretty shitty standard you have then."

He smiled, big perfectly straight white teeth. "You have no idea how you've inspired me. When Layla told me she'd met you guys, I didn't even believe her. I was totally flummoxed when Micah and Shane showed up at my gig last week."

My lip curled. I didn't need another fucking fan. I turned to Shane. "What's he doing here?"

Shane's expression darkened, and I knew I'd crossed some line. I was beyond giving a fuck. Layla stepped over, and honestly, I considered pushing her out of my way. And that thought more than anything else shook me to the core. I needed to be away from everyone. I was a total monster.

Instead of punching me in the gonads like I deserved, she laid a hand on my upper arm. "Noah. Is there anything I can do to help you?"

I don't know why that small kindness was what cracked the shell of anger that had been protecting me from the hurt I couldn't face, but right there in front of my band bros, in front of this fucking stranger who idolized me, in front of Shane's super fan girlfriend, I broke down and started to cry. If only it had been a quiet weeping, tears rolling down my face, I might have saved some pride. But I dropped to the floor, arms wrapped around her legs, cheeks pressed against her jeans, snot flowing freely. I felt like the biggest spectacle, but I couldn't stop.

She squatted down, and despite how I'd treated her, she touched my temple and gently ran her fingers back to tuck my hair behind my ear. She wrapped an arm around my neck and rocked back and forth, hushing me like the mom who hadn't even talked to me since I'd left for New York, and everything in me shattered.

I think Micah must not have realized how truly fucked I was until that moment because he came and laid a hand on my back and said, "Hey, we'll figure something out. We'll fix this."

And at this, I started to laugh, seriously laugh, because it was too fucking late, and he'd finally come to realize what I'd said earlier in the week. "Well, that's just great because now I can leave the band and go do fuck-all."

I stood up, brushed myself off, and said, "Can I please have my key card?"

Micah narrowed his eyes, but he didn't fight me. I took my key and my bags and left them to gossip about me. They might have preferred I'd taken up an alcohol addiction. At least there was a rock 'n' roll script for dealing with that. What were they supposed to say to reporters who came around asking about my emotional breakdown?

As I reached the elevator, Layla caught up to me and said, "Hey, Noah."

I was trapped until the elevator arrived, so I schooled my expression and turned to face her. My only response was a sharply arched brow. I could use my reputation as the asshole to push her away.

"When you left last week, I sat with Lucy and talked with her. I expected her to pick up and leave when you stormed away. She could have done that. She could have decided not to deal with how you were handling things."

I sucked on my teeth, waiting for her to make a point.

"She said something to me. It didn't mean much to me at the time, but I thought it might be worth something to you now."

That had my attention. "What?"

"She said, 'I'm always waiting for him to come back, but he's always walking away.' "

That was nothing new. "Not sure how difficult that is to decipher."

Layla touched my elbow. "Wait. I wasn't finished. I'm setting the context."

The elevator bell dinged, and the doors slid open. I glanced over toward the solitude I'd been yearning for.

"She said, 'It's always been too easy to chase him away.' "

"What?"

"Right? But this is the part that struck me because it was my childhood fantasy." Layla's eyes widened. "Oh, man, that's an embarrassing thing to admit."

I gritted my teeth. "Go on, please."

"Lucy said, 'There was a time Noah would climb on my parents' roof with a guitar strapped to his back to win me.' Did you really do that?"

The words unspooled me, and I smiled at the memory. "Yeah. I was determined to convince her we were right for each other. In retrospect, that was probably completely stalkery, but I was aiming for romantic."

"Do you think maybe she's looking for you to convince her again?"

"I thought I had. I was ready to quit the band and move to D.C. to be with her."

"But then you left again."

My gut tightened. "I know. That is literally the crux of the problem, Layla."

"A couple of weeks ago, when Shane serenaded me from that concert, it proved to me he was committed to me."

"I can't just serenade Lucy now."

"Why not?"

"She isn't into all this. She honestly wouldn't even see it. Or care."

"What do you think she wants?"

"Someone who doesn't exist."

At that, the naive look of hope drained from her face, and she said, "I hope you find the answer. She's clearly as in love with you as you are with her, and I would bet everything that she's waiting for you to make your next move."

I snorted. "Then she can wait. I'm out of moves."

Chapter Twenty-four

Lucy

I closed the lid on my laptop when I heard my mom coming down the stairs. She entered the kitchen and settled into a chair.

"You don't have to stop watching those videos just because I'm here. You're not fooling anyone."

"I don't know what you're talking about."

She tilted her head toward my laptop. "You think I couldn't hear that music from upstairs?"

It hadn't been that loud. She was fishing, but she was right. "I can't watch videos?"

"Not if you won't take his calls. Do you really think he wants to be on the road?"

"What difference does it make?"

"Did you know you're stubborn and unreasonable?"

"Mom!"

"You are. You always followed the rules to the letter. You got your work done. You never took a risk."

"I took a risk when I let him into Owen's life. I took a risk when I believed he wanted to stay."

She shook her head. "Noah took those risks too, Lucy. How much did you really risk by coercing him to walk away from his life? Did you honestly think he could pull that off overnight?"

"I cannot live with someone who can't commit to me. What is so hard to understand about that?"

"And how have you ever committed to Noah?"

I ground my teeth. "You know there's more at stake here."

"Do you think really think Noah is anything like your father?"

"No, I don't, but actions speak louder than intentions, Mom."

She took my hand. "Lucy, the reason your dad would never stay wasn't because of anything I did or didn't do. He couldn't stay put because he didn't truly love me, not enough. He'd try, for you I think, but I made him so unhappy. He'd pick at you sometimes because of all the things he wanted to say to me but couldn't. I'd hear him yell at you for leaving your books on the table, when what he was really saying was that I disgusted him."

I shook my head. "Did he ever say that?"

"Actually, he did."

"Why on earth did you ever let him in the house then?"

"Also for you. There was a time when you and he were thick as thieves. He doted on you, and you ate it up. I'd thought about leaving him for years, but I'd never leave you, and when you were younger, I worried you wouldn't forgive me if I took you away from him. I know your opinion of him changed over time, but as long as he was coming home, I let him. At least until you left for college. Maybe I shouldn't have done that, but I thought part of a dad was better than none."

"And you still believe that?"

"I don't know, but the difference here is that Noah is not your dad. He isn't leaving because he wants to. I believe he'd do anything if he could rearrange his life so that you were always with him, but he'd never ask you to give up your life for him. He'd never ask you to pick up and move, or go on the road with him, because you've always let him know that you never would. You've given him an ultimatum he can never satisfy, and then you act surprised when he fails. You've asked that boy to live his life split in two."

Her words hit me like a steel fist to the heart. "He shows up here once in a blue moon and moves on with the sunrise. He hasn't shown any serious intention to want to be with me in a decade, and you think *his* life is split in two?"

"I do. I think he's probably miserable right now."

"And what do you propose I do?"

"Have you ever considered meeting him halfway?"

"How? Move to New York? Join his band?" Sarcasm dripped from my tone. I hadn't fought like this with her since I was a teenager. Ironically, back then we'd fought about what a bad influence Noah was on me. "And when did you become such a fan of Noah?"

She pursed her lips, which I recognized as her losing patience with me, but I could weather her disappointment. "Since he made it plain how much he loves you."

"Everything was so clear before, and now I don't know what to do."

"You know, I said it before. You could start by talking to him instead of sneaking views of bootlegged concert footage."

I inhaled, exhaled, and said, "I just wanted to see how he's doing."

"And?"

"He's screwing up a lot. I read the comments. Fans said he's particularly dickish."

"The poor thing."

"What poor thing?" How dare she take his side?

"Like I said. He'll never be at peace."

She fished her keys from her purse and gave me an uncharacteristic kiss on the head before heading out to one of the political groups she'd joined. I turned out the lights in the kitchen and went up to check on Owen once before getting into bed with my laptop. I had a date with Netflix. I had no intention of falling back into the YouTube rabbit hole.

But as I sat on Owen's bed and straightened his blanket out, I considered Mom's words. Owen twisted the blanket up while he slept and ended up half in half out. He hadn't once asked me about Noah when I picked him up at daycare on Monday. I thought he'd be looking for him, but he'd already forgotten, and that should have made me feel better because I didn't want Owen to miss Noah at all, but I hated the reasons why he didn't miss Noah. If Noah and I couldn't work through this hiccup, it would be better in the long run that they hadn't formed a bond. But at the same time, I wanted Noah to prove he was in it for the long run so they could start to form that bond. I ached knowing how much time had already been lost.

And that was on me. Time would tell if I'd been right or wrong.

Speaking of time. Noah had been gone for a week. He'd be back in New York in a couple of weeks, and then we'd see what choices he planned to make. He needed to know I wasn't playing. I didn't want him split in two, but this *was* an ultimatum. I wanted it all: the husband, the father, the family.

♡

Noah

I forced myself to stand still even though I wanted to grab my guitar back. "No, that's not even close to right."

Dylan repositioned his hands and tried again.

"Here." I finally couldn't take it and reached over. He held the guitar out, and I showed him. "See?"

In his defense, it was a really weird chord. When he tried it again, I nodded. "Better."

After Toronto, Micah had invited Dylan to ride along with us to Rochester, promising to let him perform before the official opening act. I wanted to protest, but we'd ridden on the bus together for hours, and aside from his initial over-the-top admiration for a false god, Dylan had turned out to be pretty cool. I couldn't argue with Micah's plan to help him. We'd gotten a lot of breaks early on with people taking chances on us. Adam's band had barely met us before taking us to Europe to open for

Walking Disaster. Now whenever we went back to Europe, we often headlined those very same venues. Germany loved us.

After we'd gotten the stage set up in Rochester, Dylan had done a little soundcheck, playing one of his songs on my guitar. I'd listened for a bit from the back, and I was so impressed, I came out to stand in front of him and listen. As soon as he saw me, he broke out into "After Shock," which was a song we hadn't even released yet, though we'd recorded it in the studio and played it live. I was surprised he knew it, and when he fucked up that weird chord, I couldn't help step in and teach him.

"You're good," I said. "What else do you know?"

He launched into "Close Enough," our most popular song. It sounded like he'd played it a few times. "Do you play covers?"

"Not by choice. But I constantly get requests for other bands." He laughed. "Did that ever happen to you?"

I thought back to when we'd played smaller clubs. It had been a really long time. "Maybe."

"I guess it's the curse of the one-hit wonder. I've learned to come prepared."

I had an idea. "Stay here."

Shane had discovered a sofa in the green room where he lay back, chatting over video with Layla who'd gone back home on Sunday.

"You got a second?"

He sat up. "Can I call you back, Star Shine?"

I rolled my eyes. He was too cute with Layla. It made me want to barf all over my shoes.

He followed me out to the cavernous auditorium and up the steps to the stage. "Get on the drums and start the beat for 'Close Enough.'"

"Ugh. You dragged me out here for that? I could play that song in my sleep with one arm tied behind my back."

"Shut up and play."

I nodded to Dylan whose eyes widened at the realization that I was about to make him perform. I slung Micah's guitar strap over my neck. Micah's part was cake. All he had to do was strum and sing. We were missing the bass, but I just wanted to try something out.

Shane hit the boom-boom-pop of the opening beats, and then Dylan fucked up the first chords, the most recognizable riff of the whole song. Shane stopped playing. "What the hell are you doing anyway?"

"Do it again."

"Whatever." Shane started over, and I gave Dylan a significant look.

"Focus, man."

This time, he came in right on time and nailed it. I smiled and waited for my cue. Right about now, Micah would walk out and pick up this guitar, and the girls would go nuts. He was the true rock star of our band, and he handled it with humility and grace. I never gave him credit for that, but I didn't know how he did it.

I strummed my chords and sang into the mic, channeling Micah. I heard Shane snort behind me. I'd watched Micah long enough I could do a fair imitation. I glanced at Dylan, and he had a massive grin on his face. I wondered if this was like a weird fantasy-come-true for him. Honestly, I didn't care. This entire exercise was one hundred percent selfish.

We made it through the whole song without many more mistakes than we normally made. When the last note rang out, the sudden silence was replaced with a slow clap from the other side of the space, and I squinted my eyes to see through the dim lighting.

Micah crossed the floor toward the stage. "That was entertaining."

Caught finagling.

I wasn't going to slink away though. I took his guitar off and set it back on the stand. Dylan did the same with mine.

I stepped to the edge of the stage and sat. "Let him play it tonight."

"I know what you're doing." He crossed his arms, like he was going to have to force a confession from me.

"Yeah, and? Why can't we see how he does with a song?"

Dylan still stood behind us, probably confused about the direction of this conversation. I turned and waved him to come closer.

"Do you think you could do that tonight if we let you open the show? We could switch out right after."

His forehead wrinkled. "But why?"

Micah cocked his head. "He's trying to foist his spot on you."

"Huh?"

I narrowed my eyes. "I'm not foisting anything. I just want to see how he does. What's the harm in that?"

Micah exhaled, and it was the sound of a parent releasing years of frustration with a truculent child. "One song."

I patted Dylan on the shoulder. "Congratulations. You're starting tonight."

He said, "Uh, thanks," but he looked slightly terrified. He'd played big shows before, so this wasn't totally new. He'd told me that he'd dropped out of the music scene to go home and get his head straight after some initial success and pressure from his label. He'd faded and had been having a hell of a time clawing his way back now, despite a song that had broken the charts recently. Apparently, it was harder to get those breaks the second time around. We could help with that.

"You've got this," I said, like someone who had no ulterior motives.

Chapter Twenty-five

Lucy

Monday started out difficult. Owen fought me about going to daycare again, which made me feel super guilty as I dropped him off crying. He chose that morning to ask why Noah didn't come back. Mom promised to come get him in the afternoon, but she had an appointment in the morning, and I hated relying on her for so much anyway. I had nothing to promise Owen to bribe him to stop complaining about wanting to stay with me, and I couldn't take him with me to work, so I made eye contact with one of the daycare workers, silently pleading for her to help me out, while Owen wrapped his arms around my knees and sobbed. I considered calling in sick. Again.

As I walked away exhausted and headed to the museum, I wondered if Owen would register days like this any differently than I remembered the days when my dad abandoned me. Did Owen think I was abandoning him every day?

My heart hurt with that prospect.

When I got to my office, I found Priya waiting. She pretended to look at a watch that wasn't there, and I shrugged as I passed her and went to my desk.

"What can I help you with?"

"Where are we with the Van Gogh? Have you reached out again to the Cooper-Hewitt?"

"I emailed, but I'll call again this morning."

"It's really the first little bit of responsibility we've asked of you. You need to show us you can get things done."

It wasn't the right time to be dumping on me. "I said I'll do it today."

Once she left, I scrolled through my contacts and called up the museum, but I was told, Dajana, the curator I'd spoken to had left. I deflated. "Could you put me through to whoever is in charge now?"

"Well, that's unclear. We need to fill the position."

"Who could I speak to then?"

She patched me through to another director who transferred me to another who redirected me to a third. When I ended up talking to the first woman again, I asked, "When do you expect the position will be filled? I'm expected to arrange an exchange."

"We'll be interviewing this week, most likely."

I had a thought. "Could you email me the details of the opening? I'd be curious to take a look."

The email came a few minutes later, and I read through it. I was definitely qualified for it. I wondered if I could transfer from one Smithsonian to another. Was I really considering this? Was I willing to give up my dream job to start somewhere totally new?

I'd liked that museum, but while it was in New York, it was still pretty far from where Noah lived, so taking a job there might create a totally new problem. Although if I was willing to consider moving a couple of hundred miles to be closer to him, he could compromise by moving fifteen to be closer to my new job.

New York had been intimidating, but with Noah, it hadn't seemed impossibly scary. And Owen had loved the tall buildings. We'd never made it to the Natural History Museum. I could see how it might be exciting to live there, even though the idea of being there on my own, whenever Noah would be on the road, terrified me.

I pulled up the map, but it didn't give up its secrets. I knew nothing of New York. I had no idea about costs or neighborhoods, but Noah did. I had no idea where I'd want to live or whether Owen would be happy there. Would I want to consider a job somewhere without a ton of research?

Not to mention, if I took a job up there, I'd have to leave my mom. Then again, she was the one pushing me to consider it. I guess she could keep the town house or I'd sell it and figure out where she wanted to go next.

I shook my head. Why was I even considering this? Noah would still be on the road with the band, so would this solve anything? I'd have to trust him to meet me halfway. I still didn't know what that meant.

A part of my brain said I was being ridiculous and rationalizing any possible way to keep Noah in my life even if I had to give up everything and only get a piece of him.

Another part said that he wouldn't be leaving me if we shared a home. He'd be there whenever the band had breaks, when they were rehearsing, when they were recording. It would be hard to be alone when he went on the road, but like Mom had suggested, I could go out with him sometimes. She wasn't wrong that he wanted to be with me. I never doubted that. I only doubted that he could fulfill that promise.

It was obvious he could never truly come to me.

But the crux of the question was this: If I went to him, could we make it work?

I needed to figure out the logistics before I said anything to anyone, but the idea was there.

And then I remembered, there were other museums in New York. So many museums. Why was I limiting my options to the Smithsonian? I pulled up a job search site and typed in the parameters of New York and museum jobs and found hundreds, though most I could immediately dismiss. I couldn't do legal jobs. I didn't want low-skilled work. I landed on an opening for an Exhibitions Project Coordinator at the Brooklyn Museum. The pay was comparable, and the description sounded right up my alley.

More importantly, the Brooklyn Museum was close to Noah's apartment.

I bookmarked the site to come back to later.

With a glance at the door to my office, I popped in a pair of headphones and pulled up YouTube to search for any video from the Theater of the Absurd show in Rochester. The first one I found made my heart beat a million miles a second in panic because Noah wasn't onstage. Micah, Shane, and Rick were playing like nothing was wrong, but someone else was playing Noah's guitar. What had happened to Noah?

I stared at my phone, wondering if I should call him. Or Shane. Maybe it was time to unblock his number in case he was having an emergency. What if he'd done something stupid like gotten drunk and hurt himself?

Then the song hit the final notes, and Micah said, "Everyone give a round of applause to Dylan Black who we're just getting to know. We thought it would be fun to let him sit in on this set. Thanks, man." The audience applauded, though it was nothing compared to the uproar when Noah emerged from the shadows to take his guitar back from Dylan.

And without any fanfare, they started into another song, and the video cut off.

I went looking for others, and there were plenty. Noah seemed to be playing better, less erratically, and I couldn't believe I was relieved. After that burst of fear for his safety, it was nice to think he was coping after all.

But the adrenaline hadn't stopped pulsing through my body, and I knew that if something did happen to him, I'd regret how I never gave us a chance. I'd been living in this fantasy where someday everything in our lives would click into place, where Noah would stop belonging to his world and would dedicate his life to mine. But stealing these moments to spy on him was worse than what I'd gotten from him in that short bit of time we'd had together.

And wasn't that what he'd been saying all along? Didn't he give himself to me one hundred percent when he was with me? Wasn't that better than nothing?

I clicked the bookmark to the site with the museum job application, and without over-thinking it, I created an account and applied.

Noah

Dylan agreed to ping pong with us through Vermont and back into Canada for a show in Montreal. He got along well with everyone, even Rick, and I kept imagining him on the bus permanently. I wasn't sure if I could convince him, but I'd planted a seed anyway.

I took my guitar onto the bus, to the grumblings of the other guys, but on the way from Burlington, I asked Dylan to show me what other songs of ours he could play already. He'd only really mastered "Close Enough." He confessed that he'd learned the opening to "After Shock" when Layla told him where she was taking him last weekend. She'd made Dylan watch the bootleg recordings of it more than a few times. Still, he had the basics for a few songs, and I suggested he sit in again, but for more songs.

He eyed me. "Are you hurt or something?"

Actually, my hands generally ached while on tour, but I'd learned to cope. I just said, "I'm trying to cheat the devil."

Dylan could question that, but Micah piped up. "He's taking advantage of you."

Dylan looked even more confused. "I don't follow."

Micah turned to face me, ignoring Dylan's request for clarification. "You do realize he has a career of his own. He has songs of his own. You've heard him playing solo. What makes you think he wants to suddenly be in a band, playing someone else's songs?"

Dylan said, "Oh, hey, I'm gonna just go lie down for a bit in the back and let you guys work this out."

I held up a hand. "No, stay."

Micah scooted directly across from me. "You know he's heading back to New York tomorrow. He has his own gigs lined up this weekend. So what is your plan here?"

"My plan is to see if he has the chops to fill in for me."

Dylan's head swiveled between us, and at this he said, "Uh, what?"

Micah didn't acknowledge him. "And if he does?"

"You told me, if I found a replacement, I could leave the band."

"Wait, I'm sorry—" Dylan started to stand.

Micah's shoulders dropped, and he looked like I'd personally offended him. "You're serious."

"Did you think all of this has been a joke?"

"I was hoping that you were exaggerating."

"Well, I wasn't." I looked at Dylan. "How many of our songs do you already know?"

Dylan's mouth opened and closed, like he was surprised to suddenly be included in this conversation and had forgotten how to speak. "I don't know."

Micah rolled his eyes. "It doesn't matter. This is an academic conversation."

He turned like he was done, and I blurted out, "I'm planning to move to D.C."

Micah shook his head. "You can't move, Noah. We need you to finish recording the album. We need you nearby for rehearsals. Even if you do find someone to go on the road in your place, you've got obligations."

"Did you think I only meant to quit touring? I may have already lost Lucy for good, but if I've got a shot at winning her back, I have to quit this life. I have to show her I'm serious about her. I can't do this halfway."

"Let's not rush into anything, okay? You still have another two weeks on the road. After that, we can talk."

But I'd never been more certain of anything. Sure, I had no idea what I'd do if I wasn't playing lead guitar for a rock band. I hadn't even graduated high school before following Shane to chase a dream. We'd had to find jobs during that time when the music wasn't paying the rent, but I wouldn't want to live like that again. Maybe I'd get my GED then get a college degree. I'd be better at it this time, if I could figure out what I'd want to study.

Micah slipped to the back of the bus, leaving me under the uncomfortable gaze of Dylan who'd had all of this sprung on him without any warning.

"So how many of our songs do you know?"

He shrugged. "Look, it's flattering and all, but Micah's right. I have my own music and my own gigs."

"I'm sure you do." I gave him a wide grin. "But I could make it worth your while to stick around to the end of this set of shows."

His brows rose, and I didn't give him a chance to say no before launching into what I needed him to do.

Even if I could convince Dylan to take over for the rest of these dates and Micah didn't renege on his offer, it wouldn't solve the long-term problems Micah had listed, but one thing at a time. I had to get off this fucking bus. I had to get back to Lucy.

I gave Dylan a lot to think about and left him to figure out how he could get out of his own obligations, to figure out if he could learn half a dozen songs competently in a couple of days, if he even wanted to do this. I held a card he hadn't known he'd shown me back when he'd gushed about how much of a fan he was. I knew this would be the opportunity of a lifetime. He'd get to solidify his place with a band that he loved and also, hopefully, garner some of our fans for himself and leave at the end of two weeks with a bigger audience. He ran the risk of being vilified for not being me, of course, but I wasn't kidding myself that anyone came out to see me anymore.

For the rest of our ride, I started checking out real estate websites, looking for a rental in the neighborhood near Lucy, hoping to find a lease I could afford long enough until I could find a way to earn a living again. It was kind of exciting having no clear idea what the future would hold. It was scary, but with any luck, I'd be with Lucy and I'd get to know Owen. And we'd start a family.

The only wrinkle in all of this was that Lucy might not want to see me after I'd broken her trust yet again, but what Layla had told me had bolstered my confidence. I truly believed if I could just prove to her that I would always be there for her, she'd give me another chance.

Maybe I was stepping off a ledge into the abyss, but it was a step I wished I'd taken years earlier.

Chapter Twenty-six

Lucy

They say every day the universe expands.

Mine did on Wednesday morning when I got a call from someone at the Brooklyn Museum asking to talk to me. At the moment, I'd been sitting in Priya's office, getting lectured on the many ways I wasn't living up to expectations. When my phone vibrated, I took the opportunity to ask Priya to excuse me. I hadn't expected the call to be legit. I just wanted a pretext to bail from her probably well-deserved reprimand. But when Carla identified herself, I begged her to give me a minute so I could walk back to my office. I took another minute to pull myself together.

Then I said, "Hi. Thanks for waiting."

I'd gone home on Monday, certain I'd made a terrible mistake by applying for the job, but then I remembered I could turn it down if they even called. They'd probably already filled the position anyway, I figured. I wouldn't be the right fit. There were a million reasons why this would just be throwing an empty hook into the stream.

"Your resume was forwarded over. You've had a lot of impressive experience. You went to Georgetown?"

"Yes. Both undergrad and for my master's."

"In museum studies."

"Right." Why was I suddenly nervous?

"So may I ask you what it is about the Brooklyn Museum that most interested you?"

Oh, shit. I nearly told her *never mind* and hung up the phone. I'd never set foot in their museum. Yeah, I'd clicked around their website and loved their commitment to education, but the job was for the exhibitions. I decided to fess up.

"To be honest, there were two reasons this position stood out among others that I looked at. First, this is a position I am qualified to do, and I believe I could bring my experience and love of art to the job. I've lived and breathed museums since I was in high school, and I love visiting new museums and can spend forever getting to know one."

"What was the second reason."

"Well, this is embarrassing, but it's close to where I would like to live."

"Why is that embarrassing? This is a wonderful place to live."

"Yes, but I would be coming for a person rather than the place, and I feel like that is probably the least qualifying reason to be hired."

She laughed. "Maybe, but it would indicate your commitment to stay here. We're looking for someone who can settle into this job for a long time."

I loved that. "That's exactly what I'm looking for."

"May I ask then, this person, is this the reason you're leaving your current job? Or is there something else?"

"Honestly, I never thought I'd leave the National Gallery. This has been my dream and then my home for so long, I've been scared to move outside of my safety zone, but for this person, I'd move to the other side of the world." It had taken me long enough to realize that.

"I'm kind of jealous. That sounds like an amazing relationship. Maybe one day I'll get to meet them."

"Yeah, maybe."

"Do you think we'd be able to meet you? We don't have much of a budget, but we could put you up in a hotel for a night if you could get here."

"How soon would you need me to come in?"

"Within the next week, if possible. What about Friday?"

I'd need to take the day off, and I didn't want to tip my hand so soon after traveling up to New York. "Would Saturday work?"

Her end sounded muffled, but then she said, "Yes, that would be fine. We'll be in touch with the details."

"Sure. Talk to you soon."

I hung up, flustered from having been put on the spot with so little warning, but then I dropped my face into my palms and smiled. Saturday would be perfect. Noah would be on tour for another week, so he wouldn't be there. I could sneak up, get my feet wet, see how the job felt, if they even wanted me, and then, if everything worked out, I could surprise him with this plan. And if it didn't work out? Well, there were other museums. I could still reach out to the Cooper-Hewitt. Or maybe even the Guggenheim.

I didn't stop and consider what might happen if nobody offered me a position.

Was I being rash? Was I really thinking about walking away from this job where I'd invested so much of my life? When I'd told my mom what I'd done, she'd told me I'd been treading water for so many years, both on the job and with everything else. She'd said, "You've protected Owen, but I worry sometimes you're using your own son as an excuse to avoid taking a risk." And before I could raise the prospect, she said, "And don't even think about using me as a reason to stay here."

With all that was happening, I told myself I had no more excuses not to respond to Noah. I'd unblocked him days before, but I'd still been ignoring him. I opened my phone and stared at his last text message. It was one more plea to wait for him to get done with this leg of the tour, swearing he'd prove he'd meant what he'd said. *I'm going to find a way out of my contract,* he'd texted.

I didn't believe him for a minute, and that stopped me from writing back, stopped me from making any promises I also might not keep.

It wasn't that I didn't believe he thought he'd quit the band. I believed he'd walk away somehow. For a day or a week or a month. He'd make a huge gesture, but then reality would set in. What was he going to do with himself here? Play an acoustic set at a coffee shop? Give guitar lessons? Sit home all day resenting me more and more for taking him away from his dream while the band continued its rise? Or maybe he'd blame me if the band ended up faltering without him.

No, the only way this would work would be for me to go to him, but if I couldn't find work in New York, this whole experiment was doomed from the start.

So I held off texting him anything or getting his hopes up until I could tell him something concrete. It was only another week.

Noah

On Saturday, I ditched the band in Connecticut and took an early train back to New York, then an Uber to my place. My plan was to go home, pack as much stuff as I could, then call the landlord at the apartment I'd found and set up an appointment to see the place. I'd fly down to D.C. that afternoon, hopefully sign a lease, and then walk over to surprise Lucy.

It was a crazy scheme, but it was the best way I could think of to convince her I intended to be there for her. Big gesture.

The Uber pulled up to the curb, and as I climbed out, I checked my watch to verify how much time I'd have. It was approaching noon. I needed to hurry.

"Can you wait?" I asked the driver, but he pointed at his phone, indicating he'd already accepted another fare. Fine. I hitched my duffel bag higher on my shoulder and slammed the door.

Alone on the sidewalk, I looked around at the neighborhood I'd called home for the past couple of years. I hadn't rushed into this apartment at all. I loved how close I was to Micah and Shane without being right next door. We all had space, but we could hang out if we weren't sick of each other from all the time on the road or in the studio. Truth was, they'd become my brothers—we even fought like true siblings.

I took a minute to mourn. After all, it might be the last time I saw this apartment, at least until I came to clean it out. I breathed deep, surprised by the emotions welling up in me.

But I didn't have second thoughts. I'd find a new neighborhood, and the guys wouldn't stop being my best friends just because we were no longer bandmates. Well, Micah might never forgive me for abandoning the tour a week early. He couldn't argue that Dylan would play any worse than I had been lately, and he'd honored his word to let me take off.

I steeled myself to do what I had to do. I'd just run up and grab a few things, and then I was gone.

Searching my pocket for my keys, I suddenly remembered I'd crammed them into one of my bags. I sat on the curb and began pulling things out of my duffel. Bracelets, a hair tie, a scarf. When had I turned into a teenage girl? I flipped the whole bag over onto the sidewalk, letting guitar picks scatter. The keys clattered onto the curb, and I reached down to pick them up when a hand met mine at the same time. I glanced up, squinting against the bright light making a halo around the person eclipsing the full impact of the sun. Her shaded features were framed by midnight hair that could have blacked out the day.

My breath caught.

"Lucy? What are you doing here?"

"I was in the neighborhood, and I happened to be passing when you got out of an Uber. What are *you* doing here? You're supposed to be heading to Atlantic City?"

"The guys are, but I'm not. I was only stopping by here long enough to gather some stuff together before flying to D.C."

Where I'd hoped she would talk to me, but she was here. I jumped up. "Why are you here?"

"I got tired of waiting for you." She stood there with the most impish little grin, like she was burning to share a secret. Then she did. "Seriously though, I had a job interview."

Her words made no sense. I couldn't even form a question and heard the phrase echo out of my mouth, like it would change meaning when I said it aloud. "A job interview."

"Yeah. I realized I wasn't truly happy where I was, and I needed a change of scenery."

"What? When?" My heart started racing. Was she seriously considering it? My Lucy in New York City? The idea thrilled me and scared me. What if she hated it here? What if she hated *me* here?

"Last week, you said it yourself: There are museums all over this city. I can work here as easily as in D.C."

Why had she just now figured this out? "What about Owen? What about wanting to keep him in a stable home?"

The first cloud crossed her expressions, but she half shrugged. "I think that might have been more about me than Owen."

I wanted this. Of course I wanted this, but only if she did too.

"Lucy, you don't need to do this. I may have found a replacement. Micah said I can quit the band if I fill my spot." I didn't mention how hard he was making that in practice. I didn't mention how much it was going to cost me to break my contract. I'd made an economic decision a week ago, and I'd nearly lost my heart because of it. I'd nearly sold my soul one more time.

"You know Dylan can't actually replace you."

The hell? "How do you know about Dylan?"

She tapped her forehead. "I know things."

"You've been stalking me."

"A little bit." She leaned into me. "I missed you. I may have watched bootleg video."

I literally guffawed. "See, this is why I'm always encouraging fans to upload concert footage."

"Are you, now?"

"I used to picture you watching me. It was my weird fantasy."

"When I saw Dylan performing, I was worried something had happened to you. I didn't realize what you were doing until I noticed he'd added a new song every night this week."

"Smart, right?"

"Dylan's good, but he isn't you."

"That's exactly what Shane said when I left this morning."

"You left the tour?" She grimaced. "You need to go back, Noah. Finish this circuit at least."

And then what? Would I wake up from this dream and find myself in an endless parade of cities without her? I was ready to be done with it all and start our future together today. I took Lucy's hand. "I'm all yours. If you want to live here, we can, but I've already got an appointment to see an apartment near yours."

Her eyes widened. "Do you, really?"

"Yes. I meant what I said. I'm in this with you, however that looks. I want to be your family. I want to raise Owen together with you. Whatever I can do to make that happen, I'm ready to commit to it."

She heaved a sigh that sounded like a thousand years of pent-up frustration. "Do you know how long I've just wanted to hear you say those words?"

Was that all it took? "I'm sorry I didn't realize sooner. I'm sorry we wasted so much time."

She shook her head. "It's not your fault alone. I didn't know how to take a risk. I didn't know how to meet you halfway. But I'm ready to try now."

So many years we'd lost because we could never figure out this part of it. I'd been ready to sacrifice it all. If she wanted to compromise, I was more than happy to listen, but I didn't know what that meant.

"What does halfway look like? I can't halfway be in a band. You can't halfway live in New York City."

"I was so caught up in the belief that I needed you around all the time or not at all, that the unpredictability would be hard on Owen, but my mom made me realize that what made my childhood so difficult was the knowledge that at the end of the day, my dad didn't want to be with us. He didn't really want to be a dad. When he came home, that was the exception to his regular vagabond life."

"Yeah. I wasn't a huge fan of his."

"You mean threatening to shoot you didn't endear him to you?"

I smiled at the memory. "So you've realized I'm not like your dad?"

"I've always known that, but I worried the effects would be the same."

"And now?"

"I know it won't be easy, that you'll need to be away a lot of the time, but we'll always know your schedule. You won't appear at random times and then disappear with no warning. And we could meet you sometimes."

My eyebrow rose. "You've never done that before unless we came to you."

"Go back on tour, Noah. We'll find a way to make it work."

Easier said than done. "When I left, I told Micah I was leaving the band and moving to D.C." I could still see Micah's expression before he told me I was fucking them.

"And what would he say if you told him you'd changed your mind?"

I wasn't entirely sure. He might tell me to fuck off, that I'd burned that bridge and could live with the consequences. Realistically, he'd tell me I'd blown one of my lives, and that if I pulled a stunt like this again, he'd fire me himself. But he'd probably take me back. I doubted Dylan would hand me back the five grand I'd paid him to finish the tour, but I didn't even regret that.

None of it mattered unless I had Lucy. "What about you? What about Owen?"

"I have to head back home anyway. Assuming they offer me this job, I have to give my notice at work. I'd need time. You might as well be on the road, right?"

"And then what?"

"I don't know, Noah. I haven't really thought it through. I suppose I could find a place of my own." She slipped her hand into mine, and I wanted to melt into her.

"We'll figure it out."

"I know that now."

A weight lifted. I could picture it then. Lucy and Owen might not move in with me right away. We might find a new place together. Eventually. But this was a first step to a life where Lucy was mine again and I could keep playing in the band. I'd get to know my son. I pictured all the things we could do together, traditions we could start.

"You know there are very good schools around here."

She nearly doubled over from a laugh that seemed to catch her off guard. "Well, I'm glad you're not getting too far ahead of yourself."

There we were, standing together, face to face, like that night when I'd wandered to her doorstep, when I'd wanted to kiss her but she'd pushed my face away in the most humiliating way. I worked up my charming smolder and gave her a look I hoped would undo that aborted kiss. Her lips curved up, and I realized she was the one seducing me with those sultry eyes and a face I'd loved my entire adult life. Her tongue ran across her upper lip, and I couldn't wait another second. I bent forward to forge that connection we'd never had to work at. Her slight moan sparked a thrill that shot down my entire body.

I pulled away reluctantly. "When do you need to head home?"

"I'm taking the train back. They leave practically every hour."

"So you're not in a hurry?" I tilted my head toward the front door.

"I could stay for a bit, but shouldn't you get your ass to Atlantic City?"

Then the idea formed, and I couldn't shake it. "Come with me tonight. Come to the show. Jo might be there. And Layla for sure. There's no possible way she'd miss a chance to see us when we're so close to home. And on a Saturday."

She didn't say no. She weighed the idea over in her mind, then a small smile grew. "If I'm with you, Micah would have to play nice, right?"

"Devious. And, yes. He'd be on his best behavior."

"Let me call my mom."

I waggled my eyebrows. "Why don't you do that upstairs?"

Chapter Twenty-seven

Lucy

I followed Noah past the doorman, to the elevator, remembering the last time we'd come here with the weight of my secret between us. I'd been so worried he'd be mad at me forever, that he might not want a part in Owen's life. How wrong I'd been. The elevator doors opened, and as soon as we'd stepped in and Noah had punched his floor, he dropped his duffel bag and turned to face me with that longing that never failed to work magic.

Looking at Noah had never been a hardship. Even back before I finally agreed to date him, I loved it whenever he'd stop me in the hall to talk to me so I could enjoy the view. He was so damn pretty, but in a boyish way. That wild blond hair had always stirred the more rebellious parts of my nature. The way his sleepy eyes always drank me in, like I was an expensive guitar. His hands treated me with reverence when I finally gave in to his persistence, when wanting him overcame my every logical argument. He'd imprinted himself on me forever, and even after so many years trying to deny him, there was nobody else in the world who made me feel so much turmoil and so much peace, who irritated me and fascinated me, who challenged me and loved me unconditionally.

The bell rang and the doors slid open. Noah lifted his bag again and led me down the hall into that apartment I'd only once seen through a filter of curiosity and fear. This time, I looked around and wondered at our possible futures. Would we ever share this space? How long would we need to transition Owen to this new family dynamic? I set my own overnighter down in the kitchen and headed into the living room, past the sofa where I'd turned Noah's world upside down. I continued down the hall to that bedroom he'd shown me once on an awkward tour. Once I stepped through the doorway, I felt his hands on my shoulders, thumbs caressing the nape of my neck moments before his lips followed suit. My body ceased to be a solid, and I leaned into him, my back to his chest, his arms wrapping around me, holding me. And I didn't need to fight this. This was ours. This could be us.

He whispered my name in my ear, and his breath tickled, made me giggle, breaking the solemnity of the moment. He chuckled lightly.

I spun to face him, unable to resist sliding my hands under his shirt hem, tucking my thumbs into his waistband, manhandling him toward me, into the kiss I needed. This was the man I'd dreamed of when my waking mind tried to forget him. The man who'd given me the only other person who consumed my attention. The first man and the last man I'd ever love.

And he was here.

I turned my brain off to enjoy the way his hands form fit to my body, how his lips could feel so soft and so hard all at once, how he smelled like home. He nudged me ever so gently, and I didn't need another invitation to step back toward that enormous bed of his. When my calves hit the edge, I dropped onto my butt, eye level with his straining zipper. I slid it down, peeled the jeans down his hips, freed him from the confines of his boxer briefs, and ran my tongue straight up his shaft, loving the sound of his hiss. His hands gripped my hair, and he didn't object when

I grasped him at the base of his cock and stroked him while my mouth tightened around the head. I hadn't had the opportunity to worship Noah's body the way I'd been wanting to in years, but it was like riding a bike, or a unicycle maybe. I remembered what he liked and dragged my tongue over that sensitive spot, his moans of pleasure heightening my own need.

With my free hand, I unfastened my pants and wriggled them down. Noah's voice came out ragged as he said, "That's impressive."

I was about to impress him even more. Once my underwear followed, I kicked them off and slid a hand between my legs with a glance up at Noah who just said, "Oh, Jesus."

But my show was cut short when he sat beside me so he could take over what I'd begun, touching me lovingly, erotically, all the while kissing me, and I understood why an orgasm was called a little death because I could have died from the pleasure, but I wanted more.

I swung a leg over his, still trapped by the pants that hadn't made it past his thighs, both of us still in our shirts and socks. I didn't stop kissing him as I lined us up, but he drew his head back. "I have a condom in the drawer."

I didn't want to know about his condoms or what he'd kept them for. "Do I need one?"

"Are you asking if I've been with someone since the last time we were together?"

I said nothing.

"There's been nobody, Lucy. Who could compete with you?"

"Good." I gave him my cockiest smile as I slid down onto his cockiest part.

We both said *mmm* at the same time. I lifted his shirt, exposing the leather cord he wore like a necklace. I smiled at it. It couldn't be the same one I'd given him when he'd left for New York. Surely that one had worn out ages ago, but I loved that he wore one. The ridiculous leather wristbands were a different story, but I wasn't going to argue with a rocker's sense of style. I ran my finger down the necklace, wrapped a hand around the end of it, and pulled him into me for more sultry kisses as I rocked forward and back, taking what I could from him. He'd never resisted me or denied me anything when we were together like this.

"Tell me you love me," I whispered as I laid kisses along his cheek, across his jaw, down his neck to his collarbone.

"I've always loved you." His hands grasped my hips and urged me faster, harder. I pushed him onto his back.

"Tell me you'll stay with me forever."

"I will." His breath was labored, eyes closed, lost in pleasure.

I lifted up until he was nearly free and rocked back hard, again and again, watching the most beautiful man in the world fall apart below me, knowing this was my power, mine alone.

Always.

He opened his eyes, and in a heartbeat, I knew that my power was nothing compared to the love this man had always shown me, that I would love him helplessly for the rest of my life.

"I love you so much, Noah." It sounded almost like a sob.

He only said, "Oh," as his orgasm hit, intensifying the sensations in one sudden shock.

And then I shattered as potent drugs spread through my entire body.

I fell into him, against his heaving chest, and his arms encircled me. We held each other while our bodies floated back down from outer space, as if we could keep each other tethered. The brain candy slowly released its grip on me, and my breathing returned to normal. Then I began to realize all the weird oddities that follow chasing bliss.

The fact that Noah still had on a pair of jeans, which could not have been ideal for him.

The fact that I needed to slowly lift myself off him and make a dash to grab his T-shirt before everything spilled out. Ew.

The fact that it was the middle of the day, I hadn't called my mom, and we needed to get on the road as soon as possible.

I started laughing. Noah's face changed to indicate surprise and a question. "Are you laughing at me?"

"Kind of."

In one sudden move, I rolled over, grabbed his shirt and shoved it under my ass. "I always find this whole part so ridiculously humiliating."

He rolled toward me, and I became keenly aware of the fact that his impressive cock had returned to its primordial Silly Putty shape, and I laughed again. He smiled. "I guess I'm glad you aren't crying."

Despite the reality of the situation, everything was magical. Noah was here. There was no reason we couldn't be together like this again, every day, all the days into our future.

And then I started crying.

Noah

Lucy crying was my Achilles Heel. I gathered her to me. "What's wrong?"

She snort-sobbed. "I'm so fucking happy. I never thought—"

I hugged her tighter. "No, me either."

She pressed a kiss against my neck, and I would have loved to see where that might lead, but time had never been on our side. "We need to get going."

After two very quick, very separate showers, we got ourselves ready to go. I threw everything from my suitcase into the hamper, pitying my housekeeper who'd probably seen worse, but still. Then I packed a week's worth of nearly identical jeans and T-shirts, and then we were racing for the Uber we'd ordered sooner than we probably should have. After arriving at the Port Authority, we boarded a bus to Atlantic City.

Lucy snuggled against me. "This reminds me of that school trip kind of."

"Oh, yeah." One of Lucy's academic teams, debate or math or some other smarty pants club, had advanced to state or regionals or maybe nationals. Jesus, I should have known. She was so nervous. She begged me to come with her, and for some reason, they let me. "Better bus."

"Much." She snuggled my arm, and I felt like a hero. I knew it was asking too much, but if I could have her with me like this on the long stretches between gigs, the road wouldn't seem quite so interminable.

As it was, the trip to Atlantic City was two and a half hours of cuddles and chaste kisses. Well, sometimes not so chaste, but after the lady across the aisle cleared her throat significantly, we settled for hand holding and reminiscing. It was the shortest trip of my life.

I hadn't felt nervous about confronting Micah until we were climbing off the Greyhound and hailing a cab. On the way to the venue, Lucy took my hand and said, "He'd be insane not to take you back, but you need to apologize to him."

"Why?" Micah hadn't been my friend for the past couple of weeks.

"Because after today, you're going to have to be in a band with him, and you want to start as you mean to continue."

"Meaning?"

"As friends. Don't make him beg you to come back. Let him have this."

She was right of course. When we walked into the club, every head swiveled toward us. The variety of reactions amused me, from Rick's nonchalant shrug to Shane's eye-popping surprise. But Micah only narrowed his eyes, and I could see him digging in to make this difficult. Lucy was right. He knew he needed me, but he couldn't just reward me by letting me walk right back into the band.

I dropped my things and crossed the floor. "I—"

Lucy cut me off. "Hi, Micah. How's it going?"

He half smiled. "It's gone better."

Shane said, "Dylan's out back, puking."

"He's not ready for all the songs you left him to learn." Micah's eyes had never left me.

"Yeah," I said. "I'm sorry I left so suddenly. I didn't mean to leave you in the lurch."

"Well, you did." Micah clenched his jaw. "I thought we were in this together. Dylan's great, but what the fuck, man? This—" he swung his hand around at the four of us "—this is the band."

That was proof enough that he wasn't going to fire me. "It is. I know that. I just had something more important to take care of." I glanced at Lucy, and she laid a hand on my shoulder. "I'm really sorry. I made a mistake."

Lucy lifted her chin. "This was an inflection point, Micah. But I promise, he's committed to the band now."

Micah glanced from me to Lucy and back. "Is that so?"

I nodded. "Yeah. Everything's settled. Can we just get back to making music?"

"What about Dylan?"

Shit. Loose ends. "Let him play if he wants. Maybe I should go check on him."

I abandoned the group to head behind the club where Dylan was sitting on the ground, back against the wall. When he saw me, he said, "Oh, thank God."

He took my outstretched hand and heaved himself up.

"Man, I'm sorry I expected too much from you."

"It's okay. Now that you're here."

After that, everything became that old familiar whirlwind of soundcheck, VIP access, and finally that moment when we stepped onto the stage to the sounds of an appreciative crowd. Man, I loved that sound.

And I played better than I ever had before, knowing my girl was cheering in the audience, knowing she'd be waiting for me after the show.

I switched out with Dylan on a handful of songs, both because I wanted to get my money's worth, but also because an idea had formed in my mind, that even if I didn't quit the band, I could find another way to meet Lucy at that mythical halfway. Maybe I didn't need to go on every tour circuit. Maybe I could call in a replacement for those parenting moments I didn't want to miss.

It might not be Dylan who took my place, but if the audience got used to seeing someone else once in a while, surely they wouldn't object. Layla said the fan reaction to Dylan had been mixed. The fact I'd been so moody for the past few weeks had softened my support, but even some of my diehard fans had conceded that Dylan was different but competent. And the girls liked his dark looks. My fragile ego might have taken a hit if Layla hadn't pointed me to the slash fan fiction being written about us. The things they imagined me saying to that unsuspecting boy. He might never look me in my pretty eyes again.

When the crowd called us back onstage for an encore, I waved Dylan up with us and had him grab a spare guitar. He went with it, even though he'd been puking his guts out from the fear of performing "Josie" a couple of hours earlier. Thinking of that fan fiction, I blew him a kiss as he joined us. He winked back, and the cameras recorded it all.

Laughing, we started into the sappy love song Micah had written for his girlfriend, and I made eye contact with Lucy to piggyback on some of that sap.

I was sweaty and gross when we left the stage the final time. We disappeared into the green room to rehydrate and towel off. Three knocks on the door warned us before Jo, Layla, and Lucy came barging in. God damn but it was so good to see the only fan who really mattered looking at me like I'd never been hotter.

She flung her arms around me and gave me the kind of huge kiss meant purely to elicit wolf whistles from our tiny audience. As much as I wanted her by my side, I didn't want to drag her into all the after-show crap.

"You can wait here if you want. We have to go to a meet and greet thing for a little while."

She said, "No, sir. I am only with you until tomorrow. I'm not letting you out of my sight."

I sighed. "Just be forewarned—there will be girls. I hate it, but they'll probably try to hit on me."

"Oh, sure you hate it." She dramatically rolled her eyes.

Layla thankfully broke in. "No he really does. I can attest."

By the way Lucy tensed at Layla's attempt to vouch for me, I suddenly heard the words the way Lucy had, expecting her to swallow the insinuation and mope the rest of the night. Instead, she straight-up asked, "Did you hit on Noah?"

Layla's eyes went wide. "Nooo. I've just seen how he bats the groupies away. He really doesn't like it."

Lucy looked confused and asked her, "But you go to the meet and greets despite the groupies?"

"Of course. I like to make sure they know Shane's taken."

Shane grinned. "Not that girls would be hitting on me anyway."

Lucy wrapped a hand around my bicep. "Then I'm definitely going."

Jo touched Lucy's shoulder. "Just so you know. If you go, the fans will know you're with Noah now. You'll be in the gossip and all over their blogs. Maybe even in a bigger tabloid."

"Don't they already know that?"

Layla answered. "They already *think* that. This will put an end to speculation. You'll become one of the girlfriends."

Lucy nodded. "The sooner they get used to that, the better."

Jo smiled. "I cannot wait to see this."

"Shall we then?" Micah held the door open and ushered us all down the hall to a small room with maybe thirty people standing around waiting for us. This was a bigger venue than we normally played on our own, but so much smaller than the arenas where we'd opened for Whiplash. Still, thirty people was a pretty decent crowd, considering we'd have to take time to get selfies, sign autographs, and chat for a bit. I only recognized a few familiar faces, which didn't mean they weren't all regulars. It just meant that I didn't pay enough attention to commit them to memory.

The one face that worried me was a real super fan, the kind who would hit multiple shows in a row if they were close or who'd find ways to see us even when we'd toured farther away. I had no idea where she was from, just that she loved to hug. She was harmless as far as that went, and I normally just went along with it because it would be over faster than if I made a big deal.

I latched onto Lucy's hand.

The super fan made a beeline over to me, stopped, appraised the whole new situation, then lifted her camera to take a picture. She smiled and closed the distance between us. I braced for the oncoming physical encounter, hoping as always the grimace on my face would make plain how much I loathed all the random touching from strangers. Lucy held her hand straight out. The fan froze and did the only natural thing when a hand is extended: She clasped it.

Lucy said, "Hi, I'm Lucy. What's your name?"

And just like that, the entire situation was defused. The fan's name turned out to be Maggie, not that I'd remember that in another ten minutes. "I was in town for a conference earlier in the week and extended my trip for another day to catch the show. You guys were amazing as always." Her eyes settled on my hand clasped in Lucy's, and she said, "Could I get a picture with you both?"

Lucy laughed and said, "Of course," like the champ she was. She even went with the weird hug, and somehow I didn't mind it as much when it was my turn to hug it out with Maggie, but still, I was relieved when she looked around and said, "I was hoping to meet Dylan, too."

I indicated where Dylan stood surrounded by a couple of girls with big eyes. He didn't seem to mind it at all.

Before anyone else could circle in on us, I tugged on Lucy's hand and pulled her back away from the crowd. "Thank you."

"For that? That wasn't too bad."

"For being here. For taking a chance on me. For going on an adventure."

"We're going on the adventure *together*."

She wrapped her arms around my waist, and dozens of cameras recorded the moment when I leaned down and kissed her. Huge. For show.

And she kissed me back. Right there at the afterparty of a rock concert.

My soul had never felt so complete.

Epilogue

Lucy

I stretched my legs out, sighing at the unseasonable warmth of the fall afternoon. "You know the best thing about working at the museum?"

"No, what?" Eden sat beside me, rocking a sleeping Joshua. I remembered those days too well. I patted my belly, hoping I'd know them again.

Owen yelled, "Mommy, come push me," as he climbed onto the swing.

I stood up to cross the yard, still talking. "The best part is how nice everyone is."

I gave Owen a good push, delighting in his giggles. He hadn't had a backyard in D.C. and he loved having his very own swing set. We'd moved in here to have more space, but it was also cost effective. The rent was much cheaper than a doorman-controlled high rise by the park.

My Facetime notification went off, and I pulled my phone from my pocket, checking the screen before I answered, disappointed it wasn't Noah, even though I'd spoken to him not ten minutes before. "Hi, Mom."

"Has it happened, yet?" She sounded breathless.

"What?"

"Is Noah back?"

"Uh, no. They're running a bit late. Traffic."

The guys had been gone for longer than usual since their manager had sent them across Europe. I would have loved to join Noah on that particular tour, but I had my hands full at work, and I didn't want to disrupt Owen's new school. I glanced around the yard at my fellow tour widows: Jo and Layla. We tried to hang out together whenever the guys were on the road, and when everyone was home, well, we still hung out but with way more people. I'd never had a found family besides Noah, and this was such a bonus. Adam and Eden had surprised me by popping in, along with some other new friends, Andrew and Zion. When the other guys got back, we'd have a full house.

My mom said, "Hold the phone out so I can see everyone."

"Why?"

"Please."

I humored her and scanned around the yard, horrified when she began to sing, "It's a beautiful night." I only hoped it wasn't loud enough for anyone else to hear.

But then Jo came over and nodded along, singing the next lyric with my mom, and I kind of recognized the song. What started weird got weirder when Layla and Eden joined in. I assumed they were all humoring me for my mom behaving like a lunatic, singing, "I think I wanna marry you."

That was when the sliding door opened, and Shane stepped out. I hadn't seen anyone inside, so I nearly dropped the phone. Shane started tapping on our picnic table, giving a beat to this whole weird song, and suddenly I caught on that it wasn't an accident.

Flash mob!

My first instinct was to run into the house and hide, but Micah came out and started to harmonize with Eden. It was so beautiful, I was floored.

When Noah came out that door, I hoped he wouldn't start singing and ruin this whole thing. He played a mean guitar, but he was not a vocalist.

Owen interrupted their whole performance when he squealed, "Daddy!" and nearly jumped from the swing that I'd thankfully stopped pushing. He raced across the yard to get scooped up. The strange song died down, but before I could even ask what the hell was wrong with all of them, Noah pulled a box out of his pocket and held it up for Owen who asked, "What's that?"

Noah flipped it open to reveal a shiny ring. "What do you think it is?"

"It's a ring?" Owen looked very confused about this turn of events.

"It isn't just any ring. What kind of ring is this?"

"Is it for a wedding?" He'd seen more than one cheesy Hallmark Christmas movie with me to know about proposals.

"It is. I hope." He looked at me, then back to Owen. "How would you feel, little man, if I asked your mom to marry me?"

Owen must have known he was the center of attention because his reaction was straight out of overreaction acting school. He pressed his palms to his cheeks, mouth wide open in over-the-top shock. Then he started nodding.

With Owen on his hip, Noah crossed the yard to me, then dropped on one knee. "Lucy Griffin, I have waited my whole life to ask you this question."

"Yes," I said. I was supposed to wait for the question, but I dropped on my knees before him. "Yes."

Holy shit, a tear slid down his cheek. He was actually crying. "Let me ask this. Will you do me the honor of being my wife?"

I flung my arms around Noah's neck. Well, one arm around him, one around our son, and we must have looked like a huddle.

My mom hollered, "I can't see what's going on!"

"Sorry!"

Laughing, I retrieved the phone from behind Owen's head and handed it to Eden, so my mom could take in the whole scene while Noah slid the ring on my finger.

Adam came over beside her, holding a pair of phones screens forward, and at first I thought my mom was somehow on all the phones, watching us in triplicate, but these were different women.

Before I could parse out the meaning of this oddity, Micah was kneeling before Jo, and he sang, "I think I wanna marry you." The ladies on the phone screens were both wiping their eyes, and I finally realized these were Micah and Jo's moms, and I began to cry for real. Noah draped an arm over my shoulder and grasped Owen's hand while we watched our friends make this day exponentially more special.

Shane wrapped his arms around Layla, and I could see the rings on their fingers, glinting in the fading daylight. They'd eloped in August, but they still planned to have a real wedding. I looked over at Adam and Eden, happily married for a while now and realized how foolish I'd once been to believe that I couldn't have this with my rocker boy. How scared I'd been.

And yes, it was still hard whenever Noah went on the road, but he always came home to me. When he was here he was one hundred percent here. He even skipped out on a festival to be here for Owen's first day back to daycare. When Noah was home, he'd walk Owen there himself before heading to his own rehearsal. Sometimes, I happened to know, he'd swear Owen to secrecy, not to tell Mommy that he'd let him play hookie. Sometimes.

It was untraditional, but we'd made a home.

Noah

I stared at the swimming numbers. "I've somehow managed to make it this far in life without ever needing to use exponential notation."

The doorbell rang, and Lucy got up. "You have no trouble with musical notation though. These are just another kind of symbol." She paused in the doorway, "Think of it like when you say 2k instead of 2000. Only for exponents, instead of 1000, the symbol represents how many times you multiple a number by itself."

She ducked out of the room and left me staring at the page. I glanced at Owen who'd assembled a Tim Burton-like skyscraper out of Legos. "That looks amazing, buddy."

Voices carried up the stairs, and I took that as an excuse to abandon my GED studies. The test wasn't for another week. I wasn't panicking yet.

"Come on! I think Nana's here."

Owen unfolded himself and climbed into my lap, expecting to be carried, but my God, the kid was heavy. I settled him against me and held his back firm as I attempted to stand without falling over or dropping him. It didn't help that he was bouncing like crazy.

He nestled his face into my neck as we went downstairs, exhibiting his new shy phase. Man, I loved how good he smelled when he was all freshly washed and his hair was still wet.

When we hit the landing, Lucy's mom yelled, "Happy birthday!"

That did the trick. Owen squirmed from my arms and ran to Sara, squealing. "What did you bring me?"

"Oh, well, you'll have to wait and see, won't you?" She knelt and hugged him, then glanced up at me over his shoulder. "Hello, Noah."

I waved. "So glad you could make it."

"Wouldn't have missed it."

The doorbell rang, and Shane entered without waiting, followed by Layla.

The doorbell rang again. This time, I went to the door and greeted the parents of Jandro Chavez, Owen's new best friend.

As soon as I'd led them into the kitchen, the doorbell rang again.

Soon, the house was filled with kids, parents, shouting, and laughing. Owen led a parade of kids up the stairs to show off the pride of his life: his brand-new bunk bed. This was a practical purchase since he'd started begging us to let his friends stay over. Lucy just glowed whenever she watched Owen playing with a group of kids. I glowed watching her.

But at the end of the day, after his friends went home, when his mom had gone to work, Owen and I were best buddies. Lucy didn't know how often I skipped rehearsals and pulled him out of daycare so we could go explore the city, find new parks, discover museums, walk through interesting neighborhoods, or go on a hunt for statues or other artwork punctuating the city. I'd make a New Yorker out of the kid yet.

I snuck up behind Lucy as she pulled the birthday cake from the box. Owen had moved from *Star Wars* to *Captain America* because, in his opinion, Cap reminded him of his daddy. It made me feel proud and also an overwhelming need to hit the gym. I kissed Lucy's neck as she put the candles in. Four. Four years since Owen had been born, most of which I'd missed. I tried not to think about it since his very existence is what would eventually allow us to be together, but man I sometimes regretted it. I slid my hand around Lucy's waist, palm against her flat stomach. I sometimes imagined I felt a small swell there, but she said it was too soon, that she hadn't started to show with Owen until nearly the second trimester.

Lucy covered my hand with hers, inhaling deeply and letting it out, knowing that I was feeling same thing. We'd done this together, intentionally, and with love. We hadn't told a soul, not even Owen. Not even Lucy's mom. It was our little secret. Maybe secrets weren't always a bad thing.

I said, "Barney," and she snorted.

"No." She spun around, back against the counter so that now my hands were on either side of her, and I was reminded of one of the many times that might have led to her current situation. "Bartholomew."

We'd been working through the alphabet since we found out last week. "Yes, Bartholomew."

Her eyes blinked rapidly. "Veto."

"You skipped a few. How about Barton?"

She shook her head. "Bastian?"

"Sebastian."

We stared at each other, and both smiled at the same time. She tried it out. "Sebastian Kennedy."

"Sebastian Bartholomew Kennedy."

She swatted me.

"What are you two talking about?" We spun to find Jo behind us with a raised eyebrow.

In fact, the entire kitchen had gotten very quiet as everyone looked at us with expectation.

Lucy glanced at me, then at her mom, then back at me. I shrugged.

She took a huge breath and said, "I wasn't planning to say anything today. We just found out ourselves." She reached over and took my hand. "Noah and I are excited to welcome a new member into our family."

Family.

I loved the sound of that.

If you enjoyed this book, please consider leaving feedback on Goodreads or on whichever ebook retailer you buy books from. Reviews help authors reach readers.

And check out my other books:

Some Kind of Magic
A Crazy Kind of Love
Dating by the Book
Kind of Famous
Crushing It

Find out more at maryannmarlowe.com and loreleiparker.com

Do not miss Eden and Adam's story in

SOME KIND OF MAGIC

by Mary Ann Marlowe
Now available in bookstores and online!

In this sparkling novel, Mary Ann Marlowe introduces a hapless scientist who's swept off her feet by a rock star--but is it love or just a chemical reaction . . . ?

Biochemist Eden Sinclair has no idea that the scent she spritzed on herself before leaving the lab is designed ot enhance pheromones. Or that the cute, grungy-looking guy she meets at a gig that evening is Adam Copeand. As in *the* Adam Copeland—international rock god and object of lust for a million women. Make that a million and one. By the time she learns the truth, she's already spent the (amazing, incredible) night in his bed . . .

Suddenly Eden, who's more accustomed to being set up on disastrous dates by her mom, is going out with a gorgeous celebrity who loves how down-to-earth and honest she is. But for once, Eden isn't being honest. She can't bear to reveal that this overpowering attraction could be nothing more than seduction by science. And the only way to know how Adam truly feels is to ditch the perfume—and risk being ditched in turn . . .

Smart, witty, and sexy, *Some Kind of Magic* is an irresistably engaging look at modern relationship—why we fall, how we connect, and the courage it takes to trust in something as mysterious and unpredictable as love.

Read on for a preview. . . .

Chapter One

My pen tapped out the drum beat to the earworm on the radio. I glanced around to make sure I was alone, then grabbed an Erlenmeyer flask and belted out the chorus into my makeshift microphone.

"*I'm beeeegging you...*"

With the countertop centrifuge spinning out a white noise, I could imagine a stadium crowd cheering. My eyes closed, and the blinding lab fell away. I stood onstage in the spotlight.

"Eden?" came a voice from the outer hall.

I swiveled my stool toward the door, anticipating the arrival of my first fan. When Stacy came in, I bowed my head. "Thank you. Thank you very much."

She shrugged out of her jacket and hung it on a wooden peg. Unimpressed by my performance, she turned down the radio. "You're early. How long have you been here?"

"Since seven." The centrifuge slowed, and I pulled out tubes filled with rodent sperm. "I want to leave a bit early to head into the city and catch Micah's show."

She dragged a stool over. "Kelly and I are hitting the clubs tonight. You should come with."

"Yeah, right. Why don't you come with me? Kelly's such a—"

"Such a what?" The devil herself stood in the doorway, phone in hand.

Succubus from hell played on my lips. But it was too early to start a fight. "Such a guy magnet. Nobody can compete with you."

Kelly didn't argue and turned her attention back to the phone.

Stacy leaned her elbow on the counter, conspiratorially talking over my head. "Eden's going to abandon us again to go hang out with Micah."

"At that filthy club?" Kelly's lip curled, as if Stacy had just offered her a *non*-soy latte. "But there are never even any guys there. It's always just a bunch of moms."

I gritted my teeth. "Micah's fans are not all moms." When Micah made it big, I was going to enjoy refusing her backstage passes to his eventual sold-out shows.

Kelly snorted. "Oh, right. I suppose their husbands might be there, too."

"That's not fair," Stacy said. "I've seen young guys at his shows."

"Teenage boys don't count." Kelly dropped an invisible microphone and turned toward her desk.

I'd never admit that she was right about the crowd that came out to hear Micah's solo shows. But unlike Kelly, I wasn't interested in picking up random guys at bars. I spun a test tube like a top then clamped my hand down on it before it could careen off the counter. "Whatever. Sometimes Micah lets me sing."

Apparently Kelly smelled blood; her tone turned snide. "Ooh, maybe Eden's dating her brother."

"Don't be ridiculous, Kelly." Stacy rolled her eyes and gave me her best *don't listen to her* look.

"Oh, right." Kelly threw her head back for one last barb. "Eden would never consider dating a struggling musician."

The clock on the wall reminded me I had seven hours of prison left. I hated the feeling that I was wishing my life away one work day at a time.

Thanh peeked his head around the door and saved me. "Eden, I need you to come monitor one of the test subjects."

Inhaling deep to get my residual irritation under control, I followed Thanh down the hall to the holding cells. Behind the window, a cute blond sat with a wire snaking out of his charcoal-gray Dockers. Thanh instructed him to watch a screen flashing more or less pornographic images while I kept one eye on his vital signs.

I bit my pen and put the test subject through my usual Terminator-robot full-body analysis to gauge his romantic eligibility. He wore a crisp dress shirt with a white cotton undershirt peeking out below the unbuttoned collar. I wagered he held a job I'd find acceptable, possibly in programming, accounting, or maybe even architecture. His fading tan, manicured nails, and fit build lent the impression that he had enough money and time to vacation, pamper himself, and work out. No ring on his finger. And blue eyes at that. On paper, he fit my mental checklist to a T.

Even if he was strapped up to his balls in wires.

Hmm. Scratch that. If he were financially secure, he wouldn't need the compensation provided to participants in clinical trials for boner research. *Never mind.*

Thanh came back in and sat next to me.

I stifled a yawn and stretched my arms. "Don't get me wrong. This is all very exciting, but could you please slip some arsenic in my coffee?"

He punched buttons on the complex machine monitoring the erectile event in the other room. "Why are you still working here, Eden? Weren't you supposed to start grad school this year?"

"I was." I sketched a small circle in the margin of the paper on the table.

"You need to start applying soon for next year. Are you waiting till you've saved enough money?"

"No, I've saved enough." I drew a flower around the circle and shaded it in. I'd already had this conversation with my parents.

"If you want to do much more than what you're doing now, you need to get your PhD."

I sighed and turned in my chair to face him. "Thanh, you've got your PhD, and you're doing the same thing as me."

When he smiled, the corners of his eyes crinkled. "Yes, but it has always been my lifelong dream to help men maintain a medically induced long-lasting erection."

I looked at my hands, thinking. "Thanh, I'm not sure this is what I want to do with my life. I've lost that loving feeling."

"Well, then, you're in the right place."

I snickered at the erectile dysfunction humor. The guy in the testing room shifted, and I thought for the first time to ask. "What are you even testing today?"

"Top secret."

"You can't tell me?"

"No, I mean you'd already know if you read your e-mails."

"I do read the e-mails." That was partly true. I skimmed and deleted them unless they pertained to my own work. I didn't care about corporate policy changes, congratulations to the sales division, farewells to employees leaving after six wonderful years, tickets to be pawned, baby pictures, or the company chili cook-off.

He reached into a drawer and brought out a small vial containing a clear yellow liquid. When he removed the stopper, a sweet aroma filled the room, like jasmine.

"What's that?"

He handed it to me. "Put some on, right here." He touched my wrist.

I tipped it onto my finger and dabbed both my wrists. Then I waited. "What's it supposed to do?"

He raised an eyebrow. "Do you feel any different?"

I ran an internal assessment. "Uh, nope. Should I?"

"Do me a favor. Walk into that room."

"With the test subject?" It was bad enough that poor guy's schwanz was hooked up to monitors, but he didn't need to know exactly who was observing changes in his penile turgidity. Thanh shooed me on through the door, so I went in.

The erotica continued to run, but the guy's eyes were now on me. I thought, *Is that a sensor monitoring you, or are you just happy to see me?*

"Uh, hi." I glanced back at the one-way mirror, as if I could telepathically understand when Thanh released me from this embarrassing ordeal.

The guy sat patiently, expecting me to do something. So I reached over and adjusted one of the wires, up by the machines. He went back to watching the screen, as if I were just another technician. Nobody interesting.

I backed out of the room. As soon as the door clicked shut, I asked Thanh, "What the hell was that?"

He frowned. "I don't know. I expected something more. Some kind of reaction." He started to place the vial back in the drawer. Then he had a second thought. "Do you like how this smells?"

I nodded. "Yeah, it's good."

"Take it." He tossed it over, and I threw it into my purse.

The rest of the day passed slowly as I listened to Kelly and Stacy argue over the radio station or fight over some impossibly gorgeous actor or front man they'd never meet. Finally at four, I swung into the ladies' room and changed out of my work clothes, which consisted of a rayon suit skirt and a button-up pin-striped shirt. Knowing I'd be hanging with Micah in the club later, I'd brought a pair of comfortable jeans and one of his band's T-shirts. I shook my ponytail out and let my hair fall to my shoulders.

When I went back to the lab to grab my purse and laptop, I wasn't a bit surprised that Kelly disapproved of my entire look.

"I have a low-cut shirt in my car if you want something more attractive." She offered it as though she actually would've lent it to me. Knowing I'd decline, she got in a free dig at my wardrobe choices. We were a study in opposites—she with her overpermed blond hair and salon tan, me with my short-clipped fingernails and functioning brain cells.

"No, thanks. Maybe next time."

"At least let me fix your makeup. Are you even wearing any?"

I pretended she wasn't bothering me. "No time. I have a train to catch."

She sniffed. "Well, you smell nice anyway. New perfume?"

"Uh, yeah. It was a gift." Her normally pouting lips rounded in anticipation of her next question. I zipped my computer bag and said, "Gotta go. See ya tomorrow, Stacy?"

Stacy waved without turning her head away from whatever gossip site she'd logged on to, and I slipped out the door.

As I stood on the train platform waiting for the 5:35 Northeast Corridor train to Penn Station, I heard someone calling "Hello?" from inside my purse. I fetched my phone and found it connected somehow to my mom, whose voice messages I'd been ignoring.

Foiled by technology and the gremlins living in my bag, I placed the phone to my ear. "Mom?"

"Oh, there you are, Eden. I'm making corned beef and gravy tonight. Why don't you come by before you go out?"

I didn't know how to cook, so my mom's invitation was meant as charity. But since she was the reason I couldn't cook, her promise of shit on a shingle wasn't enough to lure me from my original plans.

"No, thanks, Mom. I'm on my way into the city to hear Micah play tonight."

"Oh. Well, we'll see you Sunday I hope. Would you come to church with us? We have a wonderful new minister and—"

"No, Mom. But I'll come by the house later."

"All right. Oh, don't forget you've got a date with Dr. Whedon tomorrow night."

I groaned. She was relentless. "Is it too late to cancel?"

"What's the problem now, Eden?"

I pictured Dr. Rick Whedon, DDS, tonguing my bicuspid as we French kissed. But she wouldn't understand why I'd refuse to date a dentist, so instead, I presented an iron-clad excuse. "Mom, if we got married, I'd be Eden Whedon."

Her sigh came across loud and clear. "Eden, don't be so unreasonable."

"I keep telling you you're wasting your time, Mom."

"And you're letting it slip by, waiting on a nonexistent man. You're going to be twenty-nine soon."

The train approached the station, so I put my finger in my ear and yelled into the phone. "In six months, Mom."

"What was wrong with Jack Talbot?"

I thought for a second and then placed the last guy she'd tried to set me up with. "He had a mustache, Mom. And a tattoo. Also, he lives with his parents."

"That's only temporary," she snapped.

"The mustache or the tattoo?" I thought back to the guy from the lab. "And you never know. Maybe I'll meet Mr. Perfect soon."

"Well, if you do, bring him over on Sunday."

I chortled. The idea of bringing a guy over to my crazy house before I had a ring on my finger was ludicrous. "Sure, Mom. I'll see you Sunday."

"Tell Micah to come, too?"

My turn to sigh. Their pride in him was unflappable, and yet, I'd been the one to do everything they'd ever encouraged me to do, while he'd run off to pursue a pipe dream in music. So maybe they hadn't encouraged me to work in the sex-drug industry, but at least I had a college degree and a stable income.

"Okay, Mom. I'll mention it. The train's here. I have to go."

I climbed on the train and relaxed, so tired of everyone harassing me. At least I could count on Micah not to meddle in my love life.

Chapter Two

At seven thirty, I arrived at the back door of the club, trailing a cloud of profanity. "Fuck. My fucking phone died."

Micah exchanged a glance with the club owner, Tobin. "See? Eden doesn't count."

"What the fuck are you talking about?" After two hours fighting mass transit, I'd lost my patience. My attitude would need to be recalibrated to match Micah's easygoing demeanor.

Micah ground out his cigarette with a twist of his shoe. "Tobin was laying a wager that only women would show up tonight, but I said you'd be here."

I narrowed my eyes.

Micah's small but avid female fan base faithfully came out whenever he put on an acoustic show. His hard-rock band, Theater of the Absurd, catered to a larger male following and performed to ever-increasing audiences. But he loved playing these smaller rooms, bantering with the crowd, hearing people sing along with familiar choruses.

Before Tobin could get in on the act, I blurted, "Can I charge my phone in the green room?"

I made a wide berth around Tobin's plumage of cigarette smoke and followed Micah down the shabby narrow back hall. Dimly lit eight-by-eleven glossy posters plastered the walls, advertising upcoming bands and many other acts that had already passed through. Nobody curated the leftover fliers although hundreds of staples held torn triangles of paper from some distant past. A brand-new poster showing Micah's anticipated club dates hung near the door to the ladies' room. That would disappear during the night as some fan co-opted it for him to autograph, and Tobin would have to replace it. Again.

The green room was actually dark red and held furniture that looked like someone had found it on the curb near the trash. And it smelled like they'd brought the trash, too. God knew what had transpired in here over the years. I tried to touch nothing. Micah flopped down on the sofa and picked up a box of half-eaten Chinese food. His red Converse tennis shoes and dark green pants clashed with the brown-gold hues that stained the formerly whitish sofa.

I plugged in my phone, praying I'd remember to fetch it before I left. I fished out some ibuprofen and grabbed Micah's beer to wash it down. I waved off his interest in the drugs I was popping. "Birth control," I lied.

Without looking up from his noodles, he said, "Oh, good. I was starting to worry you'd joined a convent."

When Micah finished eating, he led me to the front of the club and put me to work setting up his merch table. His band's CDs wouldn't sell, but his self-produced EP of solo work would disappear. Mostly for girls to have something for him to autograph. They'd already own his music digitally. A suitcase filled with rolled-up T-shirts lay under the table. I bent down and selected one of each design to display as samples.

Micah moved around onstage helping the club employees drag cables and whatnot. Not for the first time, I envied him for inheriting some of Mom's Scandinavian coloring and height, while I got Dad's pale Irish skin and raven hair. Micah repeated "one-two-three check" into the mic a few times and then disappeared around back to grab one last smoke before he had to transform from my sweet older brother into that charismatic guy who held a crowd in the palm of his hand.

Right before the doors opened to the public, one of the guys I'd seen setting up the stage stopped by the table and flipped through the T-shirts and CDs. He picked up Micah's EP and then raised dark brown eyes. "Micah Sinclair. You like his music?"

He wore faded jeans and a threadbare T-shirt from a long-forgotten AC/DC concert under a maroon hoodie. His black hair fell somewhere between tousled and bed head. I saw no traces of product, so I assumed he came by that look through honest negligence rather than studied indifference.

My quick scan revealed: too grungy, probably unwashed, poor. I resisted the urge to pull the merch away from his wandering fingers. But I wouldn't risk the sale, so I leaned in on my elbows, all smiles.

"He's amazing. Will you get a chance to hear him perform?"

"Oh, yeah. Definitely." He set the EP down and held out his hand. "I'm Adam, by the way."

I wrapped my hand around his out of sheer politeness and proper upbringing, but I couldn't help laughing and saying, "Just so you know, my worst nightmare would be dating a guy named Adam."

He quirked his eyebrow. "That's kind of discriminatory."

"My name's Eden." I waited a beat for the significance to register, but I guess any guy named Adam would've already dealt with such issues of nomenclature. His eyes lit up immediately.

"Oh. Seriously?" He chuckled, and his smile transformed his features. I sucked in my breath. Underneath the dark hair, dark eyes, and hobo wardrobe, he was awfully cute. "I'll rethink that marriage proposal. But could I get you anything? You want a beer?"

This was a new twist. Usually, the ladies were offering drinks to my brother. I loved getting the attention for a change. "Sure. Whatever lager or pilsner they have on tap."

He walked off, and I snickered. *Maybe some guys like pale brunettes, Kelly.* As he leaned against the bar, I assessed him from the rear. Tall enough, but too skinny. Questionable employment. Either an employee of the club, a musician, a wannabe musician, or a fan. Shame.

Micah strolled up. "Is everything ready?"

I forced my gaze away from Adam's backside. "Are you?"

He scratched his five-o'clock chin scruff. "That's the thing. I may need some help tonight. Do you think you could maybe sing backup on one song? I was hoping to harmonize on 'Gravity.'"

"Sure." What were sisters for? I had his whole catalog memorized, even the music from his band, although that music ran a little too hard rock for my tastes.

Micah left me alone at the merch table, and Adam returned with a glass. "Did I just miss Micah?"

He'd pulled his hoodie up so his face fell into shadow, giving him a sinister appearance. With the nonexistent lighting in the club, I could barely make out his features. This odd behavior, coupled with his interest in my brother, made me worry maybe he was in fact one of the crazy fans who found ways to get closer than normal, and not, as I'd first thought, an employee of the club. How had he gotten inside before the doors opened?

Before I could ask him, a woman's sharp voice interrupted. "Will Micah be coming out after the show?"

I looked toward the club's entrance, where people had begun to stream in. I took a deep breath and prepared to deal with the intensity of music fandom.

"I assume so. He usually does."

She didn't move. "It's just that I brought something for him." She held up a canister of something I guessed was homemade. I'd advised Micah not to eat whatever they gave him, but he never listened. And so far he'd never landed in the hospital. I knew his fans meant well, but who knew if those cookies had been baked alongside seven long-haired cats?

"I could take it back to him if you like." I made the offer, knowing full well it wouldn't do at all.

"No. Thank you. I'll just wait and give them to him later. If he comes out." She wandered off toward the stage.

I spotted one of Micah's regular fans, Susan something-or-other, making a beeline for the merch table. She looked put out that I was there before her. "Eden, if you like, I'm more than happy to man the merch."

I never understood what she got out of working merch for Micah. He didn't pay except possibly in a waived cover charge. And she was farther from the stage and possibly distracted from the performances. Perhaps it gave her status. Whatever it was, it made her happy, and I was glad to relinquish the duty to her.

"Thank you, Susan."

She beamed. "Oh, it's no problem." She began to chatter with the other women crowding up to the merch table. I overheard her saying, "Micah told me he'll be performing a new song tonight."

Adam caught my eye, and we exchanged a knowing smile. So okay, he wasn't a fan. He stepped beside me as I walked to the bar to get a seat on a stool. "So you're not the number one fan, then?" he asked.

I smiled. "Of course I am."

Before we could discuss our reasons for being there, the room plunged into near-total darkness, and Tobin stepped onto the stage to introduce the opening act, a tall blond whose explosion of wild hair had to weigh more than the rest of her.

She pulled up a stool and started into her first song without further ado. Out of respect, I kept quiet and listened, although her performance was a bit shaky, and the between-song banter didn't help. It pleased me that Adam didn't turn to me to say anything snarky about the poor girl to me or talk at all. I had to glare over at the women hanging around the merch table a few times, though. They'd shut up when Micah came on, but they didn't seem to care that other musicians preferred to play to a rapt audience, too.

In the time between acts, Adam ordered me another beer. At some point he'd dropped his hood back, but with the terrible lighting in the club, I had to squint to see his face. Normally,

I wasn't a big fan of facial hair of any kind, but Adam's slight scruff caused my wires to cross. On the one hand, I worried he couldn't afford a razor out there in the cardboard box he lived in. On the other hand, I had a visceral urge to reach up and touch his cheek. And run my finger down the side of his neck.

He caught me staring when he leaned closer to ask me how long Micah had been performing.

I wasn't sure what he was asking, so I gave him the full answer. "He's been singing since he was old enough to talk. He started playing acoustic when he was eleven, but picked up electric when he was fifteen. He formed a metal band in high school, and the first time they performed live anywhere beyond the garage was a battle of the bands."

Adam's expression changed subtly as I recounted Micah's life history, and I could tell he was reassessing my level of crazy fantardness. I laughed and said, "I told you I was his number one fan."

His smile slipped, but he managed to reply politely. "He must be very talented."

Something about the timbre in his voice resonated with me, almost familiar, and I regretted my flippant sarcasm.

Before I could repair my social missteps, the lights faded again, and the girls near the stage screamed in anticipation. A spotlight hit the mic, and Micah unceremoniously took the stage. He strummed a few notes and broke directly into a song everyone knew. The girls up front sang along, swaying and trying to out-do each other in their excitement.

Adam twisted around and watched me, eyebrow raised. Maybe he expected me to sing along, too. I raised an eyebrow back and mouthed the words along with Micah. Wouldn't want to disappoint him. Finally, Adam straightened up to watch the performance, ignoring me for several songs.

Micah performed another well-known song, then a new one, introducing each with some casual-seeming banter. I knew he planned every word he said onstage, but the stories he told were no less sincere for that. He controlled his stage presence like a pro.

Before the fourth song, he announced, "This next song requires some assistance. If you would all encourage my sister, Eden, to come join me, I'm sure she'd hop up here and lend me a hand."

The audience applauded on cue. As my feet hit the floor, Adam's eyes narrowed and then opened wide as he did the math. I curtsied and left him behind to climb up onstage to perform—Micah's support vocals once again. Micah strummed a chord, and I hummed the pitch. Then he began to play the song, a beautiful ballad about a man with an unflagging devotion to a woman. The ladies in the front row ate it up. Micah knew I got a kick out of performing, and I suspected he asked me up so I could live his musician life vicariously.

When the song ended, I headed back to the anonymity of my stool. The hard-core fans all knew who I was, but if they weren't pumping me for information about Micah, they didn't pay much attention to me. There was a fresh beer waiting, and I nodded to Adam, appreciative. He winked and faced forward to listen to Micah. That was the extent of our conversation until Micah performed his last encore and the lights came back up.

Then he turned back. "You were right. He's very talented." He tilted his head. "But you held out on me. Your opinion was a little bit biased."

"I was telling you the truth," I deadpanned. "I am his number one fan."

"You two look nothing alike. I'd never have guessed."

"We have a crazy mix of genetics."

As we chatted, the area behind us, near the merch table, filled up with people waiting for a chance to talk to Micah, get an autograph, or take a picture with him. The lady with the cat-hair cookies had nabbed the first place in the amorphous line. I scanned the rest of the crowd and discovered that Tobin had lost his bet. A pair of teenage boys holding guitars stood on their toes, trying to get a glimpse of Micah over the heads of the other fans, but he hadn't come out yet. They were most likely fans of his edgier rock band, taking advantage of the smaller venue to meet him, pick his brain about music, and have him sign their guitars. They'd still be competing with at least thirty people for Micah's time.

If I wanted to go home with my brother, I'd be hanging out a while. I could still catch a train back to New Jersey, but Micah's place in Brooklyn was closer. I decided to stay. It had nothing to do with the cute guy paying attention to me. I just didn't want to navigate Manhattan alone and drunk.

Adam leaned in and asked, "So what do you do? Are you a musician, too?"

"Actually, no. I'm a biochemist."

"Finding cures for Ebola?"

That caught me off guard, and I snorted. "No, nothing like that." I didn't know what to tell him about what I actually researched, so I half-lied. "My company's developing a perfume."

"What's it like?"

I scooted over. "I'm wearing it. Can you smell it?"

He met me halfway, eyes dilating black. I knew I shouldn't be flirting. He didn't appear to meet a single one of my criteria and, in fact, actively ticked boxes from the "deal-breaker" list. I didn't want to lead him on only to have to give him the heave-ho in the next thirty minutes.

He took my hand and kept his dark eyes on mine as he lifted my wrist up to smell the fragrance Thanh had given me. "Mmm. That's nice."

Without dropping his gaze, he brushed his lips across my skin, and an electric current shot up every nerve in my arm. I drew my hand back, shrugging off the shiver that hit me like an aftershock. "And you? What do you do?"

He laughed and scratched the back of his neck. "Well, I'm a musician."

I blinked back my disappointment. From Adam's appearance, I hadn't had high hopes, but he might've been dressed down for a night out. Way down.

On my list of suitable professions for my prospective mate, musician wasn't at the absolute bottom. There were plenty more embarrassing or unstable career choices. I wouldn't date plumbers or proctologists for obvious reasons. Salesmen either because, well, I didn't like salesmen, but also because their financial situation might be uncertain. Plus they tended to travel. My ideal guy, I'd decided, would be an architect. But there weren't many of those swimming around my apartment complex in Edison, New Jersey.

I had nothing against musicians. On the contrary, I loved them. I'd supported my brother in his career, but the lifestyle was too precarious for my peace of mind. Even the most talented had a hard time making ends meet. Traveling and selling merchandise became a necessity.

Which is why I never dated musicians.

Unfortunately, all the doctors, lawyers, and architects I encountered were usually not interested in jean-clad, concert T-shirt wearing me. This train of thought brought me around to the realization that I'd judged Adam for dressing exactly the same way.

Micah saved me from sticking my foot in my mouth when he appeared at our side. "Adam! I'm glad to see you here. I see you've met my sister." He turned to me. "Eden, do you mind if I steal him for a few?"

Adam threw me a glance. "Will you be here when I get back?"

The jolt of butterflies this simple question gave me came wholly unexpectedly. "I'll be here. I'm leaving when Micah does."

He flashed a crooked smile at me, and I traced his lips with my eyes. He was going to be trouble.

They headed toward the green room, leaving me as confused as Adam must've been when I went onstage. I didn't know who he was, or why my brother wanted to see him.

I weighed the possible options.

Option one: The most logical explanation was that Micah was hiring Adam to temporarily replace his bassist, Rick, who was taking time off to be with his wife after the birth of their first child. I congratulated myself for solving the mystery on my first try.

Option two: Maybe Adam was a drug dealer. No, other than smoking and drinking, I'd never known Micah to try a recreational drug. And surely, this wouldn't be an ideal location for such a transaction. Besides, Adam already said he was a musician. Option one was looking better and better.

Option three: Or maybe Adam was a homeless man Micah was going to take in out of charity. A homeless man who'd just bought me three beers. I rolled my eyes at myself, but then felt awash with guilt. He probably wasn't homeless, but it did seem like he might be struggling to get by, and I'd accepted three drinks I could've easily afforded. *Good job, Eden. Way to drive a man to starvation.*

Every new option I came up with to explain Adam's presence here defied logic and stretched the imagination. I gave up and watched the crowd thin. When Micah and Adam came back out, the bar was empty, save me and the staff.

Micah poked me. "We're going over to Adam's. You can come or just go straight back to my place." He bounced on his feet. I looked from him to Adam, standing relaxed up against the bar. From the looks of things, Micah had a boy crush. I might be interrupting a bromance if I tagged along.

Adam stepped toward me. "I have a fully stocked bar, and I don't like to drink alone." His smile was disarming. The whole situation seemed so contrived, and I had to wonder whose idea it was.

Micah stifled a yawn. "Come on, Eden. Just for a drink. Let's go see how the other half lives."

Did he know what that expression meant? "Okay, but let's get going. Some of us have been awake since this morning."

Acknowledgments

Every book is a leap of faith that starts as a mere seed of an idea that will never grow to fruition without a lot of encouragement to keep the confidence alive. I am forever indebted to those people in my life who let me bounce ideas off them, cry about plotting woes, and share triumphs with every milestone reached.

Thanks as always to my writing crew: Elly Blake, Kelli Newby, Kelly Siskind, Kristin Wright, Jennifer Hawkins, Ron Walters, and Summer Spence. You guys keep me sane and keep me believing that I can reach The End.

Special thanks to Elly and Kelli for your invaluable feedback and help straightening out all the things.

I'm forever grateful to you readers for coming along for the ride. Thank you to anyone who's ever reached out to let me know when they've enjoyed one of my books, especially to those who've taken the time to leave reviews on Goodreads, Amazon, etc. It means the world.

Mary Ann Marlowe lives in central Virginia where she works as a computer programmer/DBA. She spent ten years as a university-level French professor, and her resume includes stints as an au pair in Calais, a hotel intern in Paris, a German tutor, a college radio disc jockey, and a webmaster for several online musician fandoms. She has lived in twelve states and three countries and loves to travel.

Printed in the USA
CPSIA information can be obtained
at www.ICGtesting.com
LVHW040812020124
767940LV00034B/478